**DUNLEAVY FARM
KENTUCKY**

Dear Carla,

Permit me to introduce myself. I am your maternal grandmother, Octavia Whitworth Dunleavy.

When I think of the bitter circumstances under which your mother and I parted company, I feel safe in guessing that you've probably never heard of me. So I imagine this letter will come as quite a shock, but please bear with me.

My dear granddaughter, I need to see you. I have a proposition to discuss that I hope you will find most interesting....

Looking forward to hearing from you, I remain,

Yours affectionately,

Octavia Whitworth Dunleavy

A NOTE FROM THE AUTHOR

The Dunleavy Legacy marks a significant and exciting departure for me. After eleven Superromance novels written under my nom de plume, Risa Kirk, this trilogy bears my "mainstream" name—and my own—Janis Flores.

As some of you may know from my books, I own, train and love horses. What you may not know is that in addition to my contemporary novels, I've written historical romances and family sagas. I love to create strong characters who have to battle themselves and each other on their way to finding true love. Being given free rein to combine these interests in a trilogy has been very gratifying.

I hope that all my readers, mainstream and romance fans alike, enjoy the books of the Dunleavy Legacy as much as I enjoyed writing them. And remember, too: names and pseudonyms can change, but a good love story—or three— goes on forever.

Janis Flores

Janis Flores
Done Driftin'

Harlequin Books

TORONTO • NEW YORK • LONDON
AMSTERDAM • PARIS • SYDNEY • HAMBURG
STOCKHOLM • ATHENS • TOKYO • MILAN
MADRID • WARSAW • BUDAPEST • AUCKLAND

ISBN 0-373-70654-5

DONE DRIFTIN'

Copyright © 1995 by Janis Flores.

This edition published by arrangement with Harlequin Books S.A.

® and TM are trademarks of the publisher. Trademarks indicated with ® are registered in the United States Patent and Trademark Office, the Canadian Trade Marks Office and in other countries.

Printed in U.S.A.

DUNLEAVY FAMILY TREE

Alvah Dunleavy   m.1942   Octavia Whitworth
1910–1956   1916–

Meredith	Gary	Jamie
1943-	1944-1995	1946-
m.1961	m.1963	
Alan Bradshaw)	(Nancy Hansen)	
CARLA	NAN	SETH
DUNLEAVY	DUNLEAVY	DUNLEAVY
1961	1964	1967
		m.1990
		(Honey LaRue)

PROLOGUE

OCTAVIA Whitworth Dunleavy leaned on her cane as she left the main house and made her way purposefully to the paddock. For the first time in a long time old regrets were being replaced by new hopes. She'd finally done something to make amends. She couldn't remember exactly when the plan to bring the three grown grandchildren she'd never seen to Dunleavy Farm had occurred to her, but the idea had taken hold. Now all she had to do was wait.

The horse that had been grazing up on the hill lifted his head at her approach. It was the farm's famed Triple Crown winner, Done Roamin'. The great stallion neighed shrilly in greeting and started toward her. This was a nightly ritual between the old woman and the aging horse.

Three years before, the horse had been severely injured in a still-unexplained stable accident. The surgery to repair his mangled hind leg had taken a great deal of Octavia's dwindling resources, but she hadn't questioned the expenditure. Done Roamin' was more than the farm's most famous horse; he was her friend and companion. She would have done anything to save him.

Her expression was sad as she watched Done Roamin' pick his way down the grassy slope. Gone was the blazing, ground-eating stride that had gained him racing's highest accolades; in its place was an awkward, shambling gait that made her heart constrict. Abruptly she shook off her melancholy. If he'd had to, he would have come to her on three legs, so who was she to complain? Hurrying as quickly as her age and condition allowed, she went to meet him at the gate.

"We may be old and feeble," she panted as she hobbled along, "but there's still some life left in us yet, isn't there, old son?"

As though he understood, Done Roamin' neighed as he came to the fence. His shrill whinny rang out across the farm, and as an answering challenge came from another paddock, Octavia turned to look in its direction.

Done Roamin' was king, and would be as long as he lived, but it was obvious that his two sons and daughter, the last of his get, were impatient for succession. The two colts, with their half sister in another paddock, were running the fence lines, showing off for their sire.

"All in good time, my loves," she said, appreciating the way their almost-identical blood-bay coats gleamed in the sunset. She had plans for all three. "All in good time...."

Done Roamin' was waiting for her, his head arched over the fence so she could pet him. Her arthritic fingers stroked his long, silky forelock, but her eyes were faraway.

She sighed. Everything had taken place so long ago, but she could remember each event as though it had happened just yesterday. One after another, she had alienated her children and sent them away: her oldest daughter, Meredith, so beautiful and clever; her handsome son, Gary, who had so resembled Alvah, his father. And finally, her youngest and most vulnerable, her ethereal-looking, artistic daughter, Jamie.

Sometimes she wondered if things would have turned out differently if Alvah hadn't died so young. She'd been alone, with three children to raise and a horse farm to run. People depended on her; she couldn't let them down. She'd had to be strong.

But did she have to be so unyielding? Ah, that was the question. Octavia shook her head. She didn't know; all she could say was that she'd done what she thought was right, at the time.

And now, forty years later?

Her fingers still entwined in the stallion's forelock, Octavia looked again in the direction of the other paddocks. Done Roamin's two sons had tired of their game and had gone back to grazing. But the filly, Never Done Dreamin', was still gazing their way. When she saw Octavia looking at her, she snorted and stamped her foot, as if to say, *It'll be all right, just wait.*

Octavia prayed it would be as she turned to watch the older of the two colts. His name was Done Driftin', and a lot was riding on him. In a few days, the letters she'd written to each of her three grandchildren would reach them. Octavia would know by their responses if there was any hope for her and Dunleavy Farm—or if it was too late and she was just a foolish old woman.

As though he sensed her dejected mood, Done Roamin' gently nudged her arm. Octavia smiled at the gesture, thinking of some of the stallions she'd owned in the past. They had been great horses, but she never would have trusted them the way she trusted this one. Done Roamin' nudged her again, and this time she chuckled.

"Are you trying to comfort me, or do you just want your carrot?" she asked.

She brought it out as she always did, broken into pieces so it would last longer—for both of them. Then, listening to the soothing sounds of the horse chewing, she raised her eyes to the line of trees that marked the farm's west boundary.

The setting sun touched the sky with long streaks of gold and pink. The dying light seemed to hold its breath for a moment, painting the tops of the trees, silhouetting them against the skyline. She had enjoyed the sight nearly all her life, but tonight she barely noticed it.

She thought of the letters she had sent with such high hopes. Her hand trembling as she stroked Done Roamin', she wondered what her grandchildren would say when they reached their destinations.

CHAPTER ONE

"WE HAVE a letter for you, Ms. Dunleavy."

The voice came from the hallway outside the New York hotel suite Carla was sharing with her mother. Her expression bored, as she herself seemed to be so often these days, Carla turned from the view of Central Park and went to open the door. A young man in slacks and a dark blue blazer was outside, holding a silver tray upon which sat a single envelope.

"This letter was delivered for you a few minutes ago, Ms. Dunleavy," he said. "We thought it might be important so we brought it right up."

"Thank you." Carla signed for the letter and added a generous tip. She closed the door and was staring curiously at the envelope, when her mother, Meredith, emerged from her bedroom.

"Who was that, darling?" Meredith asked, inspecting herself in the foyer mirror and smoothing an imaginary wrinkle in her skirt.

"Someone from the front desk. He brought a letter."

"A letter? That's odd. Let me see."

"It's addressed to me."

Meredith rolled her eyes. "Oh, don't tell me it's from that tiresome Reggie! I thought you'd made it clear when we left London last month that it was over between you."

"I did. It isn't from Reggie. It's from someplace called Dunleavy Farm in Kentucky. How strange that the farm should have our name."

Meredith slowly turned toward her. "What did you say?"

"I said—"

"Let me see that!"

Surprised by her mother's tone, Carla showed her the envelope. Acquaintances said she and Meredith resembled each other, but she couldn't see it herself. Except for the chestnut-colored hair and the green eyes, she didn't think they looked anything alike. Meredith reached for the letter, but Carla pulled it back.

"Wait until I read it."

"Why? It's obviously a mistake," Meredith said, and paused. Much too casually, she continued, "Must be meant for some other Dunleavy."

Carla gazed at her for a moment. She knew when her mother was trying to hide something. "Have you heard of this place, Mother?"

Meredith looked away. Pretending to check the contents of her purse, she said, "I don't believe so, no."

Carla glanced at her again. It was clear that Meredith knew more about this Kentucky farm than she

admitted. She began to open the envelope and Meredith looked at her quickly.

"Why do you want to read that?" Meredith asked.
"You don't even know if it's for you."

"Let's just say I'm curious," Carla said, unfolding
the stiff, parchmentlike piece of paper. It was hand-
written. She skipped over the finely written lines of
beautiful, old-fashioned penmanship to the signature.

"It's signed Octavia Whitworth Dunleavy," she
said.

Meredith paled. Before Carla could stop her, she
grabbed the letter and quickly scanned the contents.
When she came to the signature, she muttered, "Oh,
my God."

"What is it?"

Meredith began to crumple the letter into a ball.
"Never mind. You don't need to read this. It's just
rubbish. Rubbish!"

"Mother, for crying out loud. Why are you acting
this way?" Carla prized the letter from her mother's
hand and smoothed out the page. "Who's Octavia
Dunleavy?" she asked. "Is she a relative?"

"She's no relation to me. Or to you. I mean it,
Carla. Please don't read it. You'll be sorry."

"Then I'll be sorry," Carla said.

The letter began:

Dear Carla,

Permit me to introduce myself. I am your maternal grandmother, Octavia Whitworth Dunleavy.

When I think of the bitter circumstances under which your mother and I parted company, I feel safe in guessing that you've probably never heard of me. So I imagine it will be quite a shock to hear from me after all these years, but please bear with me.

My dear granddaughter, I need to see you. I have a proposition to discuss that I hope will interest you...

Carla looked up from the crumpled paper. "This woman says she's my grandmother."

Her face set, Meredith went into the living room and sat down. Reading the rest of the letter, Carla followed.

"Well?" Carla said when she finished the contents.

Meredith was staring out the window. "Well, what?"

"Don't avoid the question. Is this woman telling the truth? *Is* she my grandmother? If she is, why didn't you ever tell me? Why did I have to find out like this?"

Meredith reached for the purse she'd thrown on the couch. She'd been trying to give up smoking, but she took out a cigarette and lit it with a snap of a gold lighter.

"Are you going to answer me or not?" Carla demanded.

"It's a long story."

"I've got plenty of time. I want to know who this woman is . . . what she is to me."

Impatiently, Meredith took a drag off the cigarette. "It doesn't matter. She's nothing to you, really. Why can't you trust me on this?"

"Because I don't think you're telling me the truth."

Meredith sighed. "All right. Octavia Dunleavy *is* your grandmother—" Her lips tightened. "Although how she ever found us here, and why she's contacting us now, I'll never know."

Carla sank into a nearby chair, trying to adjust to the news. "She didn't contact *us*. She wrote to *me.*"

Meredith looked at her pityingly. "The letter might have your name on it, but the message was definitely for me."

"How do you know that?"

Her voice hard, Meredith said, "Because I know her."

"Why didn't you ever tell me that I had a grandmother? You said we had no relatives at all."

"I was trying to protect you."

"Protect me! From what?"

"Not from what, from whom! Octavia Dunleavy is an evil old woman who would have tried to get to me through you!"

"You can't be serious, Mother. Do you realize how you sound?"

"You don't know this woman. I do."

"Well, I'm going to know her soon, it seems. She's invited me to visit Dunleavy Farm."

"You're not going!"

"Yes, I am. I think it might be...interesting."

"Interesting! You don't know what you'll be getting into. No, you can't go, Carla. I...I forbid it!"

"*Forbid* it?" Carla laughed. "Really, Mother, you can't forbid me to do anything. I'm thirty-five years old."

"But *why* would you go? You don't know her. You don't know anything about this woman."

"Well, I do know that if I visit the farm, she'll give me a racehorse. It says so, right here in the letter."

Meredith looked at her disbelievingly. "She'll give you a *horse?* That's preposterous!"

"It does seem so, doesn't it? A grandmother I didn't even know I had wants me to visit a farm I didn't know existed, and in return, she'll give me a racehorse." She paused and looked at Meredith assessingly for a moment. "Honestly, Mother, I don't see how I could refuse an offer like that."

"I don't understand how you can joke about it!" Angrily, Meredith stubbed out her cigarette. "This is too much, even for her!"

"Oh, now, Mother..."

Meredith got up and paced. "That woman has something up her sleeve, I'm sure of it. And you can bet that whatever it is, it won't be good."

Meredith's reaction piqued Carla's curiosity even more than the letter had. She was tired of sitting around this hotel room day after day. She had been bored for so long. Bored, bored, *bored*. It would be diverting to visit this backwater farm and meet the woman who was causing her mother such agitation. She had nothing better on her calendar, and if she uncovered some dark family secrets, she'd have some amusing anecdotes to tell at those dreary parties when she and her mother went back to London and rejoined the season's social whirl.

That decided, she rose and headed toward the telephone.

"What are you doing?" Meredith instantly demanded.

"I'm going to book a flight to Kentucky, and then I'm going to telegraph Grandmother Octavia Dunleavy, telling her when to expect me."

Meredith turned red. "After all I've said, you're still going to accept her offer?"

Calmly, Carla lifted the receiver. "You haven't said much of anything. Now, shall I say that two are coming, or will it just be me?"

Meredith stared at her a moment longer. Then she grabbed her purse and made for the door. Without another word, she opened it, went out and slammed it behind her.

A click sounded in Carla's ear. "Concierge," the voice said.

"Ah, good," Carla said. "I'd like to send a wire."

WADE PETRIE WAS TAKING a rare break from his chores, leaning against the paddock fence watching the colts play pasture tag, when he heard Octavia call from the front porch. She was waving something at him, obviously excited. Worried that she might tumble headfirst down the veranda stairs, he started toward her.

"It came!" she cried, holding a paper aloft.

Wade had never seen Octavia like this. "Whatever it is, it looks like good news," he said as he came up.

"Oh, it's very good news," she said. Her eyes—the vivid Dunleavy green—sparkled with joy. "It's from one of my grandchildren—Carla. I wrote to her and two others a while ago. It's been so long that I'd almost given up expecting to hear from any of them. But now Carla has sent this telegram to say she's coming to visit the farm!"

"She's coming here?" Wade tried to hide his surprise. In the three years he'd lived and worked at Dunleavy Farm, Octavia had rarely entertained visitors. And when people came, they were bloodstock agents or lawyers or bankers. As far as he knew, not one of them had been family.

"You look surprised," Octavia teased. "Did you think I was all alone in the world?"

"Well, no, I've heard a few things, Mrs. D. But you never mentioned any granddaughters before. You never mentioned anyone."

Some of the excitement faded from Octavia's face. For a few seconds, she seemed far away. "That's because they were all scattered to the four winds. I had to hire a private detective to find them." Suddenly she brightened. "But now Carla is coming to visit, and I want to ask you a favor."

"A favor?" Wade looked at her warily.

"It's not what you think," Octavia said, reading his mind. "I know what a hermit you are. You're worse than I am for never going out or getting around, except where the horses are concerned. But don't worry, I'm not playing matchmaker. All I want to ask is if you'll meet her at the airport when her flight gets in."

Relieved, he said, "Well, that I can do. Just tell me when and what time."

Octavia consulted the telegram. "She'll be arriving at Louisville tomorrow around noon."

"So soon?"

Octavia's eyes took on that faraway expression again. "It's been thirty-five years, Wade. I wouldn't call that *soon*, would you?"

"No, I guess not," he said. Thirty-five years, he thought. Just how old was this Carla? Still, it wasn't any of his business, so he asked, "How will I recognize her?"

"Now that's a good question." Octavia looked embarrassed. "I've never seen her."

Wade didn't comment. Obviously there was family history here. But he hadn't pried before, and he wouldn't do it now. He respected Octavia, owed her a lot. She had taken him on when no one else would; she had rescued him when his life had been a shambles. She hadn't asked him questions; she had just given him a job. He would always be grateful to her, more than he could ever say. It wasn't his place to ask her why she'd decided to invite a granddaughter whom she'd never seen to visit. His job was to show up and bring the woman back to Dunleavy Farm on the right day.

"Well, don't worry about it," he said cheerfully. "I've heard it said that the family resemblance is so strong, a person can spot a Dunleavy five hundred yards away."

Octavia looked at him with mock severity. "Gossip," she said. "What do people know about the Dunleavys?"

"Everybody knows about the Dunleavys," he teased. "Especially that Miss Octavia. They say she was a corker in her day."

"Still is," Octavia said saucily. Then, before she could ruin her proud pose by laughing, she turned and went inside.

WADE WAS at the airport in Louisville the next day at noon, in time for Carla Dunleavy's flight. Holding a sign that said Dunleavy Farm, he waited at the gate while the passengers deplaned. By the time the flood of people had slowed to a trickle, he wondered if she'd missed the plane. He was just about to ask the reservations clerk to check the passenger manifest, when he saw a single woman approaching.

He knew immediately she was Carla Dunleavy. She had similar features to her grandmother, the high cheekbones, the straight nose and the distinctive vivid green eyes. She also possessed, he noted grimly, the haughty manner that some people of her status and station in life assume.

He disliked her on sight. He knew her, he thought. Not personally, of course. But he knew women like her—society creatures, poseurs who made work of being seen at some fund-raiser or party or other silly function while snubbing those they considered beneath them. Which was just about everyone, he remembered, thinking of a particular woman he'd known. After that experience, he could spot stuck-up socialites a mile away.

And if he had any doubt, he just had to watch the way Carla walked. Her chin lifted, her shoulders thrown back, she moved like royalty. Unlike the other passengers who were loaded down with packages and luggage, the only thing she carried was an elegant, obviously expensive leather purse. It swung delicately from one beautifully manicured hand. The sight irritated him further.

Their first meeting confirmed his initial impression of her. Wade was stuffing his no longer needed sign into his pocket when she saw him. She paused momentarily, then approached him. Her nostrils contracting as she stopped a few feet from him, she looked him up and down, and said, "I'm going to Dunleavy Farm. My grandmother said she'd send someone to meet me. Are you the one?"

Her snide emphasis on the word *you* irked him. When he was getting ready to leave for the airport this morning, he'd debated about wearing slacks and a sport shirt. Now he was glad he'd just kept on his boots and jeans.

Hoping it would irritate her, he said cheerfully, "Yes, I'm the one. Do you have any luggage, or is that all you brought?" He pointed at her purse.

Her eyes narrowed. She suspected he was making fun of her and she didn't like it. Wordlessly, she handed him her ticket. Stapled to it were no less than four luggage checks.

"How silly of me," he said. "I should have known you'd come prepared."

"And how would you know that? We've never met."

Ah, but we have, he thought grimly. *But then your name was Annabelle. It was a different time and place, but we definitely have met.*

"You're right." This wasn't amusing anymore. "We haven't met. Come on, let's claim your luggage and get out of here. I've got things to do back at the farm."

"You didn't ask," she said in that snooty tone he despised, "but my name is Carla Dunleavy."

He'd heard the trace of an accent in her voice, but he hadn't been able to place it until now. It was British, he thought, very correct and proper.

"I know," he said, starting toward the baggage claim area without looking back. "I recognized you right away."

She was forced to follow. To his annoyance, she was able to keep up with him, stride for stride. "How did you know?" she asked.

"You have the look."

"The look?" She paused momentarily, but when he kept on, she had to hurry after him again. "What look?" she demanded.

She seemed to be challenging him to say something about the way she had treated him, so he didn't. It was as if she was spoiling for a fight, and he was not about to give her the satisfaction. He wasn't interested in knowing why she was acting this way. He didn't care about her problems, if she had any. He didn't like her manner. He didn't like her. Aside from her looks, which he grudgingly had to admit were considerable, he decided that she wasn't like her grandmother at all.

They reached the luggage carousel. The bags from her flight were just starting to come up the chute, and he glanced at her when she got in line with him.

"I told you my name," she said. "I would appreciate it if you told me yours."

"Wade Petrie," he said. Mockingly, he touched the brim of his Stetson. He'd grown up on a western ranch, where men took off their hats only for funerals, baths and when they made love—and sometimes not even then. He added deliberately, "I'm the barn manager at Dunleavy Farm."

"I see." She gave him a long, appraising stare with those green eyes and turned away just as two paisley

Louis Vuitton bags appeared at the head of the luggage chute. "I believe those are—"

"I know." Wade had already seen them. Two more in the same luxurious fabric followed, and he reached for those, too. As he pulled them off the carousel, he sensed her looking at him.

"How did you know those were mine?" she asked.

She had to ask? Aloud, he said, "Just a hunch."

She gazed at him a moment longer, a slight frown between her arched eyebrows. He knew she was trying to figure him out. He didn't care. Let her try, he thought. He was just an employee doing what he'd been sent to do.

"Shall I call a porter?" she asked, and paused. "Or do you think you can manage by yourself?"

He heard the subtle challenge in her voice and was tempted to do the macho thing and boast that he could carry all four suitcases without help. But after lifting the damn things off the carousel, he realized that even if he miraculously got them out to the truck in one piece, he probably wouldn't be able to walk upright for a week. His pride wasn't worth a bad back, so he gestured to one of the uniformed men standing to the side, then was doubly glad he hadn't tried to show off when the porter had difficulty wrestling the suitcases onto his hand trolley.

"Where to, sir?" the man asked, taking out a handkerchief and mopping his face.

Madame's carriage awaits her in the nearest parking lot, Wade was tempted to say. He'd already guessed what Carla's reaction would be when she saw the truck-and-trailer rig, and she didn't disappoint him. As he directed the porter to toss the bags into the truck bed, she stopped dead in her tracks and said coldly, "Surely you don't expect me to ride in *that*."

Wade pretended to scrutinize the rig. "Well, yeah. It's what I came in. I figured I'd go home the same way. Why, what's the matter with it?"

Carla Dunleavy was speechless, probably for the first time in her life, he thought. She looked from the truck to him and then back again. Although the vehicle was equipped to haul a nine-horse gooseneck trailer, he'd considerately brought the two-horse today. Even so, because of the big engine required to pull such a heavy load, the cab was pretty high off the ground. High enough, Wade realized, that it would be tricky for a woman wearing heels and a straight skirt to climb in gracefully. He couldn't wait.

"I don't know how I know this," she said finally, "but I'm sure you did this on purpose."

He couldn't have her thinking he'd gone to all this trouble just for her, so after he'd tipped the porter and taken out his keys, he said, "You're right, Miss Dunleavy, I did do this on purpose."

"You admit it?"

"Sure. We have to pick up a horse on the way. I figured, since I had to come all this distance, I might as well kill two birds with one stone."

Her expression was enough to turn *him* to stone. "Are you actually trying to tell me that you brought

this...this *farm* vehicle to the airport so you wouldn't
have to make two trips?''

''Well, it takes an hour and a half each way—give
or take a few minutes. And I said I had—''

''I don't care if it takes all day! What were you
thinking of? I can't ride in that!''

He was enjoying this game of pretending to misunderstand her. Now, replacing her previous cold and
supercilious expression, there was fire in her eyes and
a telltale splash of furious pink in her cheeks. It made
her seem more *real*. Was that why he was baiting her?
He used to do the same thing to Annabelle—

But he didn't want to think of Annabelle Renfrow.
Nor did he want to dwell on Carla Dunleavy. Suddenly tired of the game, he unlocked the passenger-
side door of the truck and held it open. Carla continued to look at him as if he'd lost his mind along with
his manners.

''I told you,'' she said between her clenched white
teeth. ''I'm not going to ride in that vehicle.''

He wasn't about to argue with her, so he shut the
door. ''You've got two choices, then.''

''And those are?''

''Well, you could rent a car, or...you could walk.''

''How droll. Where's the rental agency?''

''They're all inside the terminal. But—''

She had already turned away. Impatiently, she
looked back. ''What?''

He tried not to smile as he started around to the
driver's side of the truck. ''I guess I should warn you.

There's a balloon convention in town, and I don't think there's a rental car to be had for miles.''

"I don't believe you."

"Why would I lie?"

"Because for some reason I don't understand, and certainly don't wish to explore, you don't like me, Mr. Petrie."

"Did I say that?"

"You didn't have to," she said haughtily. "But rest assured, it doesn't matter, because I don't like you, either."

She reached out with those elegantly manicured fingers and opened the truck's passenger door herself. Despite himself, Wade had to admit she managed the climb into the cab quite gracefully. Then she folded her hands over the useless little purse, crossed her long legs, tossed back her shoulder-length hair and commanded, "Well, get in. Since we have to, let's get this over with."

UNFORTUNATELY FOR Carla, the drive to Dunleavy Farm was not going to be comfortable in any way. As Wade started up the truck with a roar, she glanced at him covertly. She hated to admit it, but with the Stetson pulled low over his eyes, in profile he looked just like one of those ads for the Marlboro man. All he needed was a cigarette dangling from his lip to complete the picture.

At the thought, she frowned. She didn't like him at all; why was she suddenly finding him attractive?

She looked away again. She could feel her flushed cheeks, and that annoyed her even more. She was *never* attracted to swaggering, macho types. She preferred gentlemen, with style and manners, who knew how to treat a woman. This man had treated her as if she were just another horse he had to fetch and take back to the farm.

The thought reminded her of something he'd said, and she turned to him as they pulled out of the parking lot. Her voice as stiff as her backbone, she said, "I would appreciate it if you would take me directly to the farm. My grandmother is expecting me, and I'd prefer not to keep her waiting. After that, you can do... whatever it is you have to do."

Was that the tiniest twitch of his mouth she saw? She couldn't be sure, for in the next instant he was irritating her even more by saying, "I told you, Miss Dunleavy, what I have to do is pick up a horse on the way back. It won't take long. Mrs. D. knows that we'll be a little late."

"'Mrs. D.'? Am I to assume you refer to my grandmother by that vulgar appellation?"

This time he did more than smile; he laughed aloud. "You're kidding, right? Do you talk like that all the time, or are you just trying to impress me?"

Carla's lips tightened. The man was even more impossible than she'd thought. Regally, she said, "I haven't the faintest idea what you mean."

He laughed again. "Oh, I think you do."

"How dare you speak to me that way! Why, I've half a mind to report you to my grandmother."

"Only half? I'd have thought by now you'd have a full report ready."

"Are you being deliberately rude, or is this just a normal manifestation of your coarse personality?"

"Please, we don't know each other well enough to trade compliments."

"You're an impossible man. I'm surprised my grandmother puts up with you."

"I don't know what you mean. And, as much as I'd like to continue this scintillating conversation, we'll have to table it for a while. We're here."

Carla looked up as they turned off the highway onto another road. Ahead were open iron gates that led to a farm of sorts. Wade pulled up before a big barn and cut the engine. No one seemed to be around; even the little house perched disconsolately at the end of the driveway seemed to be empty.

"Is this Dunleavy Farm?" she exclaimed. She couldn't have come all the way from New York for this!

Wade laughed at her dismay, irritating her even more. "No, this isn't Dunleavy. We're at Four Oaks, where we're going to pick up that horse."

She felt like a fool. Gritting her teeth, she said, "All right, then. Do it so we can be on our way."

He reached for the door handle. "It'll go a lot faster if you help."

Slowly, she turned to him. "Are you out of your mind? I have no intention of helping. I'm going to sit right here until you've finished your chores. Then, I hope, we can press on. If you don't mind, I'd like to get there before the next millennium."

"Oh, I get it," he said maddeningly. "You're unfamiliar with horses. That's why you don't want to help, right?"

"I was practically riding horses before I could walk," she said witheringly. "But that isn't the point. Even if I wanted to help—which I wholeheartedly assure you, I don't—I'm not dressed for the task. I doubt you've noticed, but—"

"Oh, I noticed," he said.

For the first time, she had the pleasure of seeing a flicker of appreciation in his blue eyes as he looked at her legs. But her satisfaction didn't last long. He got out of the cab and suddenly, instead of her basking in his glance, she was observing how tight his weathered jeans fit and how muscular his arms were in his short-sleeved shirt and vest. When she found herself wondering if the rest of his body lived up to the promise of what she'd seen of it so far, she brought herself up short.

This is ridiculous, she thought. She never imagined such things—especially about a man she didn't even like. She must be overtired; that's all there was to it. The flight hadn't been that long, but maybe the altitude had affected her. It was the only explanation.

Why else would she even think of finding this... cowboy... attractive? In fact, he irritated her beyond measure.

He was further annoying her now, and she glared at him and demanded, "Well? Are you going to just stand there, or are you going to get the horse?"

Mockingly, he touched the brim of his hat. "I'm on my way, ma'am," he drawled. "Just sit tight and we'll be off in a tick."

The "tick" turned out to be a full thirty minutes. As horses sometimes do, the animal Wade led out of the barn—who had no doubt been in a horse van dozens of times—suddenly took it into his head that he wasn't going to go into this one. Wade and one of the Four Oaks grooms tried everything short of carrying the creature into the trailer, but after two broken halter ropes and a shredded lunge line, the horse was no closer to being inside. With an exasperated exclamation, Carla jerked open the door and got out.

"I thought you told me you knew horses," she said. "If that's so, why can't you get the bloody horse into the van?"

Perspiration was running down Wade's face. The hard-breathing horse was at the end of his lead, looking at them both warily. Wade gestured with the rope and said, "Be my guest."

She was indignant. "Surely, you don't think that I—"

"Hey, if you can do a better job than I can, go ahead."

Thus challenged, she looked around imperiously. "All right, if I must." She spied a buggy whip leaning up against a post and went to get it.

"Oh, no, you don't," Wade called. "I won't let you beat him into submission."

"Don't be absurd. I've never beaten a horse in my life."

And with that, she hitched up her skirt and went to stand behind the stubborn animal. To show she meant business, she cracked the whip without touching its hide. The horse jumped and looked around, showing the whites of its eyes.

"Now that I have your attention, you silly creature," Carla said to it in her best British accent, "please be a gentleman and climb into the box. That's right. There's a good fellow."

And without further ado, the horse turned and marched up the ramp into the trailer, where it stood contentedly, munching the hay in the rack. Unable to hide a smile of immense satisfaction, Carla passed the whip to Wade and dusted off her hands.

"There," she said. "It's all in knowing what to do. Now, perhaps we could make our way to Dunleavy Farm."

"Sure," Wade said easily. Rude, belligerent man, he didn't even seem impressed. "But since you know so much, I'd like to ask one thing."

"And what's that?"

He shut the van doors. "Maybe you'd like to drive?"

CHAPTER TWO

AFTER THE run-down condition of Four Oaks, Carla wasn't sure what to expect from Dunleavy Farm. But a short time later, when Wade turned off the main road onto one lined with beautiful old trees, she began to relax. Even if the farm wasn't much, she thought, the way to it was certainly beautiful.

On either side of the truck, the land undulated with gentle slopes dotted with majestic old oak trees. Here and there horses grazed inside the huge enclosures.

"It's not true then," Carla said, looking at the winter brown landscape. "Kentucky bluegrass *is* a myth."

"Oh, it's no myth. In February it's just too soon to see," Wade said. "But it's not as romantic as it sounds. The blue tinge is produced by water coming up through the lime in the soil."

"You *had* to add that last part, right?"

"Did I destroy an illusion?" he asked, grinning.

"Not at all," she said stuffily, not wanting to give him the satisfaction. "It's just that I've never been to Kentucky before. Actually, it reminds me of England."

"I thought I detected a British accent. Is England your home, then?"

Were they actually having a conversation? Carla looked at him suspiciously. His eyes were on the road, but she told herself that if he could make the effort, she could, too. Anything was better than the edgy silence they'd endured since leaving Four Oaks.

"It has been home base, on and off, for the past few years. But my mother and I have spent time in Spain, Italy . . . you name it."

"Is that all you and your mother do—travel to different parts of the world?"

She should have known that the civilized portion of the discussion wouldn't last long. "Well, I wouldn't say that."

"So, what would you say?"

She began to answer, then stopped. How *would* she describe her life-style? He hadn't said the words, but he'd implied that it was idle, inconsequential . . . almost dissolute. And, she thought suddenly, that's exactly what it was. She frowned. Where had that thought come from? She'd never looked at herself that way before and it irritated her that she was doing so now. Why did she care what this transplanted cowboy with the Stetson thought?

"Not that it's any of your concern, but my mother likes to travel. And so, for that matter, do I." Then she couldn't help herself. "You might try it sometime. It's said that travel broadens the mind."

JANIS FLORES 37

"That may be true. But I'm no jet-setter. Like all us country bumpkins, I stick close to home."

How had he managed to make her sound as if she was in the wrong? Irked once more, she sat back. *For heaven's sake,* she thought. She was at ease with dukes and earls and some of the richest, most powerful men in the world. Why was this man causing her such grief? She couldn't wait to arrive at her grandmother's farm and be rid of him.

Abruptly, she asked, "How far is it to Dunleavy Farm now?"

"You've been on the way in for the last few minutes."

Astonished, she glanced back the way they had come. They'd driven so far, she couldn't see the main road any longer. When she looked ahead, she could just catch sight of some buildings through the trees, and before she knew it, she murmured, "I had no idea it would be so... big."

"Oh, I wouldn't say it's big. It's about average size for these parts." Wade paused. "Nothing like those fancy English manor estates you're used to, probably."

He was making fun of her again. To put him in his place, she said, "As a matter of fact, I have lived on some of those 'fancy' family estates. It's fascinating, you know. Some of their histories can be traced back centuries."

"That's true of all of us, wouldn't you say?"

"No, I wouldn't. It's glaringly apparent at times that some people are more civilized than others."

"You're right about that. But that's just a matter of manners, don't you think?"

Was he implying that she'd been *rude?* She looked at him indignantly and saw a flash of a dimple in his lean cheek. "Are you laughing at me?"

"Me? I wasn't laughing."

"Oh, yes, you were. In fact, you have been ever since we met at the airport."

"Do you think so? I can't think why. You haven't said anything funny, have you?"

"No, I—" He was doing it again, she realized. Her lips tight, she didn't reply. But as she sat there, she decided that as soon as she had an opportunity, she was going to report his behavior to her grandmother. Not only was he mocking her, but he'd come to get her in a horse van. Was there anything more insulting than that? If her mother had been here, she would have died of a heart attack.

She didn't want to think about Meredith, who was still angry with her for coming. They'd argued again just this morning.

"So, you're really going," Meredith had said.

Since her suitcases were standing in the entryway, Carla didn't bother to reply. Normally, she got along well with her mother; they were so close it was like being with a sister. But at times like this, Carla felt suffocated.

"You're going to be sorry," Meredith had said when Carla didn't answer.

"It's only a short visit, Mother. I don't understand why you're so upset."

"I told you. You don't know what that woman's like."

"Why don't you tell me, then, instead of insinuating all these dire things? What do you expect the woman to do? Imprison me, hold me for ransom? Is Dunleavy Farm like the House of Usher, or something? Once the gates swing closed behind me, I'll be forever doomed?"

"There's no need to be sarcastic."

"And it's not necessary for you to be so difficult. You obviously have a problem with this. Why don't you tell me what it is so we can work it out?"

But Meredith wouldn't say more, and since the bellman arrived to take her bags, Carla didn't have time to pursue the issue. She tried to kiss her mother goodbye, but Meredith turned a cold profile to her, so she gave up.

"I'll call you as soon as I get there," she said.

"Suit yourself," Meredith said with a sullen shrug. "Maybe I'll be here. Maybe I won't."

Carla took a grip on her temper. "If you're not here, where will you be?"

"Do you really care?"

It was too much. She went to the door. "You know I care. But if you get tired of the States, you can go back to London by yourself. I might love Dunleavy

Farm so much I'll decide to stay on. If that happens, I wouldn't want to hold you up."

That got her mother's attention. Whirling around to her, Meredith exclaimed, "You're not thinking of *staying* there!"

"Who knows? Grandmother *is* offering me a race-horse. It could open up an entire range of possibilities, don't you think?"

"No, I do not. Carla, you aren't serious!"

She blew her mother a kiss. "I'll be in touch. Bye."

"Carla!"

But she had already shut the door behind her.

And now here she was, riding in this degrading farm vehicle, sitting next to a man she disliked more with each passing second. Her mother was right. She didn't belong here. She was about to order the cowboy to turn around and take her back to the airport but just then the main house came into view through the trees. One glance, and she changed her mind.

The house was a magnificent two-story Georgian, painted white with a sapphire blue roof and matching shutters. Tall white pillars guarded the front, and under the overhang of the roof, a veranda just made for sipping lemonade and mint juleps ran the entire length of the house. Scattered along the veranda were chairs and a table or two, and at the end, a porch swing.

A series of high arched windows marching along the front added to the elegant appearance, and there was even a porte cochere to one side, a remnant of opulent days gone by. A wide lawn sloped away from the house, interrupted by a formal flower bed where daffodils were just starting to appear. The sight was so striking that it took Carla a moment to realize that in full bloom, the arrangement would spell out... Dunleavy Farm.

"It's not what you expected, is it?"

She'd forgotten Wade. "No, it isn't. After that place we just left—"

"You can't judge Dunleavy by what you saw at Four Oaks," he said, his eyes on her face. He stared at her a moment longer, then broke away to look up at the house. "That's why we had to stop by. Mrs. D. will deny it if you ask, but that horse we picked up was one she bought as a favor to an old friend."

Wondering why his blue gaze was having such an effect on her, she managed to say, "I don't understand."

"It's a long story. The last thing we need around here is a gelding, but Four Oaks is going through some tough times." He paused. Then, as if speaking to himself, he added, "Not that we aren't."

Carla was sure she'd misheard. The house was so beautiful; the grounds so immaculately kept that it didn't seem possible there were financial problems here. She was just about to ask him to repeat his words, when she realized he was passing the front of the house. As he began to drive around to the road that led to the barns, she asked sharply, "Where are you going?"

"I'm taking the horse to the barn, why?"

"Why?" It was obvious to Carla that whatever rapport they'd begun to develop had gone out the window. "Haven't you forgotten something?" she asked brusquely.

He looked around. "What?"

Obviously subtlety was lost on this man. "Stop this vehicle at once," she commanded. Then she changed her mind. "No, better yet, back up. I will not traipse in from the barn. You will take me to the front door—"

His eyes narrowed. "Or what?"

She narrowed her eyes right back. "Or I will speak to my grandmother and make sure you're given the opportunity to seek other employment. Really! I think I have been more than patient with you, Mr. Petrie, but this is too much."

"You honestly think I've treated you badly?"

"Indeed I do!"

He seemed to consider it. Then he nodded and said, "You know, you're right. Let me just drop off the horse, and then I'll take you around to the front again so you can make your grand entrance."

Her grand entrance! Was that what he thought? She was so incensed that she said, "Look here, don't bother. It's clear that you've taken as big a dislike to me as I have to you, so let's part company right now. You might not care, but I'm anxious to see my grand-mother—"

She reached for the door handle. Before she knew what was happening, his hand shot out and he grabbed her arm. She looked at him in angry astonishment.

"What are you doing? Take your hand off me!"

"Not until we get a few things straight," he said. His eyes under his hat brim blazed bright blue. Without warning, the air in the cab seemed stifling; she could hardly breathe. Nor could she look away from him. She hadn't realized he was so good-looking. Or maybe, she thought, he was so obnoxious that she hadn't wanted to admit that she'd noticed. Whatever the reason, she couldn't seem to look away from him, no matter how hard she tried.

"What things?" she said.

As though he suddenly realized he was touching her, he snatched his hand away. But his eyes were still angry when he said, "I care very much about Mrs. D. I don't want her hurt."

"Hurt! Exactly what are you implying?"

"I'm not implying anything. I'm saying it straight out. If you came to play games with an old woman, you can just turn around and go back where you belong right now."

"How dare you speak to me that way! Why—"

"Oh, don't come off all hoity-toity with me, Miss Dunleavy. I know all about you."

She couldn't believe this. "You don't know me!"

"Indeed I do." His glance was like a sapphire drill, boring into her. "And I'm warning you—"

"*Warning* me!" She looked at him as though he'd lost his mind. His expression indicated that he was wondering the same thing. But still, he persisted.

"I mean it," he said. "I owe Mrs. D. a lot, and I'll do anything to protect her."

"*Really!* Who are you to say such things to me?"

"I'm nobody, nobody at all. But still, I'm telling you—"

"And I'm telling you!" she said, her voice low and furious, "I don't know what your game is, and I don't care. But I will *not* have you speak to me in this manner! Octavia Dunleavy is my grandmother. I would never do anything to hurt her!"

He gazed at her a moment; she stared back. They were both breathing hard. It was a toss-up which of them was more furious. She didn't understand why he was acting this way, or why he mistrusted her without even knowing her, but she wasn't going to let him get away with it. Warning her! she thought. How dare he!

It occurred to her that they couldn't go on trying to stare each other down. Using the excuse of tugging her suit jacket into place, she broke eye contact. Then, in her iciest tone, she said, "Are you going to get the door, or shall I just struggle on my own, like I did before?"

He looked as if he wanted to tell her to go to hell. Instead, he said, "I'll get it."

Suiting action to words, he got out of the truck and came around to the passenger side. As he opened her door, he gave an elaborate, mocking bow that made her clench her teeth. She couldn't wait to be rid of this man, she fumed. How her grandmother could bear to have him around, she didn't know. But if she had her way, he'd soon be out the door and on his way.

"Watch your step," he said.

Carla was too infuriated to heed the warning. Her head high, she was getting out, when her spindly high heel slipped on the metal runner. Before she could catch herself, she was pitching forward with a startled, "Oh!"

She caught herself just as he reached for her. *Oh no you don't!* she thought. He wasn't going to touch her...ever.

But at that moment, their faces were so close, she could see exactly how blue black his eyes were. Involuntarily, her glance dropped to his mouth, and for a few insane seconds, she wondered what it would be like to feel his lips on hers.

She jerked back. Was she completely mad? She must be, she told herself, or she would have demanded that he move out of the way at once. But, as though they were both caught by this strange moment, he continued to stand there, and suddenly his expression changed. Under the brim of his hat, the black flecks in his eyes seemed to fan out and she suddenly knew that he wanted to kiss her. What would she do if he did?

Kiss him back, a little voice inside her head said.

She was appalled. What was she thinking? She hardly knew this man, and what she did know of him, she detested. She commanded herself to order him aside, but she couldn't make her voice work. The seconds ticked past breathlessly, and still he stood there. To Carla's horror, it seemed they were being pulled toward each other. As though it were happening to someone else, her pulse started to pound, and she felt light-headed. What was happening to her? She had never been so strongly affected by any man, and he wasn't even touching her.

What if he suddenly wrapped those muscular arms around her and pulled her into him, what then? Would she scream, resist, demand that he release her? Dazed, she knew that she wouldn't do anything. She almost wanted him to do it. The suspense was killing her.

"Carla! Carla, is that you? Oh my, I'm so glad to see you. It's been such a long, long time!"

With the sound of another voice, the spell—or whatever it had been—was broken. Relieved, able to breathe again, Carla turned and saw a tiny woman coming toward her. By the time she looked back at Wade, whatever she'd seen or sensed or felt in him was gone. He stood aside so she could get down from the step, and it was as though nothing had happened.

Carla realized that even though aeons seemed to have passed in that trancelike state, only seconds had gone by. She was still trying to get her bearings, when he said, "I should have warned you about that step."

She had herself under control now. "I don't know why," she retorted. "You didn't seem to care before."

His eyes glimmered. "That was before Mrs. D. came out," he said, and turned to the little woman who was coming up to them. Like a completely different man, he said cheerfully, "Here she is, Mrs. D. Safe and sound, just like you asked."

After what her mother had said—or rather, Carla thought, what she *hadn't* said—she'd expected her grandmother to be an imposing Amazon of a woman. The sight of this little birdlike creature caught her completely off guard.

Octavia Whitworth Dunleavy used a cane, but she seemed determined to play down her disability. Her white hair was carefully waved, her silk dress a vivid pink. Despite her size, the woman had real presence.

"Oh, even if I hadn't known it was you, I would have recognized you anywhere," Octavia said excitedly. "Oh, Carla, you look exactly like your mother. Welcome to Dunleavy Farm, my dear. I'm so glad you accepted my invitation!"

Carla had tried to plan what she would say to this grandmother who had ignored her existence all these years, but as she gazed down at the unmistakable happiness in Octavia's lined face, all her clever remarks disappeared from her mind. She couldn't be sarcastic and snide when the woman was so obviously glad to see her. It would be rude in the extreme.

"Thank you," she said. "It was...kind of you to invite me."

Was that the merest snicker she heard behind her? She glanced at Wade, but he was busy examining something on the truck. Her lips tightening, she turned to Octavia just as her grandmother said, "We have so much to talk about, my dear. Please, come in. Do you have any luggage?"

This time Wade's snicker was unmistakable. "She certainly does," he said.

Carla shot him another look, but Octavia seemed oblivious to the tension between them. "Oh, good," she said. "I hope that means you're prepared to stay a while."

Carla was no longer certain what she was prepared for. "I don't know yet," she said.

Wade began taking the heavy suitcases from the truck bed. "I do," he grunted. "From the looks of these, Mrs. D., your granddaughter is going to stay a lifetime, at least."

Wondering why Octavia permitted this familiarity, Carla said sharply, "Perhaps you could call someone to help you, Mr. Petrie. I certainly wouldn't want you to tax your strength."

"Wade's time is much too valuable for him to be hauling suitcases around," Octavia said blithely. "In fact, I hated to ask him to meet your flight, but my doctor—the old fogy—forbids me to drive now so I had no choice. But it worked out just fine, since Wade had to go to Louisville, anyway. I hope you didn't mind being met in the van."

Carla didn't dare look at Wade when she said, "No, I didn't mind at all." Then, because she was sure she heard him snickering again, she added, "I'm surprised that he was able to take time out of his busy schedule just for me."

"It was no trouble," the maddening man said. "After all, I did have to fetch that horse. You were on the way...sort of."

"Yes, so you said," Carla reminded him pointedly.

"Hey, no thanks are necessary. I was glad to do it for Mrs. D."

"And I appreciate it, dear," Octavia said to Wade. To Carla, she suggested, "Let's go inside. I asked Teresa to make us a lovely tea in your honor, Carla. She does make the most delicious scones I've ever tasted. Doesn't she, Wade?"

"That she does, Mrs. D."

Carla couldn't be sure, but was that a twinkle she saw in his eyes? She didn't care, she thought. She just wanted him to go away.

But to her dismay, Octavia included him. "Are you coming, Wade?"

Wade carefully avoided looking at Carla, but she was certain she saw him smirk. "Thanks, anyway, Mrs. D., but I've still got things to do. Maybe another time."

"All right. But you will set aside a few minutes later to show Carla the farm, won't you? I know it's not the best time of year, but I thought you might go for a ride." She turned to Carla. "You do ride, don't you?"

The last thing Carla wanted was to spend any more time with Wade Petrie. "Well, yes, but...but it's been a long—"

She'd been about to say that it had been a long trip, a long day... too long in this cowboy's company. But before she could make it politely clear that she wanted nothing more to do with this impossible man, he said innocently, "I can't believe you've forgotten how, Miss Dunleavy. Didn't you tell me earlier that you were riding before you could walk?"

She should have known that he'd find a way to turn her words against her. Glaring at him, she said, "I did say that. What I was *about* to say was that it's been a long day—"

"Oh, but not for you, surely," he said. "For your crowd, isn't the day just getting started?"

"What do you mean by 'my crowd'?"

They had forgotten all about Octavia Dunleavy.

"I didn't mean anything," he said. "I was talking about your... er... social set." He paused. "That *is* what you do, isn't it? Socialize?"

"As a matter of fact—"

Octavia intervened. "We can talk about riding later, can't we? In the meantime, why don't you and I go into the house, Carla. I'll have Samson bring in your bags, and we can sit and get acquainted."

"If you'll excuse me, Mrs. D.?" Wade said as if he were the politest, most thoughtful man in the world.

Octavia patted his arm fondly. "Of course. But check in later, will you, please? I also want to know how the new gelding settles in."

"Will do." He touched two fingers to his hat brim. "Nice meeting you, Miss Dunleavy."

Carla didn't get a chance to respond. Wade strolled off without a backward glance before she could reply, and she was glaring at his departing back when Octavia said brightly, "Well, my dear, shall we?"

...Just what I need—two vacant...'' Well, I'm not
about to sit around a place that feels as cold as
this one were ...in ...aiting look ...
Wrap up in this ...'' Well, anyway, here we're...

CHAPTER THREE

"I'M SO GLAD you came," Octavia said when she and
Carla were inside. "I wasn't sure you would, you
know. I couldn't be certain how much your mother
told you about me."

Carla knew there was no way to soften the blow. She
wasn't sure she wanted to. "My mother never mentioned you," she said. "I didn't even know I had a
grandmother until I got your letter."

Octavia sighed. "I should have guessed. Meredith
always was stubborn and unforgiving."

"It seems to be a family characteristic."

Octavia looked startled, then she nodded reluctantly. "Yes, I guess it does."

"Would you like to tell me what happened?"

"It was so long ago—years."

"Did it have anything to do with me?"

"No, you mustn't think that!"

Carla hadn't meant to get into this so soon, but it
was just as well. She'd thought about it on the flight
down and had reached some unsatisfactory conclu-
sions. "I don't know what to think. As I said, Mother
never mentioned you. Not only that, she always said

that my real father died soon after I was born. Is that a lie, too?"

Octavia paused a fraction too long. "No. I have no reason to believe that your mother's not telling the truth."

"Why did my mother leave?"

"Oh, my dear," Octavia said with another sigh. "If she hasn't told you, I'm not sure I should. I've always hoped that one day Meredith and I would settle things. I haven't abandoned that dream. But until then, I hope you'll let me do this in my own way and my own time. Will you grant me that?"

Carla wasn't sure she had to grant this old woman anything. But she said, "I don't seem to have any choice. And maybe you're right. It's none of my business."

"I didn't mean that." Octavia looked genuinely distressed. "It's just that...things are difficult. I know I've made mistakes in the past, but I'd like to undo some of them if I can. Won't you give me a chance?"

Carla wanted to say that it was too late, that Octavia should have begun the process long ago—*years* ago, in fact. But she couldn't say it. Now that she was actually here, things didn't seem so clear. Maybe, she thought suddenly, with families, things never were.

"I'm here, aren't I?" she said, emotions roiling. "I guess that means something."

"I guess it does," Octavia said with a shaky smile. "Thank you, my dear. You won't regret it."

Carla wanted to be sure they both knew where they stood. "I'm not making any promises," she said. "So I don't want you to think that everything is all right. At the moment, I'm not sure what I think."

"Fair enough. Now, shall we have our tea?"

At this point, Carla could have used something stronger than tea. Already this visit was shaping up to be more uncomfortable than she'd thought possible. But she couldn't leave now; it would look as if she was running away. So she followed her grandmother into the front room, where a middle-aged black woman, introduced as Teresa, was setting out a beautiful old tea service on a table in front of the couch. As Octavia inspected the tea things, Carla looked around.

The room was filled with lovely and well-kept antiques in a pleasing mixture of periods. The only family portrait was a painting over the fireplace of a stern-looking man posed stiffly with his hand on a chair. Photographs and paintings of famous racehorses hung on the cream-colored walls, and there were shelves of trophies. A glass case at one end of the room caught Carla's attention and she went over to it. Inside was a set of racing silks in royal blue and gold. Arranged beside those was a diminutive, postage-stamp-size saddle and a saddlecloth marked with the number eight.

Octavia saw Carla admiring the display. "I see you've found my treasure," she said proudly.

"What is it?"

Octavia joined her at the case. Her hand on the glass, she said, "This is the blouse our jockey wore, and the saddle he rode in all three races, when Done Roamin' won the Triple Crown."

"Done Roamin'?"

"The farm's most famous horse," Octavia told you, her eyes misting. "My husband always said that one day we would produce a Triple Crown winner, and we did. Over the years, we've sent eight runners to the Derby who had the potential to go the distance, but Done Roamin' was the one who accomplished it."

Carla knew about racing's most famous prize. The three races that formed the Triple Crown—the Kentucky Derby, the Preakness Stakes and the Belmont Stakes—were the greatest test for three-year-old Thoroughbreds that the American sport of horse racing had devised. The horses who made it to those gates were racing's elite, second to none in terms of heart, courage and sheer ability. The proof of that was the fact that, since its inception almost a hundred years before, only eleven horses had succeeded in capturing the title.

And Done Roamin' was one of them, Carla thought. She was impressed.

"I remember the day Done Roamin' was born," Octavia said nostalgically. "He was such a spindly little colt, all head and legs. His mother had been sick that winter, and several times we thought she might slip the foal. I stayed with her every night that last month before he was born. The foal was going to be the last of—''

Abruptly, Octavia stopped. Embarrassed, she said, ''But you don't want to hear the ramblings of a silly old woman, do you?''

''Yes, I do.'' To her own surprise, Carla realized she meant it. ''Please, go on. What about when Done Roamin' was born?''

They went to the couch, and as Octavia poured them both a cup of tea, she continued her story.

''The foal's grand-sire was a stallion named Donnagal,'' Octavia said, offering Carla a plate of buttery scones. Surprised at herself once more, Carla took one. Normally, she avoided pastries and biscuits. But today she didn't care. She hadn't eaten breakfast, and she was starving.

''My husband, Alvah, was so proud of Donnagal,'' Octavia went on, after she had helped herself, too. ''And the mares we bred to Donnagal cost the earth. I was furious at the expense, but I think Alvah would have sold us all before he let those mares go to someone else. He was determined to breed a Triple Crown winner, but he died before Done Roamin' was born.''

Carla was still sitting there holding the scone she'd taken. She put it down on her plate. ''He must have been quite a foal.''

''He was, all right'' Octavia said. Her eyes began to sparkle. ''I knew Done Roamin' would do us all proud, and he did.'' She paused again. ''I only wish

Alvah had lived to see Done Roamin'. But he died long before. He seemed to lose interest after Donnagal went. The romantic part of me wants to think that Alvah died of a broken heart.'' She grimaced. ''But my head knows better. It was cancer, plain and simple. It went too far because he never would take care of himself.''

''I'm sorry,'' Carla said.

''So was I,'' Octavia said sadly. ''But no one could ever tell Alvah Dunleavy what to do.'' She gestured at the portrait over the mantel. ''That's Alvah. I've always disliked that portrait because he looks so stiff and uncomfortable. He wasn't like that at all.''

Carla looked again at the portrait. It was hard to believe, she thought, but that man had been her...grandfather. Could she see a family resemblance between them, or was it her imagination?

As if she realized she had put a damper on the conversation, Octavia freshened their tea and began talking about her beloved colt again.

''I knew even when he was a baby that Done Roamin' would do us all proud.''

''What happened to him?'' Carla asked. ''Is he still alive?''

Octavia laughed merrily. ''Oh my, yes! He's twenty years old now, but still full of life, even though his Triple Crown days are long behind him. He's in his paddock waiting to meet you.''

Carla, who had always loved horses, didn't find her grandmother's remark strange; she knew people who would have kept their horses inside the house if the law allowed it. Octavia's laughter was infectious, and when she found herself smiling, too, she quickly took a sip of tea.

"Do have another scone," Octavia said, gesturing toward the plate. "Teresa is justifiably proud of her baked goods, and her feelings will be hurt if we don't finish every crumb."

"I shouldn't," Carla said, but she found herself reaching for another. Sure it was either nerves or the country air, she excused herself by saying, "Well, maybe just this once."

"More tea?"

She held out her cup. "Just half, please. It's excellent."

"I'm so glad you like it. I wanted you to feel comfortable here." Octavia's voice softened. "I'd like you to regard Dunleavy Farm as your home."

Home. The word sounded strange to Carla. She had never really had a home. Her life had been a succession of hotel rooms and guest houses and rented villas, interspersed with brief stays with her mother and whoever happened to be Meredith's current beau. When she was younger, she had yearned for the kind of stability a home seemed to provide, but whenever she asked why they didn't settle down permanently, Meredith would give her a variation of the same reply.

"But darling," her mother would say gaily, "you don't want to be like everyone else, do you? Such ordinary people, with their boring little chores. We're too interesting for that. We need excitement and adventure in our lives!''

So Carla had grown up accepting that a peripatetic life-style was the thing to have, and as a result she'd never settled anywhere long enough to accomplish anything. Oh, she had dabbled in things—buyer for an art gallery, decorating apartments and town houses for friends, managing a boutique in London, straightening out her stepfather's books for his lumber business because she was a natural at figures. But nothing had ever kept her interest, and she'd kept moving on.

Jill-of-all-trades, she thought, *mistress of none.*

She knew that if she had wanted stability in her life, a home of her own, a way to settle down, she could have had it. She'd had numerous chances to get married over the years, but with the exception of one near-miss, the closest she'd come to the altar was as a bridesmaid for different friends.

And it wasn't as though she couldn't afford a home of her own. She had never known her father, but her mother's second husband, Phillip, had treated her like his own child. Like her father, Phillip had died too soon, but not before he'd set up a substantial trust fund for her. Thanks to him, she had no financial worries. She was free to roam the world as she chose.

Abruptly, an image of Wade Petrie's face flashed into her mind, and she frowned. Now, why had she thought of him? It didn't matter if he disapproved of her nomad existence. She didn't give a fig about his opinion.

But it rankled, anyway. He'd made her life-style sound so empty and shallow, and she didn't like it.

"Are you finished with your tea?" Octavia asked. She patted the cane she had placed by her side. "I can't walk as far or as fast as I once could, but I'm up to giving you a limited tour, if you'd like."

Relieved to dismiss this unwelcome introspection, Carla started to say, "I'd like that very much, Grand..." Her words trailed off. "I'm not sure what to call you. Would you prefer Mrs. Dunleavy? Or, Octavia, perhaps?"

"I'd prefer Grandmother," Octavia said gently. "But only if you're comfortable with it."

"Grandmother," Carla repeated. It felt strange on her tongue, but it would do for now. "All right, if you like."

"I would. Now, my dear, if you will help me get up, I'd appreciate it. I'm fine once I'm on my feet. It's getting out of chairs, which seem to get lower as I get older, that gives me fits."

Carla offered her assistance. Once they were outside, Octavia asked, "What would you like to see first?"

With the farm spread out before her, Carla didn't know what to choose. A gazebo beckoned invitingly to her right, and ahead was the long driveway, bordered by the two stately lines of ancient trees whose branches met over the center in an arch. On either side of that were the pastures, and when she saw the horses, she knew what she wanted to see the most.

"Which paddock belongs to Done Roamin'?" she asked.

She knew she'd made the right choice when Octavia looked pleased. "Right this way," she said. She patted her pocket. "I've even got a carrot for you to give him."

"Are you always prepared?"

"For Done Roamin', I am. I know it sounds silly, but he's a dear friend to me."

"That doesn't silly at all. I've always been fond of horses, myself."

"Of course you have. You're a Dunleavy, aren't you? I would have been surprised if you'd have said anything else."

Carla paused, startled. It was true that she'd liked horses from the time she was old enough to sit astride a saddle, her short legs sticking out on either side of a fat little pony. But she had never thought of it being in her blood... until now. The notion unsettled her again, and she was frowning as she hurried after Octavia.

As they walked toward the paddock area, Octavia pointed out the big barns and the straight-as-a-die fences. All the roofs of the outbuildings were blue, the trim painted gold to match the Dunleavy racing colors. It was all impressive, but the centerpiece mounted in front of the main barn took Carla's breath away. It was a statue of a running Thoroughbred.

"What a lovely piece of work!"

"I thought you'd like it," Octavia said. "I had it designed right after Done Roamin' won the Belmont. It's taken from a picture of the race, when he was ten lengths in front, coming to the wire."

Carla circled the statue, which was perfectly proportioned from every angle. Although made of bronze, it was so lifelike that one could almost hear the thunder of hoofbeats, and the wind whistling in the streaming mane and tail.

"It's one of the most glorious things I've ever seen," she marveled. "I almost expect to see him breathe."

Just then, from somewhere to the right, came the ringing sound of a shrill whinny. Octavia heard it and laughed.

"And there's the old man himself," she said, "coming to greet you, just like I promised."

Carla turned toward the source of that proud, clarionlike call. But whatever she'd been about to say died unspoken when she saw the horse that was galloping...no, she thought with a pang, *lurching,* toward her.

Was this Done Roamin', the horse that had won the Triple Crown, the same stallion that was depicted in the magnificent statue behind her? If it was, the reality was so at odds with the ideal that Carla, who never cried, felt tears stinging her eyes. *Dear God,* she thought. What had happened to him? He came toward her in a shambling gait of his own design, half trot, half stumbling walk.

But as she watched him make his way down the hall, Carla realized that he was one of the most beautiful horses she had ever seen. His bay coat looked burnished in the sun; his long mane and tail looked like black silk in the breeze his movement created. But it was his *presence* that made him stand out. It was as though he knew that he was still a champion.

He came to the fence and dipped his head regally, like a king granting an audience.

Carla let her grandmother go on ahead while she composed herself. Then, willing her voice not to betray her, she said, "He's... magnificent."

Octavia reached up to give the stallion's forelock an affectionate tug. "He is, isn't he?" she murmured. As though she sensed that Carla needed time to pull herself together, she didn't look back, but said, "Why don't you come here and say hello?"

Embarrassed that Octavia had sensed her emotion, Carla joined her at the fence. "I'm sorry. I didn't mean to—"

"That's all right," Octavia said. "Lord knows, I've cried enough times myself since it happened. It's such a shame."

"What happened?" Carla asked, before she thought. Quickly, she said, "I'm sorry. Perhaps I shouldn't pry."

"No, it's all right. It's just that there's not much to tell." Octavia gave the horse a pat. "It happened about three years ago, not long after Wade came to work for me. We were right in the midst of a busy breeding season, and one morning, Wade came out to the barn and... and..." Her voice shook, but she collected herself and went on. "And found him. As you can see, his leg was broken, right into the hock. We never knew what caused it. The best we can figure out is that he cast himself somehow, and in a panic at not being able to get up, struggled so hard he just... broke it."

Carla couldn't speak. Vivid pictures of the nightmare scene flashed into her mind and she could imagine the horror of finding a horse—especially a horse like Done Roamin'—in that condition.

"There was never any question in my mind that I would do everything I could to save him," Octavia went on. "As long as he wouldn't suffer needlessly. I didn't care if I had to mortgage the entire farm. I wasn't going to lose Done Roamin', not like that. He deserved better."

"And you gave it to him," Carla said.

"I didn't do anything," Octavia told her. "He was the one who went through the operations. He was the one who had to be in a sling for nearly six months." She shook her head. "If it hadn't been for Wade..."

"Am I interrupting anything?" asked a voice that Carla recognized.

When they turned, Wade was walking up behind them, casually holding a halter and lead rope. Octavia smiled when she saw him and said, "Your ears must be burning, Wade. I was just telling Carla that I don't know what I would have done without you when Done Roamin' had his accident.''

''I didn't do anything anyone else wouldn't have done.''

''That's not true, and you know it,'' Octavia said. To Carla, she said, ''The horse was in the clinic for six months, and Wade spent every night there with him, to make sure he was as comfortable as possible. We were only able to bring him home because Wade fixed up a special stall at the farm just like the one they had at the clinic. It had a hoist for the sling and everything.''

''A man of many talents,'' Carla murmured without looking at Wade. ''Who would have thought it?''

He didn't rise to the bait. ''I just thought Done Roamin' would be better off at home. And I knew for sure that Mrs. D. would be happier if the horse was here.''

''He was right about that,'' Octavia said fervently. She gave the great stallion another pat. ''It took just about everything we had in reserve, but it was worth it, wasn't it, old man?''

As though the horse understood, Done Roamin' let out another whinny. Carla had to smile when she heard answering calls from all over the farm. ''It sounds like everyone agrees,'' she said.

Octavia laughed in response before saying to Wade, ''Did you come to take Carla on that riding tour?''

Instantly, Carla tensed. It seemed Wade did, too. As though on cue, they spoke at the same time.

"Oh, I can't—"

"Oh, I don't think I—"

"It won't take that long," Octavia said, blithely dismissing all objections. "It will be good for both of you. Wade, don't forget to take her up by the stream. I haven't been there in ages, but as I remember, it's beautiful this time of year with the wild daffodils just showing up."

Wade tried one last time. "Mrs. D.—"

As though she hadn't heard, Octavia flapped her hand at them. "You two have a nice time now. Carla, I'll see you at dinner."

What could she say? "Yes, Grandmother," Carla said, and glared at Wade.

THIRTY MINUTES LATER, Carla was riding a big gray gelding up the hill behind the main barn. She didn't know how Wade felt, but she was so uncomfortable at this enforced togetherness that she finally said, "You didn't have to do this, you know. I could have come by myself."

Wade checked the horse he had saddled. It was a high-spirited chestnut, a colt that was so full of himself that a lesser rider would have had difficulty staying aboard. Carla had already noted that Wade rode as if his jeans were glued to the saddle. *So the man knows how to ride,* she thought. It didn't change how she felt about him.

"I had to take this colt out for a little exercise, anyway," Wade said. "It didn't make any difference to me if you wanted to tag along."

Tag along? "We both know that if my grandmother hadn't insisted, I never would have agreed to come."

"So we were both in a bind."

She'd had enough of this man. "In that case, Mr. Petrie, please feel free to ride on ahead. The farm isn't so big that I can't find my way back by myself."

"No, we can't do that. Mrs. D. would skin me alive if she found out I left you to fend for yourself."

"I can take care of myself."

"I'm sure you can. But orders are orders."

"I certainly won't tell if you don't."

"Tempting, but no. Take the path to the left here, if you don't mind. Mrs. D. wanted me to show you the stream, and it's through these trees."

Carla wanted to wheel her horse around and go back the way she had come. She wasn't worried about her ability to handle the gray she had chosen. But her pride wouldn't allow her to give in first. If he could endure this mandated outing, she thought with gritted teeth, so could she. She turned the horse to the left.

A few minutes of silence later, Carla knew that if she hadn't been so tense, she would have enjoyed the ride. They'd been climbing since leaving the barn area, and when she looked back, the entire farm was spread out below them. From this distance, the house and barns looked almost minuscule, the horses in their pastures as small as toys. Her eyes found Done Roamin's paddock, and without realizing it, her expression turned sad.

"What's the matter?" Wade asked, twisting in his saddle when she stopped.

"I was thinking about Done Roamin'."

He rode back to her. As he looked down at the stallion's enclosure, he said, "Sometimes I wonder if we did the right thing saving that horse."

"If you had doubts, why did you do it?"

"*I* didn't do it. Mrs. D. did."

"But my grandmother said that you spent every night with him at the clinic. You built a special stall for him at the farm so he could come home."

Under his hat brim, his glance met hers. He seemed about to say something, but then, his expression changed. Their brief truce vanished, and he said with that irritating casualness, "It was no big deal. I was paid to do it."

Before she could reply, he started off down the track again. She looked after him for a few moments, wondering why he seemed so determined to make her dislike him. Despite what he'd said just now, she didn't believe for a minute that he'd devoted so much time to Done Roamin's recovery simply because he'd been paid to do it.

Or was it that she didn't *want* to believe it? It was a sobering thought.

Her expression grim, she turned her horse and went after him. When she caught up, he said, "You ride well. That horse can be a handful."

Surprised by the unexpected compliment, she said, "I should know what I'm doing in a saddle. I've had enough lessons. Whenever mother wanted to get rid of me so she could spend time with another of her man friends, she'd hire a riding instructor. I think I've spent half my life on horses."

"I see."

Already regretting that she'd told him something so personal, she said, "You ride well yourself."

"My experience comes from growing up on a ranch. We didn't have fancy riding lessons, just broncs that had to be bucked out every morning before we went out to ride fence and herd cattle."

"Isn't it strange, then, that you ended up here, in Kentucky."

"I could say the same thing about you. This little backwoods place doesn't seem your style."

She looked at him sharply. "You don't know anything about me."

"Only that your grandmother invited you here, and you came. That's all."

"You obviously have a problem with that," she said stiffly.

He shrugged. "I've known Mrs. D. long enough to know that what she wants, she gets."

"I've no intention of discussing my grandmother with you," Carla said haughtily, and then proceeded to do just that. "I have noticed, however, that for reasons I simply cannot fathom, she seems fond of you."

"Does that bother you?"

"I don't feel one way or another about it. I was merely making a comment."

"It sounded more like a criticism to me."

"Really? Then perhaps it was."

"Are you always so touchy?"

"Are you always so offensive?" she countered.

"Always. It's a protective mechanism."

She looked at him scornfully. "And what do you think you need protecting from?"

"Women like you."

"You certainly have an inflated opinion of yourself!"

"On the contrary. For instance, I know exactly where I stand with you."

"Oh, really? And just where is that, might I ask?"

"You don't like me very much, do you?"

"I really couldn't say," she sniffed, "since I haven't given it a moment's thought."

"Oh, come on. I can't believe that."

"You really are insufferable!"

"Yeah, but curious. Go on. Tell me."

"All right, if I have to give an opinion, I'd say that you're one of the most arrogant, patronizing, supercilious men I've ever had the misfortune to meet. Furthermore, I can't imagine why my grandmother puts up with your insolence. Fortunately for both of us, I don't intend to stay long. But while I am here, the farm certainly seems to be big enough for us to avoid each other."

She'd made him angry, she was happy to see. His jaw tightened as he said, "I'll see that it is."

"Good. In that case, I'm going back now. You don't need to accompany me. I might be an idle, superficial socialite, but I think I can find the way myself."

"Wait a minute."

She had already started to turn her horse. "What?"

"You had your say, now I'll have mine."

She raked him up and down with a glance. "I don't think we have anything more to discuss."

"Don't try to pull the princess act with me, because it won't work. I told you, I know your kind."

"And I know yours!" she said furiously. "Goodbye, Mr. Petrie. I devoutly hope we don't meet again!"

She put her heel so sharply into her mount's side that the horse leaped forward. As quick as the movement was, Wade was even faster. Without a moment's hesitation, he reached down and grabbed her bridle, jerking the startled horse to such a sudden halt that Carla almost lost her balance. Enraged, she looked at him.

"What the *hell* do you think you're doing?"

"Trying to stop you from killing yourself."

"What? Get out of my way!"

"Not until you calm down!"

"Give me my reins," she said tightly. "Or I'll—"

"What? Slash me with your riding crop? Now, that would be a little melodramatic, don't you think?"

"You are intolerable!"

"And you're too sly for your own good. Just what are you doing here, *Miss* Dunleavy? Trying to ingratiate yourself with an old woman who desperately wants a family? Because if that's your game—"

"How dare you!" she cried. "You have no right to say such things to me! No matter *what* you think of yourself, you're just a—"

She'd been about to say hired hand, but just then she heard the sound of hoofbeats rapidly approaching. Quickly, she turned in the saddle. Coming up the hill was one of the most beautiful horses she had ever seen. He was the same deep bay color as Done Roamin', but he was much younger. Even so, he had the same air about him, the same... presence. Transfixed, she watched as the colt galloped straight up to the fence and let out a high, challenging whinny, like Done Roamin' had done.

At the sight, she momentarily forgot her quarrel with Wade. "Good lord," she said. "Who's that?"

"That," Wade said tightly, "is Done Driftin'. He's the colt your grandmother wants to give you."

Carla heard something in Wade's voice and tore her glance away from the horse to look at him. "I...didn't dream—"

"Yeah, well, now you know." Wade narrowed his eyes. "Don't hurt her," he said. "Because I swear to God, if you do, I'll make you sorry."

Before Carla could reply, he sent his horse forward. Shocked by the threat, Carla watched him until he disappeared over the rise. Gradually, she became aware of the colt again. Done Driftin' was prancing back and forth along the fence, showing off for her, and as she stared at this wondrous creature, she forgot Wade and felt something stir inside her.

The stallion Done Roamin' was beautiful, she thought. There was no other horse like him in the world. But this colt... this was the horse of dreams.

Just then, Done Driftin' stopped and looked directly at her. Before her dazzled eyes, he lifted his beautiful head and let out another ringing challenge.

Or was it a greeting?

It didn't matter which it was. She still had her doubts about this visit; she disliked Wade Petrie more with every word they exchanged. She didn't know how she felt about Octavia Dunleavy, or what she thought of Dunleavy Farm. But as she watched Done Driftin' beginning to run the fence again, she was sure of one thing.

She couldn't leave now.

CHAPTER FOUR

A WEEK AFTER Carla arrived at Dunleavy Farm, Wade was in his office at the main barn going over the books for the month. When he realized he'd added the same set of figures three times with as many different results, he switched off the calculator and sat back with a scowl.

This is ridiculous, he told himself. Where was his mind? He glanced out the window. *Up at the big house, that's where.* Disgusted and restless, he tossed his pen aside and got up to stretch. He had a lot of room to do it, for the office was almost Spartan in decor. He didn't like clutter, and his only luxury was the comfortable chair. Shelves behind the desk held stud books, breeding charts and neatly stacked horse-related magazines and books. Not much to indicate a lifetime spent working with horses, he thought suddenly.

The awards he'd won, along with numerous "win" pictures that had once filled an entire wall at his stable in California, were piled in one of the closets in his bedroom at the barn manager's house, where he lived now. He'd given some excuse when Mrs. D. had asked him once why he didn't put up the pictures, but the truth was that he hadn't wanted any reminders of the past. And, after what he'd done, he had no right to display awards.

When he came to Dunleavy Farm three years ago, he'd been about as low as he could go. The days when he'd owned his own training stable were gone—vanished in a cloud of conflict and foolishness that had resulted in the threat of a lawsuit. A lawsuit he'd avoided by the skin of his teeth. Mrs. D. had taken a chance on him when she'd hired him to manage her barns, and because he'd been starting over—and having to prove himself all over again—he hadn't wanted any reminders of past glories to haunt him.

He didn't want to dwell on the past. Pouring another cup of coffee from the machine near the desk, he went to the window, blowing on the hot brew. Out of nowhere, a picture of Carla Dunleavy floated before his eyes. He hardly knew her, but it seemed that ever since she'd arrived, he couldn't get her out of his mind.

He shook his head. He'd seen a lot of people ride in his time, but he'd never seen anyone ride a horse with as much skill and finesse as she did. He had deliberately saddled a difficult horse for her the day they'd been forced to go riding together. He'd known that the gray wouldn't hurt her, but he'd hoped it might put her in her place.

Instead, he thought, Carla had put him in his. She'd not only controlled the animal with ease, but she'd looked damned beautiful doing it. He didn't care how many lessons she'd had in her youth; no amount of training could instill that natural grace. Whenever he thought of her astride that gray, he felt something stir inside him that he didn't like.

He turned away from the window. He had to stop thinking about Carla Dunleavy. He had enough on his mind. Besides, he'd lost his head once; wasn't one lesson enough?

He went back to the desk and sat down. He had finally persuaded Mrs. D. to sell two colts, and he took out the bills of sale he'd received last week for them. Both had gone to a farm in Maryland, and Wade had volunteered to deliver them himself. Carla had been here for three days by then, and even though he'd only caught glimpses of her since their ride, he had to get away for a while. Perhaps she'd be gone when he returned.

Coward that he was, he'd turned a two-day trip into four. But when he got home this morning, any hope that Carla had grown bored and had taken off vanished when he saw the midnight blue sports car in front of the house. He knew without a doubt that the car belonged to Carla. The only question was why Mrs. D. allowed it here. Octavia had firm ideas about loud, fast cars around horses; the only reason she let him have his motorcycle here was that he kept it in the shed at his house and didn't drive it near the barns.

But when he saw that little blue convertible, his jaw tightened along with his insides. Against his will, he imagined how she'd drive that car. She'd be quick and precise and expert, downshifting on curves, taking the straightaway with enough speed to start the adrenaline flowing. He could even see her behind the wheel, that silky chestnut-colored hair blowing out behind her, her cheeks blushed from the wind and those green eyes glowing with a hint of recklessness that some men found irresistible.

But not him. Oh, no, not him. After his unhappy experiences with women, he preferred females who were down-to-earth. The last thing he needed was another episode like the one he'd had with Annabelle.

"Damn it," he muttered. He didn't want to think about Annabelle Renfrow, but now that she'd popped into his mind, he couldn't get her out again. He tried to will the memories away, but Annabelle was like an itch that couldn't be scratched.

He'd done everything he could to forget her, but even after all this time, he could still see her as clearly as if she were standing right in front of him. Annabelle, with the flaming red hair and the vivid blue eyes. She and Carla Dunleavy didn't look anything alike, but he knew that under the skin they were sisters. His infatuation with Annabelle had ruined his life.

"I want her to run," she'd said petulantly on that last disastrous night. They were at the track, in the trailer he kept instead of a house, because he could be closer to the training barn, on call around the clock.

"I want her to run," Annabelle had repeated.

They'd been in bed at the time, Annabelle sitting up with the sheet barely clinging to her naked breasts.

They'd just made love for the second time that evening, and as exhausted as he was, he was also hungry.
He hadn't eaten anything since a hastily grabbed sweet
roll that morning, and he'd been about to drag himself out of bed to see what was in the kitchen when
Annabelle had made her announcement. Immediately, the atmosphere in the room had chilled.

He remembered not answering for a moment, debating how to handle the situation. One of the most
prestigious distaff races in the country was going to be
run the next afternoon, and he had two fillies entered. One of them belonged to Annabelle.

Warily, he'd turned to look at her. At the sight of
her naked back—she had a beautiful back—he'd felt
renewed desire. He knew he shouldn't have seen her
tonight, but when she'd come around to the track that
afternoon, beckoning with those blue eyes, promising
wonderful things with those pouty lips, he couldn't
refuse her. She was like some narcotic to him; he
couldn't resist her.

With her there in his bed, horses were the last subject he wanted to discuss. He'd even forgotten he was
hungry. Even after making love twice, he wanted to
hold her in his arms and feel her soft flesh against him.
Her glorious red hair fell nearly to her waist, and he
longed to bury his face in the sweet-smelling strands
and dream of ways to please her. He reached for her,
but she shifted away impatiently. He knew the signs,
and he fell back against the pillow, his hand over his
eyes.

"Annabelle," he said, "we've talked about this—"

"We're going to talk about it again until you listen to reason."

"There's nothing to discuss."

"And I think there is. I want Queen Mab to run tomorrow, and that's all there is to it."

Queen Mab was one of Annabelle's many horses, a fast three-year-old who had come back from her morning work with a slightly filled front ankle. Mab had a good chance of winning the distaff, he thought—if she went to the gate tomorrow. Although the vet had checked the filly thoroughly and pronounced her fit, Wade felt uneasy. When he'd said he thought they should scratch the race, Annabelle had reacted badly. It seemed she was still angry.

He understood her disappointment; what he couldn't condone was *why* it was so important to her that Queen Mab race the next day. He'd known that it wasn't just because the filly could win; the reason was that she wanted to impress her friends.

"My whole crowd is coming just to watch the silly thing run," she said petulantly. "How will I explain it if you scratch her?"

Wade had always known that horses were just an amusing diversion to Annabelle, but the offhand way she dismissed one of the best fillies in the country infuriated him. "Don't explain," he said. "Just tell them that your trainer didn't like the look of Mab's ankle."

Pouting, Annabelle crossed her arms over her ample breasts. She had a good figure and she knew it, sometimes brazenly parading in front of the trailer's open windows in the nude. She didn't care if anyone saw her, but he did. He'd already broken one of his cardinal rules by getting involved with a client.

"The vet said she was all right," Annabelle pointed out.

"He has his opinion, and I have mine. As your trainer, I think it's better to be safe than sorry."

"Well, I don't," she said. Without further ado, she threw back the rumpled sheet and got out of bed. Her mouth a tight line, she gathered her clothing and went into the bathroom. He could tell by the way she walked that the discussion wasn't over, so he was dressed and waiting by the time she emerged. Fully clothed, but not on even ground, they faced each other.

"I want her to run," Annabelle repeated obstinately.

"And as your trainer, I advise against it."

She put on that supercilious expression he detested. It transformed her face, making her look pinched and superior. In her best finishing-school tone, she said, "I own the horse, Wade. If I say she'll run, she'll run. You do what *I* say, not vice versa."

That was the moment he'd relived a thousand times. She had given him the opening; all he had to do was walk through it. The words were right there. He knew what he should say, but he couldn't make himself say it. Annabelle Renfrow owned and raced thirty horses. He had them all in his barn right now. He knew that if he took Queen Mab out of the race tomorrow, he could expect the filly and her stablemates to be gone by afternoon. It was a lot of horses to lose in one blow, but even so, he should have stood his ground. The fact that he hadn't still made him feel ashamed.

Suddenly, as only she could, Annabelle changed right before his eyes. Gone was her arrogant, over-bearing manner; in its place was the Annabelle that drove him crazy. Her voice low and sultry, her eyes half hidden under her thick lashes, she came to him and put her hands on his chest.

"It'll be all right," she murmured, her lips against his cheek. "Trust me, Wade darling. Haven't I been around horses all my life?"

Her hot, moist lips moved to his jaw, then his neck. Gently, she bit him with her small, even white teeth. "And after she wins, we'll have a party to celebrate." Her fingers drifted to his groin. He was already swelling, and she cupped him in her hand. "Just the two of us...."

Suddenly, the office seemed too confining. He had to get out and forget things for a while. He grabbed his jacket, and five minutes later he was on his way into town with the bank statement. But as he threw a leg over his motorcycle, he was reminded again of that little midnight blue sports car parked up by the house. Annabelle had driven a Wedgwood blue Jaguar, custom painted to match her eyes. As far as he was concerned, the only thing different about Carla Dunleavy was that the car she'd chosen wasn't green.

CARLA WAS on the phone in the guest bedroom when she looked out the window and saw Wade driving by on a motorcycle. Since he'd only come in a while ago from a long trip to Maryland, she wondered where he was going now. She followed his progress until the trees along the driveway hid him.

Annoyed that she'd been interested enough to wonder, she turned away. She didn't care what Wade Petrie did, or how he spent his time. It was all the same to her if he came or went or just stayed in his little office down in the main barn.

Was it? She flushed, remembering how when he'd been away, she hadn't been able to resist going down to glance into his office. But it had been a quick look, and she hadn't gone all the way in.

Not that it would have done any good, she thought. The office had as much personality as a sterile operating room. He hadn't had any mementos anywhere, not even a picture on the desk . . . nothing.

Nothing to tell you what he's really like, you mean, came the thought.

Nothing to show me what qualifications he has to run this farm, she qualified.

And why do you care?

Ah, that was a good question. When she first came to Dunleavy Farm, she hadn't anticipated staying longer than a few days—perhaps only an hour or two, depending on how well the meeting with her grand-mother went. She had even brought most of her lug-gage with her so she wouldn't have to slink back to New York and face her mother; she could just go on to her next destination, wherever that might be.

But now her clothes were hanging in the closet or had been folded in drawers by the efficient Teresa, and she still hadn't decided when to leave. And even more telling, whenever she looked at her riding boots in the corner, she felt warm all over.

As for Wade Petrie, she couldn't understand it. She didn't even like the man, yet she couldn't stop think-ing of him. What *was* it about him that was so in-triguing? It couldn't be his manner; she had never met anyone so rude and obnoxious. He seemed to go out of his way to annoy her, and enjoy doing so.

But still. . . .

"Carla?" said a voice at the other end of the line. "Carla! Are you still there? Is something the matter? Do we have a bad connection?"

"No, the connection is fine. I just got . . . distracted for a minute. Where are you, Mother?"

"I'm in Acapulco. I want you to join me. You know you love it here."

Carla couldn't think of an easy way to say it. "Mother, I'm not leaving Dunleavy Farm right now."

When all she heard was a faint buzzing on the line, she wondered if they'd been cut off, after all. Then Meredith finally said, "I beg your pardon?"

She knew that tone. "Now, Mother, surely you can get along by yourself for a few days, can't you?"

"Getting along by myself isn't the point," Meredith said sharply. "Oh, I knew this would happen if I let you go down there! It's—"

"In the first place, you didn't *let* me come here, Mother. I accepted Grandmother's invitation myself. And in the—"

"Oh, so it's *Grandmother* now? Who thought of that? No, don't tell me. It was that woman, wasn't it? I might have known she'd try to get into your good graces by playing on nonexistent family ties!"

"Don't you think you're being a little harsh? I know you and Grandmother had your differences—"

"You don't know anything about it, so I'll thank you to keep your uninformed opinions to yourself! Unless—" Meredith paused before going on even more angrily, "Unless, she's already filled your head with lies. I wouldn't put it past her, meddling old woman that she is!"

"Mother, for heaven's sake. Will you listen to yourself? Grandmother isn't like that. In fact, she hasn't said anything at all about you."

"Oh, really? Why do I find that so hard to believe?"

"I don't know. Maybe you should tell me. After all, I know so little about our family."

"Our family is you and me!"

"So I thought—until I found out I had other relatives. A grandmother, for instance. It makes me wonder who else you've been hiding all these years."

"I don't like your tone, Carla. I resent these veiled accusations."

"And I resent the fact that you never told me about Dunleavy Farm!"

"There was nothing to tell! I left when—"

When Meredith stopped abruptly, Carla said, "Go on. You left . . . when?"

"Never mind. I don't want to talk about it."

"Well, that's too bad, isn't it? I think the time has come for us to discuss a few things."

"I have no intention of discussing the past with you. If I'd wanted you to know anything, I would have told you before now."

"Why are you being so stubborn? What's the secret now? I know about the farm, I know about Grandmother. What more do you have to hide?"

"I told you, nothing!"

"Maybe I'll just ask Grandmother about that."

"You do what you have to. But I'm warning you, be prepared. You think Octavia Dunleavy is a nice old woman who just wants to get to know her granddaughter. Well, I know better."

"Are you sure about that? After all, it's been so long since you've been home."

"Dunleavy Farm is not my home!"

"It was."

"And *was* is the operative word. Oh, I can see that you're determined to be stubborn about this. Well, I guess you're just going to have to find out the truth yourself."

"I intend to."

"Fine. But while you're there, think of this. If that woman is so *nice,* why did she allow all these years to pass without trying to contact you? You think she has something to give you. I happen to know she wants a lot more in return."

"And what might that be?"

"She got you there, didn't she? You told me you were only going to stay a day or two. Now it's been a week. Tell me, Carla, what's keeping you there?"

Without warning, an image of a man in jeans and a Stetson hat pulled low over his eyes flashed into Carla's mind. *Oh, no,* she thought. It wasn't Wade who was keeping her here.

"Well?" Meredith said. "Aren't you going to answer me?"

"It's no secret, Mother. I've never been to Kentucky before. And despite what you say, Dunleavy Farm is a lovely place. A real showpiece."

"So, you're enamored of Dunleavy Farm," Meredith said sarcastically. "It's hard to understand, since you've visited some of the most beautiful horse farms in Europe."

"I know." Carla couldn't explain it even to herself. "I guess it's because this place is the only thing in my life that comes close to... home."

She should have known how Meredith would react. Right on cue, her mother erupted. "*Home?* Have you lost your mind? Dunleavy Farm is the last place in the world any of us could ever call home. What has that woman done to you? You have to leave there immediately. I don't want you under her influence any longer!"

"Grandmother hasn't done anything to me, Mother," Carla said calmly. "I'm a grown woman—"

"Who's acting like a child!"

"I think you're the one who's being childish. I've tried, but I'm out of patience. If you have something to say about my grandmother, or about the farm, I wish you'd say it. Otherwise, I'll see you—"

"When?" Meredith demanded. "I won't wait for you forever!"

"You can leave Mexico whenever you choose. I told you not to wait for me."

"But—"

"My mind is made up. I'm going to stay a while longer."

"But why?"

"Well, for one thing, there's Done Driftin'."

"Done Driftin'?" Meredith repeated sharply. "What's that?"

"Not what—who. He's the colt Grandmother is going to give me if I stay the month."

"What?" Meredith was outraged. "I know you're angry with me, Carla, but... a month! You can't intend to stay that long!"

"Well, you're right—I didn't, at first. But now..."

Carla thought of how thrilled she'd been at her first sight of Done Driftin'. Even now, she could hardly keep her eyes off him when he was out in the paddock. In fact, she and the colt had developed a little ritual of their own: whenever she came out to the fence, he lifted his head and called to her, his entire body vibrating with the force of his greeting. But he never came running, as the stallion did for Octavia; to Carla's secret amusement, Done Driftin' was too independent for that.

"I'll buy you a horse," Meredith said desperately. "I'll buy you a half dozen, if you like! Oh, Carla, you can't listen to that woman—"

"I wish you'd stop calling my grandmother 'that woman.' If you can't refer to her as your mother, at least call her by her name!"

"I don't want to call her anything, and neither should you. I can't tell you how upset I am, Carla. We've been so close all these years. I expected better from you."

"I'm sorry you're disappointed, but I'm not doing anything wrong. And since you won't tell me what the problem is between you and Grandmother, I don't think we have anything more to talk about."

"Neither do I. If you come to your senses, I'll be here until the seventeenth. After that, I don't know where I'll be. But one thing is for certain, it won't be at Dunleavy Farm."

Carla started to say something, but her mother had already banged down the phone. Wincing at the clang in her ear, she replaced the receiver. She debated calling Meredith back, but she knew it wouldn't do any good. They were both too upset to have an intelligent discussion; she'd wait a few days and then try again.

Feeling restless and dissatisfied, she wandered over to the window again. When Meredith had demanded to know what was keeping her here, her instinctive response had been her fascination with the farm. But as soon as she'd said it, she'd wondered if it was true. While Wade was away, she'd explored a little on her own. The land itself was beautiful, but to her distress, she had discovered evidence of a subtle decline.

She'd noticed things that she hadn't seen when she first came: sheds with peeling paint, horse stalls that weren't bedded as deep as they could have been, tack that should have been replaced, but instead had been repaired.

And there were things inside the house that weren't quite right. Carla had noticed several blank spots on the walls, indicating that paintings had been removed—and sold? And she'd noted bare spaces in an étagère containing a jade collection which was now obviously incomplete. She hadn't gone so far as to count the silver or the lovely old Spode in the sideboard, but she suspected that if she did, pieces would be missing from those sets, too.

At first, she told herself it wasn't any of her business what her grandmother did with her belongings. After all, she didn't know if Octavia had given these things away or if she'd had to part with them. Certainly, she couldn't ask. But the more she thought about it, the more intrigued she became. She remembered what her grandmother had told her about how much Done Roamin's accident had cost. At the time, Carla had been so absorbed in the story that she hadn't thought to question why the accident had happened in the first place.

Now she wondered.

She knew horses cast themselves in stalls all the time. Big, clumsy creatures in such a small space, they sometimes miscalculate, lie down too close to a wall and then can't get up. But Done Roamin' had shattered what would be the equivalent of a knee joint in a human. How could he do that much damage to himself without anyone hearing him?

She frowned at the thought. Octavia had told her that because the manager's house was being painted at the time, Wade had been living in the apartment above the barn. He should have heard something, but apparently he hadn't. Was it possible that he—

No, she wouldn't even think it. No matter how much she disliked the man, she could not believe that he had anything at all to do with Done Roamin's accident.

And that's what it was, she told herself firmly: an accident. She hadn't been here; she didn't have all the details. She was not going to let her imagination run wild just because Wade Petrie was rude and difficult.

Without intending to, she looked toward the little house where he lived.

Her expression unreadable, she stared at the cottage a long time before she finally turned away to dress for dinner.

CHAPTER FIVE

"YOU'VE HARDLY TOUCHED your dinner," Octavia commented after watching Carla push the food around her plate. "What's the matter, dear? Don't you feel well?"

Carla couldn't repeat her argument with Meredith, so she said, "I'm fine, Grandmother. Just a little tired, I guess." She managed a smile. "Although why I should be, I don't know. I haven't done a thing since I got here. It must be the country air."

"Maybe so. But on the other hand..." Octavia paused, then asked tentatively, "Perhaps you're... bored?"

"You know, normally, I would be. But right now, I'm not."

"Maybe you just needed a rest."

"From that endless round of parties and soirees, you mean?" Carla said ruefully. She shook her head. "I hardly think so."

Octavia took a sip of tea from a cup so delicate, Carla could see the level of the liquid through the china. When she had first commented on the lovely pattern of forget-me-nots entwined with fern, Octavia had told her that the set had belonged to *her* grandmother, who had brought it over from Ireland when she came to America. To avoid breakage, everything had been packed carefully between layers of handmade quilts.

As she had several times during her visit, Carla felt wistful. Her grandmother had such a history. The house contained so many treasures. The china was just one example; the ornate silverware that her grandmother's great-grandmother had owned was another. There was so much tradition here that Carla felt she could stay years and never see or learn about all of it. Mementos were everywhere.

Just today she'd found out that her grandmother had had a sister named Ursula, who had died when she was just seventeen. Octavia had showed her a set of hand-embroidered towels and pillowcases that Ursula had sewn while attending a convent school in Chicago. The delicate linens were folded in tissue paper that still smelled faintly of lavender, and even though Ursula had been so young at the time, the sewing was the most exquisite Carla had ever seen.

Such things made her want to learn more about this family she'd known nothing about. She and Meredith had moved around so constantly that they hadn't kept much memorabilia. She hadn't realized what a lack that was in her life until she arrived at Dunleavy Farm.

"Do you like your life-style, Carla?" Octavia's voice brought Carla back to the present.

"It's the only thing I know. I never really thought about it, I guess."

"I can't believe that. You're too intelligent not to have realized you were frittering your life away."

"It hasn't really been like that, Grandmother," Carla said defensively. "I've tried different things. It's just that nothing has ever interested me long enough to stay with it."

"And now?"

"I don't know," she said slowly. "Ever since I came here, things have seemed . . . different."

"Different? How so?"

"If I try to explain, it will sound too ridiculous. Besides, I'm not sure myself yet. Grandmother," she said suddenly, "I don't want you to take this the wrong way, but you didn't have to . . . to bribe me to come for a visit. Offering me a horse was—"

"A lure. I admit it." Octavia's green eyes, so much the color of Carla's own, rested on her granddaughter. "But be honest now. Would you really have come if I hadn't?"

"I'm not sure. Maybe I would have. I have to admit, finding out I had a grandmother was startling. I might have come just out of curiosity." She smiled. "Still, offering the colt was a clever touch."

"I didn't intend to be clever. I thought about it for a long time, and even though you didn't know me, I wanted you to have something—something that meant a lot to me—from Dunleavy Farm. It was inexcusable to wait so long to contact you, I know. But I hope it isn't too late for us."

Carla thought of her mother's reaction during their phone call earlier this evening and wondered if Meredith would ever come to grips with her own past, as Octavia was obviously trying to do. When she remembered her mother's angry tone, she doubted it.

"I think we should talk about Done Driftin', Grandmother," she said. "Now that I've seen him..." She shook her head. "I can't accept him. It's too much."

"You don't like him?"

"Like him? He's the most beautiful horse I've ever seen. With the exception of Done Roamin', of course."

But as a gift, it was too much. Carla might have felt differently if she hadn't seen all the evidences of cost-cutting around the farm. But Done Driftin' was a valuable horse, and she knew he'd bring top dollar at any sale. She couldn't allow this sentimental gesture to rob Octavia of a future; it wouldn't be right.

Octavia laughed. "Tactfully put, my dear. But you're right, Carla. Done Driftin' is one of the stallion's best sons. In fact, he reminds me of Roamy when he was young. He has the same arrogance, the same presence. If he has the same speed this year as he did at two, there won't be many who will catch him. You'll see soon enough."

"You're going to put him back into race training?" Carla felt torn at the idea.

"It's time," Octavia said. "And if ever a horse was born to race, I think it's Done Driftin'." She paused. "What do you think?"

Reluctantly, she said, "I guess you're right."

"I know how you feel. It's one thing to see a colt like that in pasture. It's another to have him in training, where his every move is regulated around the clock. The truth is, I've always had mixed emotions about it myself."

"But you've raced horses all your life. If you felt that way, how could you continue?"

"Because long ago, I realized that the alternative—not seeing them run at all—would be even worse," Octavia said. "Even now when that flag goes up, my pulse goes with it. And when they turn for home, I don't think there's a more glorious sight in the world." Octavia stopped. "Listen to me," she said. "I sound like an advertisement."

Carla laughed. "The best kind, I think. You convinced me."

"Then you agree Done Driftin' should go back to the track?"

"Well, it's not really up to me."

"Yes it is, dear. I realize I said you could have him if you stayed a month, but I know you now, and I want you to have him—regardless of whether you stay the month or not. So you might as well start making decisions now about his future. If you decide against it, you can always bow out."

Carla leaned forward. "I appreciate what you're trying to do, but Done Driftin' is too valuable to...give away like this, Grandmother. I can't accept him even if I wanted to."

"*Do* you want to?"

"Please don't ask me—"

"Do you want to?" Octavia asked again.

When Carla thought of *her* colt going to someone else, she felt a pang. "Well, of course I do," she said, before she could stop herself. "I'd be a fool to refuse such a magnificent horse. But you don't have to—"

"You're right," Octavia said. "I don't. I want to do this, Carla. Why won't you let me?"

Carla thought again of all those signs of decay she'd seen around the farm. She knew her grandmother felt strongly about giving her the horse, but she couldn't take advantage of an old woman.

"I appreciate the offer, I do. But can't we compromise? I have money, Grandmother. Why don't you let me buy—"

Octavia's face changed. Stiffly, she said, "There's no need to be insulting. I realize that I have a lot to answer for, but if you want to punish me for past omissions, please don't do it by throwing a gift back into my face."

Carla was appalled. "I didn't mean—"

Octavia rose from the table. "Good night."

Carla shot to her feet, too. "Grandmother, wait. I didn't mean to offend you. Please, that was the last thing on my mind! I just— I just—"

"You're a beautiful, sophisticated, cultured woman, Carla," Octavia said. "But you have a lot to learn about the art of graceful acceptance."

Alarmed that she might have destroyed this fragile relationship, Carla said, "Please, forgive me. I never should have—I didn't mean . . ."

To her horror, she was near tears. She tried to get herself under control. "I'm sorry, I don't know what's come over me," she said. "I never meant to insult you. I don't know why I offered to buy Done Driftin'. It's just that . . . ever since coming here, I've felt . . ."

"What?"

"I don't know." Helplessly, she looked at her grandmother. "I can't explain."

Octavia was silent a moment. Then she said, "Come into the living room with me. We're going to talk about this."

Carla didn't want to make a greater fool of herself than she already had, but she couldn't resist when Octavia took her arm and pulled her along. They went into the living room and sat down on the sofa.

"Now," Octavia said. "What's all this about?"

"I didn't mean to offend you, Grandmother. It's just—" She stopped, wondering how she could tell Octavia why she had offered to buy the colt. Saying that she didn't think her grandmother could afford such a gift would only make things worse.

"Just what? You can tell me, my dear."

"Can't we just say I made a mistake?" Carla asked desperately.

Octavia watched her for a moment, then she said, "I think I understand. You don't think I can afford to give you the colt."

"Oh, that's not—"

"Of course it is," Octavia said calmly. "You're not stupid. You've been around the farm. I know you've seen signs here and there that we don't keep things up like we once did."

Carla felt so uncomfortable that she had to blame someone and the first person she thought of was Wade.

"It's all Wade Petrie's fault," she said.

Octavia burst out laughing. "Wade! Why do you say that?"

"Well, he's the farm manager, isn't he? Isn't it his job to make sure things are kept up?"

"Wade is the *barn* manager," Octavia corrected. "His job is to see to the horses. But Carla, even if he did manage the farm, he couldn't spend money that isn't there."

"You see!"

"Now, now, everything's going to be all right. We've fallen back a little, I admit. But we're not destitute, believe me."

"I know, Grandmother," Carla said, although she had her doubts. "But—"

"No buts," Octavia said gently. "I wouldn't lie to you. I told you what I did when Done Roamin' got hurt, didn't I? Well, the farm is still recovering from that episode. I did something that Alvah always told me not to do, and that was to dip into my reserves. I had no choice. And I know that if Alvah had been here, he would have done the same thing himself. So now I'm cutting back here and there. I've even—" she looked significantly at Carla "—sold a few horses. Thanks to Wade, that is."

Carla was horrified. "Wade knows about your financial situation?"

"Don't sound so shocked. Wade is more than just the help, you know. He's also a friend."

Friend was the last word Carla would have used to describe Wade Petrie. But she didn't want to argue about the man, so she said, "I'd like to be your friend, too. Is there anything I can do to help?"

"As a matter of fact, there is."

"What?" Carla said eagerly. "I'll do anything. Anything I can, anyway. I'm afraid I don't know very much about American race pedigrees, but—"

"What I have in mind doesn't involve pedigrees. Now, you mustn't feel obligated in any way, but I was thinking that maybe you could help me with the farm's bookkeeping. You said that you used to help with your stepfather's business accounts—"

"That's true, I did."

"Well, after I had to fire Walter Remy—"

"Who's he?"

"*He* was the farm manager until I caught him with his hand in the till last year. Since then, I've been doing the books myself. But I don't have the patience I used to, and it shows." She looked hopefully at Carla. "Would you be interested in helping me? Just until you get things in order again."

Carla didn't hesitate. "When do we start?" she asked.

"How about tomorrow?"

"Tomorrow it is. Just point me in the right direction and I'll take care of it."

"You're an angel."

Carla flushed, pleased. "What else can I do?"

"Now that you mention it, there is one other thing."

"What's that?" Carla asked. She was so eager to help that she completely missed the satisfied look in her grandmother's eyes—until it was too late.

"I've been invited to a horse sale and party next week," Octavia said. "Would you come with me? I know you'll think I'm being a silly old woman again, but I really would like to show you off."

"Oh, Grandmother—"

"Please. It would mean so much to me."

How could she refuse? "In that case, I accept."

Octavia's eyes twinkled as she warned, "It's formal."

Carla feigned indignation. "You don't think a dyed-in-the-wool socialite like me would travel without a formal gown, do you?"

"I should have known," Octavia said with a laugh. "By the way, there's just one more thing..."

"What's that?"

"Wade is coming, too. But that shouldn't be a problem, should it?"

"Problem?" Carla said, trying to disguise her dismay. "Of course not. Why would you think that?"

BUT IT WAS a problem on the night of the party when Carla began dressing. Trying to tell herself it was because she always prided herself on how she looked, she took extra pains with her appearance. But she knew the truth was she wanted to look so outrageously gorgeous that she'd knock Wade Petrie's hat right off.

Face it, she thought, as she stood before the closet trying to decide what to wear. *You're attracted to the man. You don't like it, and you want to make him pay for it.*

It wasn't fair, but that was beside the point. She habitually lost interest in a man the instant she snared him, and tonight was her chance to reel Wade Petrie in. When she tossed him back, she'd be cured of this inconvenient maddening preoccupation with a man she didn't even like.

With that in mind, she took out two dresses. One was crimson satin with beads and sequins weighing down the low-cut bodice; the other was a simple but sophisticated one-shouldered gown in a deep shade of purple velvet. She held them up, debating. The red dress was definitely flashy and sexy; the velvet sleek and sensual. Which would it be?

Twenty minutes later, Carla eyed herself in the mirror. There was no doubt about it: the slinky purple velvet clung in all the right places. With all she'd been eating lately, it had been touch and go for a minute as she was pulling it over her hips, but when she'd examined herself from all angles, the dress still fit perfectly. Even so, she was going to have to stay away from Teresa's beaten biscuits. She had long ago honed her willpower, but those flaky delicacies were nearly impossible to resist.

She was almost ready. The gown's single bare shoulder mandated that she pull her hair back on that side, so she fastened it with a brilliant diamond clip. As she turned her head, the jewels caught the light and suddenly all the flash seemed a bit much. She wanted to impress Mr. Wade Petrie, she thought, not blind him completely.

She reached for the clip, then paused. *Blinding* him was one thing, she thought with a sly smile. *Dazzling* him was quite another. She decided to leave the clip where it was.

It was time to get her wrap and meet everyone downstairs. Octavia had told her that Wade would be driving tonight, but at the idea of relinquishing even that much control to him, she had offered to chauffeur her grandmother in her own rental car. Octavia had laughed.

"That fast little thing you drive? Oh, no, thank you, my dear," Octavia had said. "Assuming for a second that I could manage to get down into that low seat, I'm sure I could never get out of it again. No, we'll take my sturdy old Rolls. It's ancient like me, but real class never goes out of style, does it? Besides, it wouldn't be the same if I didn't arrive in that car. It's ferried me to more functions over the years than I can count."

Carla had tried another tack. "Yes, but Wade might not like the idea of driving."

"Oh, I don't—" Octavia had stopped and looked at her keenly. "Why, Carla Dunleavy," she'd said, "are you really asking how it's going to look if we arrive with the hired help?"

"No, that's not it at all!" But she'd felt herself turning bright crimson and knew she'd only make it worse by trying to explain. The problem wasn't Wade's position, or lack of it: it was the man himself.

Reminded of that exchange tonight as she checked her lipstick for the last time, she frowned and stepped back. A self-assured woman in diamonds and sophisticated purple was reflected in the mirror, and as she stared at herself, she thought how convenient her mask was at times. Who could guess that beneath all this glamour she was riddled with questions and doubts?

She was reaching for her wrap when a thought occurred to her. She probably wasn't the only one hiding behind a facade. If she wore a disguise, she was sure Wade did, too. He wanted everyone to believe that he was just a simple homespun cowboy who had wandered over from the plains, but she doubted that. He wasn't meant to be a barn manager, even if it was on a farm like this. She was sure of it.

Now that she thought about it, she recalled Octavia's mentioning that Wade had owned his own training stable once. If that was so, why had he surrendered a high-profile, exciting career for a humdrum life at Dunleavy Farm? A man like Wade was destined for challenges, and training highly strung Thoroughbreds was one of the greatest. She had sensed from the moment she'd met him that he wouldn't hesitate to put everything on the line.

Had he crossed over that line? she wondered suddenly. Was that why he'd retreated to a farm far away from where the action was? Uneasy at the thought, she switched off the bedroom light and went downstairs.

AT THAT MOMENT, Wade was in the living room, trying to stretch his neck in an unfamiliar shirt collar. When he saw himself in the ornate mirror by the door, he grimaced.

Whoever invented the tuxedo, he mused, *should be hunted down and shot.*

The damned bow tie not only looked ridiculous, it wouldn't stay straight. As for this cummerbund, he wanted to strangle the designer with it. Furthermore, in deference to Octavia, he'd left the old Stetson home. Despite being trussed in this getup, he still felt naked without his hat.

Or was his problem that he really didn't want to go to the party tonight?

Scowling, he turned away from the mirror. He hated parties and social occasions; they reminded him too

much of the past. When he'd had his own stable, he'd
been out all the time. Horse owners liked to be feted
and told how wonderful their runners were, whether
they were or not, and he hadn't minded the ego strok-
ing and game playing when he had a talented horse in
the barn. And he could certainly celebrate with the
best of them when one of them won. But then he'd
met Annabelle, and suddenly everything changed.

His scowl deepened at the memory. The parties
Annabelle took him to weren't celebrations at all, he
recalled. They'd been hard-drinking, hard-partying
gatherings for bored socialites who had nothing better to do with their time. It hadn't taken him long to
get his fill of it, but by then he'd been trapped. Annabelle had had an inexplicable hold on him, and she
wouldn't let go—not until everything fell apart.

At the thought, he muttered a curse. He couldn't
blame Annabelle; what had happened had been his
fault. If he'd been thinking with his brain instead of
another part of his anatomy, he would have broken off
the affair long before it destroyed his life.

But he didn't want to dwell on Annabelle and what
might have been. He was just running his finger inside his collar to stop it from strangling him, when
Octavia appeared and rescued him.

"Why, Wade," she said from the doorway, "how
very handsome you look."

He started to tip his hat to her before he remembered he wasn't wearing it. "Thank you, Mrs. D.," he

responded gallantly. "And might I add that you're looking lovely tonight yourself."

She laughed and came into the room. "I'm happy to see that chivalry isn't dead, after all. Shall we go?"

He tried to be oh-so-casual as they headed toward the foyer. "Does this mean that your granddaughter isn't coming?"

"No, it does not," said a voice from the stairs.

When Wade turned and saw Carla standing on the third step from the bottom, his jaw dropped open. He had never seen a more beautiful woman in his life than Carla Dunleavy in that purple dress. He couldn't take his eyes off the vision on the stairs.

The gown clung to her curves—such curves!—like nothing he'd ever seen, and the sight of that bare shoulder could drive a man wild. Diamonds flashed in her hair and on one slim wrist, but it was the smile she turned on him that turned his insides to mush. He knew he was staring like a fatuous idiot, but he couldn't help himself. He couldn't have looked away from her if his life had depended on it.

"Good evening, Grandmother...Wade," she said.

Wade thought her voice sounded even huskier than usual, but with his heart pounding like a bass drum, he could have imagined it. He tried to answer her, but his mouth was too dry, so he just nodded.

Carla came down the last three steps, the gown shimmering provocatively every time she moved. *Whoever designed that dress,* he thought dazedly, *should be awarded a medal.*

"Would you mind, Wade?" Carla purred.

He jerked his eyes down. He was in such a state of disarray that he didn't know what she meant at first. Then he realized dimly that she wanted him to help her with her wrap. His fingers numb, he took the cape, but when she turned her back to him, he caught a whiff of her perfume and almost dropped the garment.

What was that scent? he wondered. He'd never smelled anything like it. The fragrance seemed to hold out promises of...he didn't know what. He got a flash of hot, steamy nights, and the glow of perspiration between smooth, creamy breasts. Just for an instant, he heard throaty laughter and tasted ice-cold champagne. Then the image vanished, leaving him feeling...bereft.

"You look beautiful, Carla," he managed to say. "And that perfume..."

"Do you like it?" she asked softly. She smiled as she moved away, leaving behind another tantalizing whiff. "It was made for me some time ago by a perfumer in New Orleans. We called it White Sapphires."

For a moment, he couldn't answer. The scent was going straight to his head. At last, he said, "It suits you."

Carla lowered her long lashes. "I'm glad you think so."

Wade was thinking about a lot more than Carla's perfume as he escorted the two women out to the car. Samson, Teresa's husband and Octavia's man-of-all-chores, had spent the afternoon washing and waxing the vintage black Rolls. Parked out front now, it gleamed like a luxurious relic of days gone by. Wade opened the back door and Octavia climbed in. Carla was about to follow, when her grandmother waved a hand.

"Why don't you sit in front with Wade, dear?" she suggested. "After all, even though he's being kind enough to drive us tonight, he isn't really our chauffeur. It wouldn't be right for him to be up there all alone with no one to talk to. And this way, I'll be able to have the back seat to myself. It's these arthritic old knees, you know. They give me fits if I don't have enough room."

Since the back seat in the old car was long enough for tiny Octavia to lie full length on it and still not reach either end, Wade looked at her suspiciously. Octavia merely smiled.

"Shall we go?" she said. "We don't want to be late."

He glanced at Carla, who looked as if she'd prefer turning around and going back into the house. Was it because she didn't want to sit up front with him? Well, he didn't like the idea, either, but what could he do, pick her up and seat her there, anyway?

Disturbed even more by the sudden, tantalizing image of Carla in his arms, he decided it was time to get going. He opened the front passenger door and waited. Carla had no choice but to get in, and as she seated herself in front, he caught another whiff of that perfume. That stuff was deadly, he thought, and quickly shut the door.

CARLA PERCHED tensely on her side of the car, as close to the door as she could get without actually sitting on the handle. Gone was her intention to impress Wade with her glamorous sophistication; instead, she was mortified to realize, *she* was the one who was feeling a little dazzled.

It's a sin for any man to look that handsome in a tuxedo, she thought. Her heart was pounding and she felt light-headed. If she felt this way now, what would the rest of the evening be like? The night hadn't even started yet.

Distantly, she realized that Octavia was talking. Guiltily, she started to listen in time to hear "...known Trent Spencer and his late father for years, of course. It was such a shame when Trent and his wife separated. They had that darling little boy—what was his name? Do you know, Wade?"

As though he'd been lost in thought, Wade started at the question. "Uh...it was before my time, Mrs. D.," he said.

"It's not important, I guess. It was so...wait a minute, I remember now. It was Derry. Derry was the name of Trent's son. Isn't that right, Wade?"

"If you say so, Mrs. D."

"Well, anyway, it was so sad when the wife and the boy moved away," she said wistfully. "I admit we're rather insular around here and don't take kindly to strangers, but the Spencer family was different. For one thing, Trent knows horses. And I guess he wasn't such a stranger to these parts," she added reluctantly. "His grandfather did own the local feed store even before he bought ChangeOver Farm."

"ChangeOver," Carla repeated. "Isn't that the place next door?"

"If you call a hundred acres away 'next door,'" Wade said, eyeing Octavia in the mirror. "And don't let Mrs. D. fool you. Those *outsider* Spencers have owned the place for over fifty years."

"Yes, but they weren't *originally* from here," Octavia emphasized primly. "As I recall, that family came from Pennsylvania."

"Oh, I get it," Carla said. She dropped her voice conspiratorially. "You mean they were ... *Yankees.*"

"Yes, that's right, they were," Octavia retorted, not in the least abashed. "You may laugh, but in the old days, things like that were important."

Trying not to laugh, Carla looked over her shoulder. "Am I going to meet this Yankee usurper tonight?"

"Oh, yes. I think you'll like him, too. Trent is—"

But just then, they drove through the gates to Candlewood Farm, where the horse auction and party were being held. Lanterns lighted the drive in, and when they came to the house, the entire place was ablaze with light. Two young valets were kept hopping, and after Wade helped her from the car, Octavia grasped the sleeve of one youth before she surrendered the Rolls.

"That car is older than you are, young man," she said severely. "I've taken great care of it all these years. So if I come out and find just one scratch on it, I'll know who to blame."

The valet grinned. "Oh, don't worry, ma'am. I'll guard it with my life. You don't see cars like this anymore."

"You certainly don't," Octavia stated as she positioned herself between Carla and Wade. "Now," she said, "let's go look at some horses."

Carla had been to many horse sales, both in England and on the Continent. But she had never attended a sale like the one at Candlewood Farm that night. It turned out to be a mock auction for the Jockey's Relief Fund, and to her surprise, she joined in the fun.

She couldn't understand it. Normally, she shunned affairs like this. But before she knew it, she found herself participating in a spirited bidding war for a nondescript filly who clearly didn't want to be the center of attention. Every time Carla raised her rival's bid, the crowd applauded and the filly kicked out with both hind feet. Everyone was laughing and having a good time—especially Octavia, whose face was pink as she cheered her granddaughter on.

At last, the auctioner paused to wipe his streaming face. The mock auction was being held under a huge striped tent, but heaters positioned around the space warmed the night air, and he'd been working hard. To laughter from the audience, he finally tucked his handkerchief in the breast pocket of his tux and went on with his rhythmic patter.

"All right, ladies and gentlemen, this is the last sale of the night, so let's made it a good one," he said. "Remember all proceeds go to benefit retired jockeys and injured jockeys. And the successful bidders get the satisfaction of knowing they've contributed to a worthy cause. We've got two bidders now, but anyone can join in. So what am I bid, what am I bid? The last hand up said forty-five hundred. Shall we make it an even five and put it to bed?"

Carla's rival on the other side of the tent had been the last to bid. As the auctioneer looked comically from him to her and then back again, she caught her competitor's eye and smiled. He smiled in return, and just before the gavel came down for the third time, she raised a hand. The auctioneer immediately went into action.

"And we have a five, five, *five*, ladies and gentlemen! Shall we make it five-five? five-five, five-five, five-five? No? Anyone else? You, sir?"

The man who had been bidding against Carla laughed and shook his head. He was good-looking, she thought, with black hair going silver at the temples that gave him a distinguished air. She smiled again as he backed away, and a few minutes later, the relieved filly was being led from the ring.

"Well done, my dear," Octavia said in her ear as people began to crowd around to congratulate and meet her. "I'm proud of you for joining in."

"It was for a good cause," Carla said, and meant it. But all the while she was acknowledging introductions and accepting greetings from the people who came up, she was covertly looking around for Wade. He'd been right beside them when the auction started, but he'd disappeared.

Her annoyance grew the more she searched. But since the last thing she wanted to do was betray her interest in Wade Petrie by asking anyone where he'd gone, she finally gave up and concentrated on meeting her grandmother's friends.

"Hello, yes...how do you do? It's a pleasure meeting you..."

It seemed as if everyone in the tent came up to meet her. At last, her distinguished-looking rival appeared. Somehow, she wasn't surprised when Octavia introduced him as their neighbor, Trent Spencer, an investment banker.

"That was quite a bidding war," Trent said while they were shaking hands. "I figured I'd better get out while I still had my head."

Carla smiled. "What you mean is, you lulled me into a false sense of security and then left me holding the bid."

He smiled, too. "It was for a good cause, wasn't it?"

"Indeed. And I enjoyed it."

"So did I. And it's nice to meet you at last."

"At last?"

"Oh, we've all heard rumors about Octavia's granddaughter visiting Dunleavy Farm. But no one's seen you, so we thought it was just gossip."

"My, that was quick. I haven't been here that long."

"News travels fast here."

"Yes, so I've heard." She glanced mischievously at Octavia. "Grandmother was just telling me recently that you're practically a stranger yourself."

Trent's dark eyes danced, but he said solemnly, "That's true, I'm afraid. The Spencers have *only* been in this part of the country for a mere seventy-five years."

"Yes," said Octavia briskly. "But your time didn't count until your grandfather bought that farm."

"It's a good thing Mom and Dad aren't here to hear you say that. Come to think of it, Granddad wouldn't be too pleased either," Trent said with a smile.

Both Carla and Trent laughed, and soon after that, they followed the crowd to another tent where a sumptuous buffet and a bar had been set up beside a wooden dance floor. Trent excused himself and Octavia was claimed by an older couple, leaving Carla alone. All the excitement had given her a headache, and she needed some air. An exit was nearby, and she was sidling toward it, when Wade appeared.

"Leaving so soon?" he asked in that mocking tone she disliked.

She started to answer, but just then a group of people trooped in. Whatever she'd been about to reply vanished from her mind when Wade instinctively put his hand on her arm to guide her out of the path of the newcomers. To her horror, that simple touch made her feel breathless.

It must be the crowd in here, she told herself. The press of people trying to get through the door was suffocating; the atmosphere was making her light-headed. That was all there was to it.

But it seemed aeons before the group made its way past and Wade was free to move away; by then she really did feel faint.

"Are you all right?" he asked.

She had to pull herself together. "I'm fine," she said, her head swimming. "I...I just need to sit down a minute."

"Let me find you a chair."

The last thing she wanted was for him to develop a sense of gallantry that would keep him nearby. "No, that's all right," she said, but he'd already taken her elbow and was leading her outside.

Mercifully, there were chairs close by, and she sat down in the first one she saw. "I don't know what's wrong with me tonight," she said. "I felt perfectly fine when we left the house...."

He had remained standing. "Maybe it's all the excitement."

"Oh, surely not—"

"Well, I don't know. It's not every night someone gives so much money to a charity she's probably never heard of before."

He sounded angry, and she looked up. "You don't approve of the auction?"

"It's none of my business."

His response irritated her—as so many things about him seemed to do. "Why are you acting this way?" she asked. "It was for a good cause."

"And you're really into good causes, right?"

"Are you being sarcastic?"

"Me? Gosh, no, ma'am. I'm just the hired hand, remember?"

She stood up, her earlier wooziness completely forgotten. "What's the matter with you?"

"Nothing's the matter. I just don't like parties."

"Then why did you come to this one?"

"Because Mrs. D. asked me."

"And do you always do what my grandmother asks?"

"I owe Mrs. D. a lot."

"Yes, so you said." She thought of what Octavia had told her about Wade's former occupation and couldn't resist. "You didn't say why."

"No, I didn't," he replied evenly.

She flushed. "Perhaps I shouldn't have asked."

"Yeah, maybe you shouldn't have. Why are you so interested, anyway? Have you been talking to someone about me?"

She stiffened. "I know it will be a shock, but I really don't spend my time discussing Wade Petrie."

Her sarcasm seemed to be lost on him for he said, "I'm glad to hear that. Because as far as I'm concerned, my private life is my business."

Now she was angry. "That's true. As long as it doesn't affect my grandmother or Dunleavy Farm."

"You should talk," he countered belligerently. "What are you still doing here? I thought you'd planned to stay an hour or so and be on your way. Or was that just a ploy?" he asked suddenly, eyes narrowed. "You did have a lot of luggage."

"For your information," she said between clenched teeth, "I *always* travel with a lot of luggage. I like to be prepared for anything."

"I see. Well, just make sure that you're not taking advantage of—"

Before he could complete the sentence, Octavia joined them. Seemingly oblivious to any tension, she said brightly, "Oh, there you are, my dears! I've been looking all over for you. Am I intruding?"

"Not at all," Carla said, giving Wade a glacial stare before she turned to her grandmother. "We just came out to get some air."

"Yes, it was stuffy in there," Octavia agreed, fanning her face with her handkerchief. "Where did you go, Wade? You left before the end of the sale."

"I saw enough," Wade said, standing stiffly beside Carla. "Besides, you see one sale, you've pretty much seen them all."

"Did you know Carla bid on a horse?" Octavia asked.

"I heard she added quite a sum to the jockey association."

Carla didn't miss his dig at her. Frostily, she said, "As Trent said, it was for a good cause."

"That reminds me," Octavia said. "Have you discussed Done Driftin' with Carla yet, Wade?"

"Done Driftin'?" Carla repeated. She turned to Wade. "What about him?"

"He'll have to go into race training soon if he's to be ready for the season. He really should have been at the track months ago," Wade said.

"That's my fault," Octavia confessed guiltily. "I didn't want him to go until I heard from you, Carla. I thought if you did visit the farm, you'd want to see him."

"I'm glad you waited, Grandmother. But now that I *am* here, maybe it's too late for him to start."

Octavia chuckled. "You sound like a mother hen with her first chick."

To Carla's surprise, she did feel that way. But for Wade's benefit, she said pointedly, "Well, you did say Done Driftin' was mine, Grandmother. Can I help it if I feel protective?"

"I can't blame you," Octavia agreed. "But are you saying that, now that he's yours, you don't want to race him after all?"

Carla hadn't thought that far. In fact, she realized she'd been trying not to think of the implications of her grandmother's gift. If she formally accepted the colt, it would mean that she'd have to make some kind of commitment to Octavia and the farm. Was she ready for that?

Confused and uncertain, she made the mistake of turning to Wade. "What do you think?"

He looked directly at her. "Why do you care what I think? You're going to do what you want to, aren't you?"

His response annoyed her so much that she immediately said, "Yes, I am. Grandmother's right. I think I should put the horse in training." Then, just to show him who was boss, she added, "I can always change my mind later."

Anger flashed in Wade's eyes, but to Carla's disappointment, all he did was shrug as if it didn't matter. "It's your call," he said. "I just work here."

"Good," Octavia said. "I'm glad that's settled. Now, I hate to say this, but I'm a little tired, and I think I'll go on home. But don't let me spoil your evening," she added. "I'll call Samson to come and get me if you two want to stay here and dance a while."

Carla suddenly became aware of music drifting out from the tent. But the last thing she wanted was Octavia to push her and Wade onto the dance floor, so she said quickly, "I've had enough, too. I'll just go home with you, if you don't mind, Grandmother."

Wade made it unanimous. "I'll call it an evening, too. You two wait here while I bring around the car."

IT WAS A SILENT RIDE on the way home. To his intense
annoyance, Wade couldn't get Carla out of his mind.
She had looked so beautiful tonight that it had been
difficult to keep his hands off her. When those people
had pushed through the door, and he'd guided her
aside, it had been a real battle not to take her in his
arms and kiss her right there.

Just in time, he'd remembered how much he disliked her—and how well she fit in with that well-heeled
crowd where he had learned he didn't belong. He'd
watched as she'd joked and laughed with everyone and
when she'd blithely written out a check for five thousand dollars in the name of a charity she knew nothing about, he'd been reminded forcibly of Annabelle.

Not that Annabelle would have given that much
money to a good cause, he thought cynically. For Annabelle Renfrow, the only good cause she'd had was
herself. Even so, the two women were still sisters under the skin. Money meant about as much to them as
horses did; he'd seen that in Miss Carla Dunleavy tonight.

Damn, he wished Octavia hadn't given Done Driftin' to Carla. She could pretend confusion over what to
do about the colt, but he knew from bitter experience
that people like Carla Dunleavy would act as the spirit
moved them. If it amused her for a while to race the
colt, she would. If she decided—God forbid—to make
a hunter or jumper out of him, she'd do that, too. She
wouldn't think of the horse or her grandmother; she'd
please herself. People like Carla always did.

He had to stop thinking of her, he told himself. But the drive back to the farm seemed endless—especially when he caught a whiff of Carla's perfume. As the tantalizing scent filled his nostrils, his hands tightened on the wheel, and he wished to hell he was home again.

CARLA SAW Wade's hand tighten on the wheel. Against her will, she remembered how that same hand had felt tonight when he'd taken her arm. Her entire body seemed to grow warm at the recollection, and she hated herself. How could she feel any attraction for this man? He disliked her; she despised him. And all he had done was touch her. It wasn't as if he'd swept her into his arms and kissed her until she was senseless.

Maybe she should just pack her bags and leave. What was keeping her here, anyway? She had never stayed so long in one place; it was past time to move on.

Glumly, she stared out the window. How could she leave before Done Driftin' started training? He was her horse if she wanted him. How could she go away and not learn how he took to the track?

And what if he entered a race and won?

No, she couldn't leave now. She'd been here this long; it would be foolish to go when things were just starting to get interesting. She'd only stay long enough to see how the colt ran, *then* she'd be on her way. She had to give him a chance, didn't she?

OCTAVIA SAT in the back seat, quiet and content. She saw the covert glances between Carla and Wade when each thought the other wasn't looking, and she smiled to herself.

Her granddaughter could do a lot worse than Wade Petrie, she thought. Despite all the rumors about him, she knew he was a good man. Oh, she'd heard the stories about Wade and that no-account Renfrow girl, but rumors had always swirled around Annabelle. She thrived on trouble, and that's what she got.

Without warning, Octavia thought of her oldest daughter, Meredith, and Gary and Jamie, her other two children. She'd sent out her letters to her three grandchildren, but so far Carla was the only one who had replied. She hadn't heard yet from Gary's daughter, Nan, in Montana, and she hoped that the reason Seth, Jamie's son, had been silent was that he and Honey moved around a lot, and his letter hadn't caught up to him.

Or maybe she was just an old woman still fooling herself, she mused sadly, and was glad when the car finally pulled up at the house.

CHAPTER SIX

"I CAN'T IMAGINE why I ever agreed to this," Carla grumbled while climbing into the cab of the truck very early one Friday morning, almost two weeks after Done Driftin' had gone to the track for training. The sky was still dark; the clock on the dashboard read five to four. She sat back with a grumpy sigh and closed her eyes.

Wade got in behind the wheel. As they drove out, he said, "You were the one who wanted to see Done Driftin' work out."

Briefly, Carla opened one eye. "Yes, but when I said that, I didn't realize we'd be out in the dead of night. Who trains horses in the pitch black, anyway?"

"It won't be dark by the time we get there. Besides, racetrack people get up early."

"Bully for them. I wonder if anyone has ever asked the horses how they feel about being up before the crack of dawn."

"Are you going to complain the entire way? Because if you are, tell me, and I'll take you back right now."

"Don't tempt me. This is insane. I never get up at this hour. In fact, until this morning, I didn't realize there were actually two four o'clocks in every day."

"Oh, really? With your life-style, I would have thought that's about the time you get home from your dates."

Carla wasn't going to rise to the bait. "That just goes to show how much you know about me. Now, if you don't mind, could we have a little peace and quiet? I'm up. I'm dressed. I'm on the road at this ungodly hour. But nowhere does it say that I can't sleep the rest of the way."

"Fine with me. I'd rather have silence than grousing. We've got a way to go. Do you think you can keep quiet until we get there?"

"It'll be a struggle, but I'll try," Carla said, settling into a more comfortable position. "Wake me when we arrive, if you please. Perhaps by that time, the sun will at least have made a pretense of getting up, and I'll be able to see my horse without using a flashlight."

Wade didn't answer. After a few minutes of silence, broken only by the purring sound of the truck's big engine as they headed down the interstate, he reached for the radio. He was about to turn it on to keep him company, when he glanced at Carla to see if she really had gone back to sleep.

It certainly looked like it. She had put her coat over herself for a blanket and was nestled under it, her eyes closed, her head leaning against the doorjamb. The position looked uncomfortable, and he wondered if he should gently pull her over so she could rest against his shoulder.

He jerked back. What was he thinking? Getting close to this high-and-mighty porcupine of a woman was the last thing he wanted to do. He should be counting his blessings that they had managed, these past few weeks, to put aside the swords and shields and reach this new level of—what? It couldn't be considered friendship. Maybe he'd call it a wary truce. They talked when they met; they'd even had a decent conversation or two. But, as if by unspoken agreement, they avoided any tack that would lead to angry words.

Not that he liked her any more than he had when they'd first met, he thought hastily. Just because they had reached this precarious understanding didn't mean that she had changed. She was still the same spoiled, bored socialite she had been when she'd arrived.

And yet...

Who would have thought she'd still be here? When he had gone to get her at the airport, he would have bet money that she wouldn't last two days at Dunleavy. But now she seemed in no hurry to leave. In fact, Mrs. D. had delightedly confided in him that Carla had developed such an interest in the place that she'd taken over the account books. He didn't know how he felt about that, but as he and Carla had agreed—on this one thing only—it wasn't his business.

Of course, Done Driftin' had a lot to do with Carla's staying. In the beginning, when Octavia had told him what she intended to do with the colt, he'd decided she was being a lonely, foolish woman caught up in dreams. After all, that colt, along with two other offspring, was probably the last of old Done Roamin's get. As such, Done Driftin' was a valuable animal, especially if he proved to be as good as his preliminary training reports indicated. He was already worth a lot of money, and yet Octavia, who was clearly in need of funds herself, had just given him away.

Now the colt was at the track. Since Wade no longer had his own training stable, they had put him with an old friend of Octavia's, a respected trainer named Dwight Connor. Wade knew Dwight from the "old days," and he'd approved of the choice. Connor was a good trainer, one of the best. If anyone could bring out the talent in Done Driftin', it would be Dwight.

It seemed they'd chosen well. The trainer had phoned last evening to say it would soon be time for the colt's first race this year. Which was why he and Carla were on their way to the track so early this morning. An official clocker was going to time the colt's morning work, and after that, they'd decide which race to enter. If Done Driftin' was as fast as they all thought he was, the horse could go down in the record books.

Wade glanced at Carla again. That was, if the new owner kept the colt at the track.

She certainly seemed preoccupied with every aspect of Done Driftin's training. She wanted to know everything there was to know: what the colt ate and when, how much he was exercised, what kind of shoes the farrier used on him, when the veterinarian came to check on him. No detail was too small. Sometimes he thought she had collected enough information to write a book on the subject.

He grinned, thinking how glad he was that he wasn't the colt's trainer. Dwight was at his wit's end when he'd called last night. Wade knew it wasn't funny, but he had to laugh anyway. He might have lost his own stable, but he recalled all too well the hand-holding that trainers were so often required to do where owners were concerned. What Dwight had told him made him smile and feel nostalgic at the same time.

"Uh, Wade," Dwight had begun hesitantly, "would you mind answering a question? I don't want to step on any toes here, so if I'm out of line, just say so, okay?"

"Sure. What's the problem?"

"Well . . . how well do you know this granddaughter of Mrs. Dunleavey's?"

Wade had guessed what was coming. "Enough to know that the lady not only speaks her mind, she's got a lot on it. Is that what you mean?"

"I don't like to say anything against a client, you understand. But Wade, this lady is driving me crazy!

She wants a complete journal on that colt, from the time he gets up in the morning to when we turn the lights out at night. Now, I've had owners who were interested in their horses before, but this is too much. I've got two dozen runners in training. I don't have time to write up a status report every time the horse takes a—''

"I understand, Dwight," Wade said. "I think she's just anxious—"

"Anxious! No disrespect, but she's going to drive us all around the bend. My assistant trainer won't answer the phone because he thinks it's her again, and two of the grooms are about to have nervous breakdowns because they think she'll show up unannounced and find a stray wisp of straw in the colt's mane, which she says wouldn't happen if the horse were groomed properly. Is there anything you can do to help us?"

Wade knew Carla, and doubted it. But Dwight sounded so harassed that he had to say something. "You know how new owners are sometimes," he said soothingly. "She'll calm down."

"When?" Dwight's voice rose. "Lord help us if the colt loses his first time out. She'll probably fire the lot of us right on the spot. And if he ever gets hurt..."

"He's not likely to get hurt, not the way you bring your horses along," Wade reassured.

"But anything can happen. You know that."

Without warning, Wade had a flash of a filly running all out, then going down. He blinked quickly, trying to get the picture out of his mind and concentrated on what Dwight had just said.

"Carla . . . er . . . Miss Dunleavy understands that," he said. "After all, she knows horses."

"That she does," Dwight agreed reluctantly. "And she sure picked a good one. That colt is taking to training like nobody's business."

"He's settled in, then?"

"Settled in! It's like he's been here for years. He's rarin' to go, in fact. It's going to take a locomotive to hold him back." Dwight paused a moment. Then he said, "It was a good decision to rest him a while, Wade. But then you know horses, you always did."

Wade tensed. He always felt uncomfortable whenever someone even obliquely mentioned his training days. He wanted to get off the subject as quickly as possible.

"I can't take credit," he said. "Done Driftin's a good colt. Smart and eager. You can't ask for a better combination than that."

"True. And that brings me to the reason I called tonight. We're going to be clocking the colt tomorrow, and I wondered if you all would like to come down and watch."

"I wouldn't miss it," Wade said without hesitating. "I'll ask, but I think Mrs. D. will probably wait for the race. Have you told Carla about it yet?"

"No, I thought I'd call you first to find out what kind of reception I might get. I don't think she likes me much."

"She doesn't like me much, either," Wade said with a laugh.

"Swell. I was hoping you'd act as a go-between."

"Sorry."

"Okay, then. I guess I'll see you tomorrow morning about five-thirty, six. Oh, and by the way, Wade—"

"Yes?"

"Don't be surprised if this colt knocks your socks off."

"He's that good?"

"Good?" the trainer had said. "He's better than anything around here on four feet."

So now he and Carla were on their way to see just how good her colt was. Wade stretched and looked at the dashboard clock. It was almost five. He glanced across at Carla.

She hadn't changed position, except that the coat covering her had slipped off her shoulder. Without thinking, he reached over and tucked it into place. Carla stirred, and he snatched his hand back as though he'd been scalded. Annoyed by his reaction, he grabbed the wheel with both hands just as Carla yawned and sat up.

"Are we there?" she asked.

"Almost. I said I'd wake you up, didn't I?"

She rubbed her neck. "I wasn't really asleep. It's too uncomfortable trying to sleep in a truck."

"Obviously you've never transported horses for any distance."

"No, I can't say that I've had that dubious pleasure."

"Once you've done that, you learn to sleep anywhere, even standing up."

"An achievement to admire. But thanks, anyway, I'll pass."

As she reached for her purse and pulled out a comb, Wade noticed for the first time what she was wearing. He shook his head. No ordinary jeans and blouse for her; instead, she was decked out in suede pants, silk blouse and soft leather boots.

"What are you staring at?" she asked abruptly. She pointed with the comb. "Shouldn't you be paying attention to your driving?"

"You're right. I was just wondering why you wore those boots."

She looked down. "What's wrong with them?"

"They won't last five minutes on the backside. You need mukluks or something."

"Oh, wouldn't those be attractive."

"Maybe not, but they'd be a damned sight more serviceable than those flimsy things."

"Why are you so concerned about my footwear?"

"I'm not. Maybe we should just change the subject."

"Maybe so."

Wade decided it was safest to discuss horses. "When I talked to Dwight last night, he said that Done Driftin' has settled in real well."

"Yes, he told me the same thing," Carla said. She replaced the comb and took out a tube of lipstick. "I was glad to hear it. Some horses are upset by all the track activity. They never do adjust to it."

"How do you know that?"

She'd pulled down the visor to use the mirror. Giving him a sideways glance, she said, "I know a lot of things."

He couldn't argue that. "What else did Dwight tell you?"

"Among other things, he told me how fast Done Driftin' is."

Was that a genuine note of pride Wade heard in her voice? "We'll see," he said.

"Yes, we will. In fact, I'm so sure of him that I'll bet you he'll go six furlongs in...let's say...one-eleven and change."

Where did she get that track jargon? he wondered. "You're crazy. That would be a decent time for an experienced horse in an actual race. It's impossible for a morning workout."

"Not for Done Driftin'," Carla insisted. She slanted another glance at him. "What's the matter—chicken, or too cheap to bet?"

It was that challenging look in her eyes that did it. "Neither," he said. "Name your price."

"Loser buys dinner."

He hadn't thought they'd bet anything but money. Instantly, visions of him escorting Carla out in that purple gown filled his head. Before he knew it, he was saying, "You're on."

She smiled, Cheshire catlike, as she settled back against the seat. "Good," she said. "I like a man who puts his money where his mouth is."

"Just make sure you're ready to pay up when you lose," he retorted.

"Oh, I won't lose." There was laughter in her voice. "One of the grooms told me that Done Driftin' already breezed that distance the other day in one-twelve."

Breezed meant a horse hadn't been working that hard, just galloping easily. Wade didn't show it, but he was impressed. How much better could this colt do when he was running full out?

"You cheated," he said.

"No, I'm just informed. Can I help it if you're not?"

This seemed a good opening to try to help Done Driftin's beleaguered trainer. "Now that you mention it," he said, "Dwight told me you were very interested in the colt's schedule."

"He doesn't think owners have a right to inquire about their horses?"

"I didn't say that." The last thing he wanted was to get the man into trouble. "But you might lighten up. After all, Done Driftin' hasn't been in race training that long. Everyone needs a little time to adjust, including the trainers, the grooms . . . and the horse."

When she didn't answer immediately, he knew he'd made her mad. *Well, so it goes,* he thought. He wasn't going to apologize for saying something that had needed to be said, so he kept his eyes on the road and just drove.

But she surprised him by saying, "You're right. I always put people off. I don't know why, because I don't really feel the way I come across."

He was so startled by what she'd said that he nearly missed the gate at the backside of the track. They had arrived, and after the guard recognized him and waved him through, he quickly parked the truck. Then he turned to her and said, "I didn't mean—"

"Yes, you did," she said quietly. "It's all right. It's something I've lived with all my life."

Now he really felt like a heel. "I just—"

"You know, it's funny. Normally, I don't care what people think of me. But ever since I came here, it's...different."

Dawn had imperceptibly broken while they'd been on the road, and Carla suddenly looked so fragile that he wanted to pull her into his arms. But he didn't, because he knew her vulnerability was an illusion. Just because she was in a mood now didn't mean that she'd welcome his attentions. On the contrary, she'd probably break his arm if he tried to touch her.

"Different?" he asked cautiously. In the soft, rosy light, her eyes were very green, her skin like porcelain. Her chestnut hair looked burnished, and he had to fight an impulse to take a fistful and bury his face in it. With an effort, he kept himself on track. "In what way?"

"I don't know why I said that. Forget it."

"I don't want to forget it. Tell me."

It was one of their rare moments of communication. He could see her debating about what to say—especially to him—but finally she said, "It's hard to explain, but ever since I came here, the feeling has been growing in me that..." She stopped. "Never mind. I don't know what's wrong with me. Let's just chalk it up to early-hour madness, all right?"

He was so fascinated by her face that he just sat there and watched when she reached for the door handle. When he realized that she was about to get out, he reached across and grasped her arm. "Wait."

"What?"

"You started to say something a moment ago," he said. "I'd like to know what it was."

"You'll think I'm being silly."

He took a deep breath. "I think a lot of things about you, Carla Dunleavy, there's no doubt about that. But one thing I never think is that you're silly. Now, what is it?"

She bit her lip. Then she said, "I don't understand it. I've never felt this way about any place. I never thought I would. But ever since I came here, the feeling has been growing in me that the farm is...home." She looked at him almost defiantly. "I told you it would sound silly."

He held her gaze. They were almost close enough now on the seat to kiss, and he knew that if he looked at her mouth, he wouldn't be able to resist. So he said, "It doesn't sound silly at all. I feel the same way about it."

"You do?"

He sat back, trying to give himself breathing space. But she'd made a painful confession to him; he could do no less for her. He said, "I don't know what it is about that place. Maybe it's the land, maybe it's the heart and the courage of that old stallion. Any other horse would have given up after what happened to him, but not Done Roamin'. And not Octavia Dunleavy, either. They make the farm what it is, a place to restore the spirit—"

It was his turn to stop talking. *Where had that come from?* he wondered, chagrined.

"You do understand," Carla said, marveling.

He was too embarrassed to reply. It wasn't like him to be poetic. "Well, enough of that," he said to cover his embarrassment. "We'd better start moving or we'll be late. After getting up so early and coming all this way, you don't want to miss that workout."

Carla seemed as relieved as he was to have something concrete to do. They got out of the truck, slamming doors together and shoving hands into pockets. On the way to the barn, they studiously walked several paces apart. Wade was relieved to see that Done Driftin' was being tacked up when they arrived, and he was about to call out to the grooms, when the horse caught sight of Carla and let out his shrill neigh of greeting. Everyone turned to look, and Dwight Connor quickly appeared at the doorway to his little office. He saw Wade and Carla and came out grinning.

"I see you made it, Ms. Dunleavy," he said.

"I wouldn't have missed this for anything," Carla replied. She turned to give Done Driftin' an affectionate pat. "He looks just fine."

"He does, doesn't he?" Dwight said, sounding pleased at the praise. "But I can't take credit for it. He just bloomed on his own. Some horses fall off a little in weight when they first come, but not him. He's been set from the get go."

"Then let's see what he can do."

Dwight's regular jockey appeared just then, pulling on gloves as he emerged from the tack room. They had already been introduced, and as he approached, Carla said, "Good morning, Ian. Are you ready to give my colt a little workout?"

Ian McKenzie had been riding horses since childhood. Rumor had it that he had one of the best sets of hands in the business. He also had a gold front tooth that showed when he grinned.

"Let's do it," he said, tooth glinting.

Done Driftin' seemed even more eager to go than the little crowd that surrounded him. After Dwight effortlessly tossed the jockey into the saddle, the colt pranced on the way to the track as everyone else followed. After a signal to the clocker to indicate that Done Driftin' was out on the track, Ian trotted out to

begin the warm-up. Dwight, Wade, Carla and the
grooms took up strategic places at the rail.

After jogging halfway around, Ian let Done Driftin' lengthen his stride into a long-legged canter. As she
watched, Carla felt her heart quicken. The colt's
ground-eating stride was a sight to see, but she knew
he was nowhere near clocking speed. Trying to calm
herself, she observed the other horses who were
working out this morning. One horse and rider galloped by in front of them, the exercise girl standing
straight up in the stirrups while leaning back on the
reins. Down the track, two horses seemed to be dueling it out, their riders crouched low over the animals'
necks as they sped around a turn. Not far from them,
a striking gray horse was cantering sideways as his
rider tried vainly to straighten him out, and some distance away was a group of three horses who were being walked back to the barn after their workout.

Carla looked again for Done Driftin' and immediately spotted him and Ian. As she did, Wade took her
arm.

"Here they go," he murmured.

Carla tensed as Ian crouched low in the saddle,
asking the colt for speed. As though the jockey
had put the horse in gear, Done Driftin' seemed
to...stretch out. Tail streaming, he flew down the
track, close to the rail. Within seconds, he was going
so fast he was almost a blur. Carla drew in a breath,
knowing she would never forget that sight. She had
never seen anything so beautiful in her life.

"Lord," Wade breathed, beside her.

Carla couldn't look away from her colt. Without realizing it, she grabbed Wade's hand and gripped it. On her other side, Dwight was clutching a stopwatch, muttering to himself. Done Driftin' flashed under the finish line just then, and Dwight bellowed in delight.

"Man, can that horse run!" he shouted.

"How fast?" Wade asked.

Dwight looked down at the watch again. When he saw the time, his florid face turned crimson. "I don't believe it!"

"What? What?" Carla cried.

Dwight tried to answer, but nothing came out. He showed them the watch, but his hand was shaking so much from excitement that she had to grab it to read the face. When she saw the time, she turned excitedly to Wade.

"I told you, didn't I?" she crowed.

Wade grabbed the watch from her. When he saw the hands, he looked at Dwight, who was grinning from ear to ear.

"Lord," Wade said again.

Done Driftin' had just breezed six furlongs in exactly one minute eleven seconds.

WHEN THE JOCKEY finally cooled out Done Driftin' enough to meet them by the rail, his face was bright red and he asked excitedly, "Did he fly, or was it my imagination?"

In answer, a grinning Dwight held up the watch. The clocker had confirmed the trainer's unofficial timing, and when Ian saw the numbers, he let out such a wild whoop that people down the rail glanced their way. None of the elated group noticed as they trooped back to the barn behind the steaming, blowing horse.

While the groom took over the happy chore of walking Done Driftin' until the animal could be bathed and put back in his stall, Carla, Wade and Dwight talked strategy in the office. After what he'd seen today, the trainer thought the colt was ready to race.

"When?" Carla asked.

Dwight consulted the racing schedule and named a race the following Saturday. Pleased at the prospect of seeing how Done Driftin' would do against competition, Carla said she couldn't believe it was going to happen so soon.

Dwight was still grinning. "He's ready, Ms. Dunleavy. That colt is just busting out of his skin, wanting to run. What do you think, Wade?"

Carla turned to Wade, who seemed a little embarrassed at being consulted. "You're the trainer, Dwight."

"Okay, we'll enter him."

Carla couldn't leave before she made sure Done Driftin' was all right. The colt was in his stall, and when she stopped outside the door and he saw her, the barn rang again with his shrill whinny. She laughed, pleased that the horse had acknowledged her.

"You did a good job today," she murmured when the animal came over to the stall door. She reached up to pet him, but when he nuzzled her hand, she remembered that she hadn't brought him a treat from home. She'd meant to, but they'd left so early that she'd forgotten. She knew Dwight kept carrots in the feed room and was just turning to head back that way, when she realized Wade was right behind her.

"Oh! I'm sorry," she said, almost bumping into him. "I didn't see you there. I was just going to..."

Her voice trailed off at the look in his eyes. They were standing so close that he took up her entire field of vision, but even so, she couldn't have looked away from him if she'd tried. *One more step, and she'd be in his arms,* she thought suddenly, and was wondering what to do, when Wade held up something.

"Is this what you were looking for?" he asked, his voice sounding strange.

Incredibly, it took her a few seconds to recognize that he was holding a carrot. She looked at it blankly for a moment. Then she realized he must have gotten it for Done Driftin' and she took it.

"Th-thanks," she said, stammering. "I meant to bring one from home—"

Pull yourself together! she told herself. She couldn't stand here like an idiot, staring into this man's eyes and wishing he would...what? Kiss her? But that was insane. They were in a public place, he was her grandmother's barn manager and—

So what?

I'll tell you what.

It had nothing to do with who he was, or what job he held at the farm. She knew what Wade thought of her; the point was what *she* thought of him. She was never going to forgive him for implying that she'd come to Dunleavy Farm with the nefarious purpose of taking advantage of her grandmother in some way. How did she know that he wasn't trying to do the same? Just what *was* his interest in the farm, anyway? Why was he there as barn manager, instead of training horses, as he should be?

CARLA WAS SO EAGER to tell Octavia the thrilling news about Done Driftin' that she didn't even argue when Wade gave her the keys to the truck and asked if she wouldn't mind driving back by herself. In fact, if the truth were known, she was relieved that he wasn't coming with her. The morning had had too many *moments* when she'd looked into his eyes and felt . . . she didn't know what. She only knew that she wanted to get away from him for a while. She hoped that all these confusing feelings about him were due to excitement and that once she was alone, she'd come to her senses.

But she did remember to ask, "If I take the truck, how are you going to get home?"

"I'll catch a ride from someone," he said, avoiding her eyes. "Don't worry about me."

She tried not to. But, perversely, as she drove back to Dunleavy Farm, she couldn't stop thinking about

Wade and wondering if he had the same conflicting feelings about her as she had about him. Had she just imagined what she'd seen in his face this morning?

"Oh, to hell with it," she muttered. She was not going to allow Wade Petrie to ruin her excitement about Done Driftin'. Her colt had done magnificently, and she couldn't wait to tell her grandmother.

Octavia met her at the door. "Well?"

Now that she was back home, Carla forgot her problems with Wade and grinned from ear to ear. As she took her grandmother's arm and pulled her gently into the front room, she said, "Have I got a story for you!"

She'd just finished telling Octavia the tale, when the phone rang. A few moments later, Teresa appeared in the doorway.

"A telephone call for you, Ms. Dunleavy," she said to Carla. "It's your mother."

"My mother?" Uncertainly, she looked at her grandmother. "Maybe I shouldn't—"

"Of course you should," Octavia said. She took hold of her cane and slowly stood. To Carla's sudden distress, she seemed to have aged ten years. "You go ahead, my dear. We can discuss Done Driftin's racing career later."

Carla felt torn as Octavia went from the room. She wanted to follow her grandmother, but she couldn't let her mother hang on the line. She watched Octavia's departing figure, then went to the phone.

"Mother? Why are you calling? Is something wrong? Did anything happen?"

"Nothing happened, I'm just fine. But I would appreciate a hello."

"I'm sorry. But this is sort of a bad time. Can I call you back?"

"No, you cannot. I'm going out right now. In fact, the only reason I called is to tell you that I'm leaving Acapulco for the East Coast tomorrow. I wanted to know what flight you'll take so we can meet and return to London together."

Carla was dismayed. "You can't be thinking of going back already!"

"Already? It's been weeks! Now, I've been understanding long enough. I want you on the first plane out of there. We'll meet tomorrow at the—"

"I can't make it," Carla said.

"I beg your pardon?"

"You heard me. I can't leave tomorrow."

There was a silence. Then Meredith said icily, "All right, then. When would be more convenient for you?"

It was difficult, but Carla stood her ground. "I don't know. I'm not sure I want to go back to London."

"What?"

"Listen, Mother, you don't understand—"

"You're right about that, I don't. Oh, I knew *that woman* would turn you against me! What has she been saying, anyway? I want to know."

"She hasn't said anything. In fact, we don't even talk about you."

"Oh, really?"

"Yes, really! I know I can't expect you to understand, but some exciting things have been happening here. Remember the horse that Grandmother gave me? Well, today—"

"I don't want to hear it. Now, are you going to meet me or not? I'll give you two days, but that's all. I can't imagine what possible reason you'd have to stay longer than that. We'll talk about this later."

"No, we'll talk about it now," Carla said sharply. "I told you, I can't leave now. Done Driftin' is going to race next Saturday, and I'm not going to miss it."

"That's ridiculous! You never expressed such an interest in horse racing before!"

"I never owned my own racehorse before. Now, I'm sorry you don't understand, but that's the way it is. I'm not leaving, and that's final."

There was another chilly silence. Then Meredith said, "I don't know what's happened to you, Carla. You haven't been the same person since that woman got her hooks into you. It's obvious that since you won't leave, I'll have to come and get you."

Carla was sure she hadn't heard right. "You're coming here?"

"Yes, I am."

"But you said you'd never come to Dunleavy Farm."

"Things have changed," Meredith said coldly. "That woman ruined my life. I'm not going to allow her to ruin yours. I'll call again with my flight information. In any case, expect me soon."

"But—"

"You *will* come to pick me up at the airport, I trust? That is, if she hasn't turned you completely against me by now."

"Of course I'll come," Carla said, trying for patience. "But, Mother, you have it all wrong. Grandmother would never—"

"We'll see," Meredith said. She hung up without saying goodbye.

Just then, Carla realized that Octavia was standing in the doorway. When she saw the look on her grandmother's face, she knew there was no need to tell her that after all these years, her oldest daughter was coming home.

CHAPTER SEVEN

CARLA WAS LATE. At the very time that Meredith's plane was touching down in Louisville, she was still on the road to the airport, stuck behind an eighteen-wheeler that refused to move over so she could pass. By the time she arrived at the airport, parked and ran into the terminal, the flashing On Time sign opposite her mother's flight number indicated that the plane had been on the ground almost forty minutes. *She was in trouble now,* she thought as she turned and headed toward the gate. How was she ever going to explain this?

She didn't have time to worry about it. Meredith was waiting for her, and from the woman's expression, she wasn't happy about her daughter's tardiness.

"Where have you been?" she demanded as Carla rushed up. "I've been waiting almost an hour in this hideous airport."

"I'm sorry, Mother," Carla said, trying not to pant. "I know it's inexcusable, but I lost track of time."

"What? What do you mean, you lost *track?* How is that possible? I told you three days ago when I planned to arrive."

Carla couldn't confess that she'd become so absorbed in working on the farm's accounts that she had completely forgotten the hour. In fact, she recalled guiltily, if Teresa hadn't come to remind her, she'd probably still be sitting at the desk in the converted sitting room that served as the office, wondering again how Octavia could have gotten herself into such a financial mess.

But now wasn't the time to think of that, she knew, and said hastily, "Well, we're both here now. And as soon as we get your bags, we can be on our way."

"I'm not so sure," Meredith said. "I've changed my mind. I think it might be best if I just left now."

"Leave? What are you saying? You just arrived!"

"I know. But already I don't like it." Meredith looked around disdainfully. "I'd forgotten how... provincial it is."

"For heaven's sake! You haven't even left the airport."

"I don't have to," Meredith said peevishly. "It's all coming back to me. In fact, the more I think about it, the more I realize how ridiculous this is. I can't imagine why I felt compelled to come. If you don't want to return to England with me, I can't fight you. You're an adult, even if, in my opinion, you're acting like a recalcitrant child."

Carla had vowed on the way to the airport that, no matter what Meredith said, she would not lose her temper. "Why don't you stay for a while, Mother?

Give it a chance. You might find that you like it here after all these years."

"I doubt that," Meredith stated flatly. She looked around again, her nostrils pinched. "Still, I did come all this way, so we might as well get it over with."

Without giving Carla a chance to respond, she turned and began walking toward the baggage-claim area. Behind her, Carla counted to ten, then followed. When she caught up, she said, "I'm glad you came. I have so many things to tell you."

"If it has to do with that woman, I don't want to hear it."

"Would you please stop calling her 'that woman'? If you can't manage 'Mother,' why don't you just call her Octavia?"

"I'd prefer to call her nothing at all," Meredith said tartly. "The only reason I'm here is to prevent her from destroying your life, as she did mine."

Carla abandoned the cheery pretense. "All right, instead of dropping all these dire hints, maybe it's time to tell me what happened between you. Then I'd know what to avoid and we'd all be happy."

Meredith's expertly made-up eyes flashed. "I didn't come all this way for you to make fun of me in public."

"I'm not making fun of you! It's just—"

"I said I didn't wish to discuss it. Now, shall we get my bags or not?"

Carla took a deep breath. "I'll get the bags," she said. "Where are your claim checks?"

Meredith wasn't mollified. Coldly, she swept past. "Don't bother. I can manage by myself."

Meredith Dunleavy traveled with even more luggage than her daughter did. As she looked around for a porter to load it all onto a baggage cart, Carla was uncomfortably reminded of her own arrival at this very airport. So many things had changed—she, most of all. Now she couldn't blame Wade for thinking her insufferable that day; she *had* been a real witch. If she'd been in his place, she would have left him standing right here in the middle of the airport.

Suddenly, she couldn't bear her mother's attitude any longer. She came forward just as Meredith was exclaiming to the confused porter, "No, no, no! What's the matter with you? I told you not to put that on the bottom of the pile!"

"Here, let me take it," Carla said. To her mother's surprise and the porter's obvious relief, she reached for the elaborate makeup case. Ignoring her mother's expression, she said to the man, "The car is just outside." To Meredith, she said, "Mother, if you'll follow us..."

Without waiting for a reply, she led the way out. Meredith managed not to say anything until the luggage was stowed and they were on their way, but they had barely hit the interstate before she erupted.

"And just *what* was that all about?"

Carla changed into the fast lane. She knew there was no point in playing innocent, so she said, "Things work differently here, Mother. Life goes at a slower pace.''

"Really, do you think you have to tell *me* about the *pace?* I spent my youth in Kentucky, if you recall.'' Meredith looked out the window. ''More's the pity.''

"Now, Mother—''

"And I would appreciate it if you gave me a little credit,'' Meredith said, turning to Carla once more. "You act as though I haven't traveled out of my backyard, when I've been around the world.''

"All I was trying to say was that the man was doing the best he could under the circumstances.''

"And what circumstances were those, might I ask? If you're implying—''

"I'm not implying anything, Mother. He *was* trying—''

"Well, when did you become so understanding?'' Meredith interrupted. "You never cared about such things before. You've changed, Carla, and I don't like it. I don't know what it is, but it certainly isn't—'' Meredith's mouth tightened "—*Octavia's* influence. She treats everyone like a servant. When she deigns to notice them at all, that is.''

This was the opening Carla had been waiting for. She'd hoped that the hour's drive to the farm would give them an opportunity to discuss the past.

"I've been meaning to talk to you about that,'' she said.

"About what?''

"The farm. Why didn't you ever tell me about it?''

"I didn't see the point."

"You didn't see the *point?* For heaven's sake, Mother! It's where you grew up!"

"Yes, but it's not my home."

"That's a strange attitude."

"I have my reasons."

"I suppose you do. But I'd like to know what they are."

"I don't wish to discuss it. If you want to know anything, why don't you ask your *grandmother?*"

"I did. She said it was up to you."

"Well, that's a surprise. I would have thought she'd take any opportunity to put herself in the best possible light."

Carla tried another tack. "I realize this might be difficult for you, but it is for me, too. Can you imagine what it's like growing up believing we had no family—"

"We had family. It was you and me!"

"That's not what I meant, and you know it!"

"I know what you meant, and I told you, I don't want to talk about it."

Carla knew that further conversation would be futile, but as she drummed her fingers impatiently against the steering wheel, she wondered why this was so important to her. Her mother was right: until she'd come to Kentucky, she'd never thought of any other family but Meredith. Why was she suddenly wondering how it would feel to be surrounded by uncles and aunts and cousins? She was an adult; if she hadn't missed having relatives when she was a child, why did she feel the lack now?

It was the farm, she realized. It had taken hold of her and wouldn't let go. It wasn't simply the land, or the horses, or even the house—she'd lived in places that were more beautiful. The difference was that the history of Dunleavy Farm was *her* family's history; that's what made it so special.

Every day she discovered more things about her heritage, things that were giving her a sense of time and place she hadn't had before. There were all those pictures of famous horses that had been born and bred at Dunleavy Farm; there were the trophies and ribbons and plaques all attesting to the contributions the Dunleavy family had made to racing over the years. And of course there was Done Roamin' himself. Every time she saw that brave old horse with her grandmother, she didn't know whether to cry or break into a cheer.

She couldn't understand it. She had *never* been sentimental or emotionally sloppy; it wasn't in her nature. But each night when Octavia went out to the paddock gate and that stallion came down the hill for his treat, Carla knew she was witnessing something special, something she had missed all these years. Done Roamin' represented an accomplishment, a lifetime of achievement, and Octavia had a right to be proud. What had she, Carla, done with her time except dabble? She had no real accomplishments she could point to, no achievements she had won on her own. The realization made her cringe.

Meredith interrupted her thoughts. "She wants something from you, Carla. That's why she sent for you. I've tried to tell you that."

"Well, it's interesting that you interpret it that way, Mother. Especially since she's the one who gave me a gift—a very valuable horse."

"She can afford it."

Could she? Carla wondered. She thought of all the red ink she'd found since she'd taken over the farm's accounts. She'd discovered that Octavia hadn't exaggerated when she'd said that she'd spent most of her reserves on Done Roamin's veterinary bills—in fact, Octavia had underestimated the financial drain. Carla had discussed the situation with her grandmother.

"How could this have happened?" she'd asked. She'd shown Octavia the columns of numbers that were increasingly pointing to disaster. "Don't you have a financial consultant, or a farm manager, or at least, an accountant to advise you?"

Octavia had waved away her concern. "What do I need an adviser for? I've been running this place all my adult life, and I intend to go on until the day I die."

"But—"

"Now, I admit those silly tax forms have become so complicated that I'd never think of trying to file on my own. But as for the rest, it's nobody's business but mine."

"Grandmother—"

Octavia had patted her cheek. "I should have said, it was nobody's business but the *family's*. Now that you're here, of course I'll take your advice. Do you have some suggestions? Is that what this is about?"

Carla hadn't been ready to commit herself at that point, so she had stalled by saying, "I don't know, Grandmother. I haven't been through everything yet."

"Well, you go right ahead and take your time. I'm sure you'll find everything in order."

But that was the problem, Carla mused. Everything *wasn't* in order. In fact, from what she'd seen, the farm's financial status was so shaky that not even the money from the horses Octavia had recently sold would do much to stem the red tide.

How could Octavia be so oblivious to the truth? Her grandmother was eighty years old, but she still had a mind as sharp as a tack. Was Octavia deliberately blinding herself to the situation, or did she think that somehow, miraculously, it would all just...work out?

Even Wade seemed to be aware that something was amiss, she thought with a frown. He'd been pleased about the sale of those horses, but as he'd said to Octavia, the farm was still supporting too much stock. And now that she had the figures, Carla agreed with him. It was obvious now why he'd made that remark about the farm's going through tough times the day they'd brought home that gelding from Four Oaks. How was Octavia going to manage if she kept buying horses and giving others away?

But she couldn't get into all that with her mother right now, so she said, "Whether Grandmother can afford it or not is beside the point. What matters is the gift."

"It was no *gift*, you may be sure of that," Meredith retorted. "Octavia Dunleavy never *gave* anything away in her life. Not without wanting something in return."

Carla looked at her mother in exasperation. "And what do you think she wants this time?"

"It's obvious. I've told you before, Carla. Why do you insist on being so dense? The answer is staring you in the face. She wants you."

"That's ridiculous."

"Is it? You think about it. The woman is eighty years old, and what does she have? A farm that's losing money faster than she can stop it—"

Carla gave her a sharp look. "How do you know that?"

"Because it always has, that's why. Because Mo— because your grandmother has never had a head for business." Meredith's voice rose. "Because she loves those damned horses more than she loves anything else!"

Carla heard something in her mother's voice that she'd never heard there before, and glanced across the seat. As though she'd betrayed herself, Meredith quickly turned away from her.

"Never mind," she muttered. "I didn't mean to say that. It's all past history and doesn't matter anymore."

"Fine," Carla said. "But you're right about the financial health of the farm. From what I've seen, it needs a money transfusion, and fast."

Meredith whipped around. "You're not thinking of contributing!"

"Well, what if I am? It's my money—"

"Good Lord, you're just as bad as she is! And don't look at me like that! I suppose you didn't think I'd find out about that check you wrote at that stupid charity ball! You could have at least told me. I couldn't believe my ears when the accountant called to ask me about it. I had a good mind to tell him to put a hold on it."

Carla almost stopped the car. "You didn't do that, did you? Mother, you had no right!"

"You don't have to shout. I didn't do it."

"Well, why did you bring it up? And why are you acting this way? Are you nervous—"

"Me, nervous!" Meredith laughed shrilly. "Where did you get such an idea?"

"Oh, I don't know. Maybe it's because you haven't been home in so long."

"I told you, Dunleavy Farm is *not* my home! I left it behind when—"

When Meredith stopped abruptly, Carla said, "You might as well tell me. You know I'm going to find out sooner or later."

"Oh, all right!" Meredith snapped angrily. "I don't know why you're so obsessed with it, but the truth is that I left home because your sainted grandmother disapproved of your father. She didn't want me to marry him. And when I did, she hired a fancy lawyer and had the marriage annulled. She didn't care that you were already on the way. She just did it. Now are you happy? How do you feel about her now?"

Carla looked in angry disbelief at her mother. "Why didn't you tell me this sooner? All this time, you let me think that he was—" She stopped. "Is he still alive? Do you know where he is? Did you even love him?"

"Of course I loved him!"

"Then how could you have let this happen? Why didn't you fight for him? Why didn't you—"

"Because he left, that's why!" Meredith cried. "Your grandmother threatened him, or bribed him, or...something! The fact is, I never saw him again, and it's all her fault! Now leave it alone, Carla. I don't want to talk about it anymore!"

But Carla couldn't leave it alone. "You can't just drop it like this! I have a right to know everything about him! After all, he was my father!"

"Then ask your grandmother!" Meredith shouted furiously. "She's the one to tell you. I've told you all I know!"

"All right, I *will* ask her!" Carla shouted back. "Don't think I won't!"

"Then you'd better get ready because we've arrived."

Carla had been so involved in the argument that she had turned automatically onto the long driveway. As they passed under the huge canopy of trees and the beautiful old house emerged from around the bend, Meredith's voice cut like a knife.

"I see nothing's different," she said acridly. "But then, why would I think it would be? With Octavia Dunleavy still in charge, everything was bound to stay the same."

Carla didn't answer as they pulled up to the front door. But as she got out and followed her mother up the steps, she couldn't help thinking that, after what she'd seen and learned these past few weeks, everything at Dunleavy Farm had changed.

Octavia was waiting in the front room when they went inside, and as Meredith paused on the threshold and Octavia slowly and painfully stood up to greet her, Carla looked from one to the other and felt her heart sink. She knew immediately that her own confrontation would have to wait. Time obviously hadn't softened feelings between her mother and grandmother. Their estrangement seemed to be even more bitter, and right before her eyes, her loving grandmother turned into a stranger.

Meredith spoke first, "Hello, Mother. I knew you wouldn't have, but I'm pleased to see that you haven't changed a bit."

It was a moment before Octavia replied. Without taking her eyes off her daughter, she said in a voice that Carla barely recognized, "Would you please leave us alone, Carla? Your mother and I have a lot to talk about.''

''There's no need to send her away,'' Meredith countermanded. ''Whatever we had to say, we said long ago.''

The last thing Carla wanted was to be put in the middle. ''I do have a few things I need to attend to,'' she said. ''I'll see you later for tea....''

Neither woman moved as she backed out of the room, pulling the sliding doors closed behind her. Outside, she took a deep breath. As she went down the porch steps and looked back at the house, she felt as if she'd just escaped from prison. Already she had a pounding headache, and her mother had arrived less than two hours ago.

CHAPTER EIGHT

CARLA HEADED toward the paddocks so she could distract herself by watching the horses. The sight of the placidly grazing animals usually calmed her, but not today. Deep in thought, she sensed rather than heard someone coming up behind her, and turned to see Wade Petrie leading a horse in her direction. She frowned. Weren't things bad enough today, without having to see him?

She'd been avoiding Wade ever since they'd gone to see Done Driftin' at the track. She just didn't know how to handle her conflicting emotions about him. For the first time in her life, it seemed, she was being thrown for a loop by a man. Should she ignore him? Should she treat him like an ordinary employee when they both knew he wasn't? Should she tell him she wanted to talk about it?

No, she'd decided. What would she say? It was galling. She, who had never given a thought to conversing with anyone, be it a sheik or an emir, or even a king or two, was forced to admit that she didn't know how to talk to her grandmother's barn manager. What was happening to her?

And now, after successfully evading him for almost a week, here he was, not two feet from her. Since it was too late to escape, she took refuge in aggression.

"Why didn't you say something?" she demanded. "I don't like people sneaking up on me like that."

He smiled. Damn the man! she thought. She hated it when he smiled. It made him even more attractive than he already was. Those dark blue eyes of his crinkled at the corners, and when he pushed the brim of his hat back a little, he resembled one of those cowboy heroes, just coming in off the range. Was it any wonder that she had reacted so strongly to him? she wondered helplessly. When a man looked like this, what woman could resist?

Then she stiffened. Well, *she* could, she told herself sternly. She wasn't a silly teenager with a crush; she was a grown woman, and there was no excuse.

"Well, I'm sorry I startled you," he said. "I thought for sure the way this colt was dancing around, you'd hear us."

"Well, I didn't," she said peevishly. "I was thinking about something else."

"So it seems." He gestured toward the gate she was blocking. "Look, do you mind? I'd like to put this horse out before we lose daylight."

Oh, wasn't it like him to be sarcastic! She moved out of the way—but not far enough. As he passed by her, she caught the hint of his after-shave. Immediately, the scent tantalized her. Sharp and spicy and sexy as hell—

much like the man himself. Praying her face wouldn't betray her thoughts, she watched as Wade unclipped the lead rope. The colt dashed across the pasture, heading for another group of three-year-olds bunched together down by the fence. "I don't think I've seen that one before," she said. "Who is he?"

Wade watched as the horse reached the others and the little herd wheeled as one and took off across the grass. "His name is Done Cryin'," he said. "He's been at the vet hospital being treated for a lung infection."

Carla shaded her eyes with one hand to look. The colts were still running, kicking and bucking—all with the exuberance of youth. It was a sight to behold, and she smiled—until she realized that she and Wade were standing side by side. If she moved two inches to the left, their arms would touch.

"He's a beauty," she said, trying to concentrate on the colt's lines—the long, fine legs, the muscled hind-quarters and wide chest that were hallmarks of the racing Thoroughbred. But with Wade right beside her, what she really wanted to do was concentrate on *his* long legs, *his* muscles and *his* chest. Hastily, she asked, "Has he raced before?"

If Wade was as aware of her as she was of him, he didn't betray it by even a flicker. "Yes, last year. Just like Done Driftin'. In fact, he's from the same crop of foals. Now that he's fit again, he'll go back to the track."

"It would be a shame if he didn't," she said. As though a silent signal had been given, the exhilarated colts had bunched together once more and were running in the other direction. Done Cryin' was in the lead and as Carla watched him extend his stride effortlessly to increase the distance between him and the others, she added, "He looks like he's got potential."

"That he does. But there's a big difference between training at the track, and running in a pasture." Wade glanced at her from under his hat brim, his eyes crinkling. "Still, I think that when he gets the chance, he could even beat your colt."

"Beat Done Driftin'? Never!"

"A little defensive, aren't we?"

"I don't have to defend my colt. His record will speak for itself."

"Well, I don't know. Done Cryin' is one fine horse, and their sister is just as good."

Caught off guard, she said, "Their sister?"

Something softened in his eyes. "Her name is Never Done Dreamin'. She's the last of the foals Done Roamin' sired before his accident."

Carla couldn't believe she'd been here all this time and hadn't heard about these horses. First it was Done Cryin', and now this elusive filly with the magical name. "Where is the horse, then?" she demanded. "Why haven't I seen her?"

"How do you know you haven't?" he asked slyly.

She was positive. "Oh, I'd know," she assured him. "Done Roamin' stamps all his get with that tremendous presence he has. When you see one of his foals, there's no doubt who the sire is."

Wade stared at her a moment, then he glanced away. "You certainly do know horses. You're right, she's been away."

As pleased as she was by the unexpected compliment, Carla told herself to stay focused. She would *not* think about the reluctant admiration she'd just seen in Wade's eyes, or how strong his hands looked as he fiddled with the rope he was still holding. They'd talk about something safe... like horses.

"Where has this filly been?" she asked. Suddenly she grasped Wade's arm. "Is she hurt?"

"No, no, it's nothing like that." He didn't glance down, but under her fingers, his muscles tensed. "We sent her down to Cathcart Farm right before you came. They've got a swimming pool and she needed to build up her stamina."

She realized she was touching him and quickly dropped her hand. "Are you sure that's all?"

"I'm sure," he said, and seemed to make up his mind about something. He looked at her and started to say, "Carla—"

But just then, the front door slammed loudly up at the main house. Startled by the sound, they both turned to look. Carla gasped.

"What in the world?" she exclaimed.

Meredith had come out of the house and was running down the front steps. Before Carla could even call out, Meredith threw herself into Carla's rented car and started the engine with a roar. She pulled away with a screech of tires, gravel spraying as she disappeared down the driveway.

Wade whistled. "Was that your mother?"

Carla couldn't believe what she'd just seen. Tight-lipped, she said, "It was."

"Do you think we should go after her?"

We? For a moment, she felt a glow that he wanted to help. Just to be with him, she almost said yes. But she knew that going after her mother was the last thing she wanted to do.

So, her eyes on the now-empty driveway, she shook her head. "No. Assuming we could even catch her, it wouldn't do any good. Not right now, anyway."

"I'm sorry."

"So am I." She couldn't help herself. Bitterly, she added, "They haven't spoken for thirty-five years, so I guess it was unrealistic to expect them to end this ridiculous feud today."

"Is there anything I can do?"

Carla jerked her eyes to his face. "No, but thanks for the offer. I guess this is something that Mother and Grandmother are going to have to work out themselves. I just wish I hadn't left the damned keys in the car."

"It wasn't your fault." He hesitated, then tried again. "Carla, about—"

But he was interrupted once more, this time by Teresa's frantic appearance on the front porch. "Miss Carla! Mr. Wade! Oh, come quick!" the housekeeper screamed. "Something's wrong with Mrs. Dunleavy! Oh, please, she needs help!"

Carla and Wade looked at each other. Then, as one, they turned and ran toward the house. Teresa held the front door open for them with tears streaming down her face. Wade took one look at her and rushed ahead, but Carla paused.

"What is it?" she asked. "What happened?"

"I don't know...I don't know—" Teresa sobbed. "I came into the front room to fetch the tea things, and Mrs. Dunleavy was... was..."

"What?" Carla cried.

But the housekeeper just burst into renewed weeping and couldn't answer. Carla didn't waste any more time; she jerked open the screen door and ran inside. Wade was already in the front room, bending over a prostrate Octavia. He heard Carla's footsteps and looked over his shoulder.

"I think she's had a heart attack. Call for help while I start CPR."

She snatched up the phone and dialed 911. Her hands were shaking so badly she nearly dropped the receiver, but somehow she managed to hang on long enough to make the emergency call. With the promise of help on the way, she threw the phone down and ran to Wade's side. By this time, he was busy counting and didn't pause. She stood there tensely, counting with him, her eyes on her grandmother's face. Octavia wasn't just pale, she thought desperately. She was gray to the lips.

She had to ask. "Is she—"

"Not yet," Wade said between breaths. "We'll have to wait."

It was the longest wait of Carla's life.

Finally, when she was sure she'd start to scream if help didn't arrive soon, she heard the sound of sirens and ran to let the paramedics in. Quickly, efficiently, they took over, and almost before she knew it, Octavia was in the ambulance on the way to the hospital. Carla and Wade followed in one of the farm trucks.

"She'll be okay, she'll be okay," Wade kept saying on the way. "She's a tough lady. I know she'll come out of this just fine."

All Carla could do was sit on her side of the seat, her hands clutched so tightly in her lap that her knuckles were white. When Wade noticed and put a hand over hers, she tried to smile, but her face felt too stiff.

What would she do if the worst happened? she wondered again and again on that long, interminable drive. All these years, she'd thought that she didn't have any family but her mother. Now that she'd found Octavia, she realized how empty her life would be if she lost her. They were just getting to know each other. What would she do if Octavia died?

"SHE'S NOT going to die," the doctor told them an endless time later.

Carla and Wade were in the waiting room—and *waiting,* Carla thought, was exactly what they'd been doing. It seemed that she'd looked at the big wall clock ten thousand times since Octavia had been rushed to the cardiac care unit; the hours had passed so slowly that she was sure everyone had forgotten about them. Finally, the doctor had come in. When he'd smiled slightly as they got to their feet, she'd felt as though she could breathe for the first time since she'd entered this awful place. *If he was smiling,* she'd told herself, *then the news must be good.*

"She's still not out of danger," the doctor warned. "The next twenty-four hours will tell us more. But right now, it looks like the attack was mild and there was little damage."

"Thank God!" Carla exclaimed. Without warning, her legs felt weak, and she had to sit down again. Wade came to stand beside her, and when he put his hand on her shoulder, she squeezed his fingers gratefully. This was no time for pretense.

The doctor was a young man whose name tag identified him as Bob Glassman, M.D. She asked him, "Can I see her?"

Dr. Glassman shook his head regretfully. "I'm sorry, we've given her medication to help her rest. She shouldn't be disturbed tonight. But don't worry, we'll take good care of her," he added. "The best thing you could do for Mrs. Dunleavy is to go home and get some rest."

"I can't go home!" She shook her head vehemently for emphasis. "I want to stay here."

"I really think it would be best," the doctor insisted gently. "It's ten o'clock. You look bushed."

"I can sleep here," she said.

Dr. Glassman shook his head. "We'll call you if there's the slightest change. I promise."

"But—"

"I promise," he repeated gently. "Now, go home and try to get some sleep."

Carla felt much too tense to rest. "I'll go home," she said shakily, "but don't make me promise that."

He smiled. "Well, do what you can. Come back and see her in the morning. We'll know more then."

"All right. Thank you."

Once the doctor was gone, Carla wondered if she had the strength to get up. The worst was behind them—or so she hoped, but she felt so numb.

Wade seemed to sense her precarious emotional state, for he said softly, "Come on, Carla. Like the doctor said, you can't do anything more tonight. Let's go home."

Carla didn't realize until then that his hand was still on her shoulder and that she still had a grip on it. She wondered at first why such a simple gesture on his part was so comforting, but then she realized it was because she'd felt it so rarely. Her stepfather had died when she was barely in her teens and since the rest of the men in her mother's life seemed to come and go like the seasons, she had learned not to depend on a man for reassurance.

Until now.

She didn't like this change in her feelings toward Wade; it made her uncomfortable. Or maybe, it was only because she was tired. The day had been such a strain from beginning to end that she could hardly think straight.

"I guess you're right," she said. "It's just... What if something happens?"

"The doctor said he'd call. Come on now, there's nothing we can do here." He paused. "Unless you want to try to locate your mother again?"

At the mention of her mother, Carla forgot her weariness. She'd called Teresa at the house numerous times to give the worried housekeeper an update on Octavia's condition, and to ask if Meredith had come back, only to learn each time that there had been no sign, no call, nothing. From the moment Meredith had flashed down the driveway in Carla's car, it was as though she had vanished.

"Where could she have gone?" she'd demanded rhetorically of Wade each time she called the house. "She hasn't been home for years. Who could she possibly know around here anymore?"

"I don't know, Carla," he'd said soothingly. "But she'll show up, and when she does, Teresa will send her right over here."

But now it was time to go home. Her face set, Carla said, "No, I don't want to try to reach her again. I've already tried a dozen times, and that's enough. When she comes home—*if* she comes home—she'll just have to deal with the situation then.''

"What do you mean, 'if'?" Wade asked when they started out to the parking lot.

Carla was too weary and upset to care what she said. "For all I know, she took the car and headed back to the airport. She could have already been halfway over the Atlantic while we were sitting in the hospital wondering if my grandmother was going to live."

"You don't really think that, do you?"

Carla didn't know what to think at this point. She hadn't said anything to Wade, but during that long, tense wait, she kept picturing Meredith slamming out of the house. *What had happened between her mother and her grandmother to precipitate Octavia's heart attack? What had Meredith said? What had Octavia asked her after so many years?*

The questions whirled around and around inside Carla's head until she was so confused, she didn't know what to believe, much less what she really thought. She knew how her mother felt about Octavia, but she couldn't believe that Meredith would have deliberately run away if she'd known Octavia was in trouble.

So where was she? Where could she be all this time?

Carla didn't want to think about it anymore. She and Wade climbed into the truck to go home, and as he started the engine, he said, "Why don't you stretch out on the seat and get some sleep? The doctor was right—you do look like you're on your last legs. I'll wake you up when we get back.''

Carla shook her head. "No, as tempting as the offer is, I'll just wait until we get home." She smiled faintly. "Besides, you look as tired as I feel. If I fall asleep, who's going to keep you awake?''

"Maybe you've got a point," he said, stifling a yawn as they drove out of the parking lot. He shook his head to clear it. "I didn't realize just how tense I was until that doctor came in and said that Mrs. D. was going to be all right.''

"I know what you mean.''

She was just putting her head back against the seat and closing her eyes, when suddenly, she began to shiver. The more she tried to control it, the worse the shaking became. She crossed her arms in front of her, but it didn't help. Her teeth started to chatter.

Wade noticed and turned up the heater. When he realized that the hot air blasting out of the vents wasn't doing much good, he gestured. "Here, get next to me. Maybe that will help.''

The last thing she wanted—or needed—was to get closer to Wade Petrie than she already was. But she couldn't control this shaking, and she was so cold! Scooting across the seat, she huddled next to him.

"I'm s-s-s-s-sorry," she stammered. "I d-d-d-d-don't know what's come over me. It's not that c-c-c-c-cold out. . . .''

He put his arm around her and pulled her closer into his warm side. "I think it must be a reaction to the strain. Mrs. D. gave us quite a shock."

She looked up at him. In the faint green light from the dashboard, his lean, handsome face was shadowed and drawn. He had never looked better to her.

"It d-d-d-didn't affect you this way," she managed to say.

His arm tightened around her. "Inside, I'm shaking too."

That was the moment when Carla accepted that this man meant more to her than she'd wanted to admit. The knowledge washed over her like a warm summer rain. Suddenly, she wasn't cold anymore.

INCREDIBLY, she must have dozed, for the next thing she knew, Wade was shaking her gently and saying, "Hey, sleepyhead, we're home."

Disoriented, she sat up and looked around. They were parked in front of the house. "Did we just get here?"

"No, we've been sitting here a while. I didn't want to wake you up."

She pushed her hair back. "Some companion I am. As I recall, I was the one who was supposed to keep you awake."

"You've had a hard day. I knew you were tired."

He reached for the door, but she said, "Wait—"

He turned to her. "What is it?"

She didn't know how to explain, but she knew that this intimacy she felt would vanish when he got out of the truck. Outside, she'd once again be Carla Dunleavy, idle socialite, while he'd be Wade Petrie, barn manager and employee. But here in this warm, private cocoon, she was just a woman with feelings for him that had nothing to do with who they were to the rest of the world.

And she knew he had feelings for her; she could see it in his face, in his manner tonight, in the way he'd held her all the way home. Who knew what tomorrow would bring? If she didn't act on her feelings now, maybe she wouldn't get another chance.

Carla knew that she wasn't exactly herself, but she didn't care. If the strain and worry of the past hours had taken a greater toll on her than she realized, so be it. She was tired of always being proper; she was sick to death of pretending she didn't need anyone or anything to make her complete. She needed someone to hold her, to comfort her, to make the ugly realities of the world go away, even for a few short hours. She needed a man, she thought longingly. And then: *No, she needed a man named Wade Petrie*.

But it seemed that the habits of a lifetime were too strong to break, after all. When she wanted to tell Wade what she felt at that moment, all she did was stare at him and say helplessly, "I wanted to thank you for all you did today. For Grandmother and . . . for me."

"Oh, it wasn't—"

"Yes, it was," she said quietly. "You saved my grandmother's life, and I'm more grateful than I can ever say. Thank you is such a meaningless phrase for what you did. I wish I could tell you—" She stopped and shook her head. "Never mind. Just...thank you."

"Carla, I—" he began, then changed his mind. "Oh, hell!" he said instead, and reached for her.

They met in the middle of the seat. As their lips merged fiercely in a hard kiss, he wound his fingers in her hair, holding her tightly. Sensation flooded through her; she had never, she thought dazedly, felt like this. It was as though Roman candles were going off inside her, setting every nerve on fire.

"Oh, Wade!" she murmured, her lips moving under his.

His answer was to press her back against the seat. His other hand came up to cup her breast, and when she felt his touch, she uttered a soft cry that resonated with the guttural sound that emanated from him.

He lifted his head. In the faint illumination from the porch light, his eyes looked almost black. Hoarsely, he said, "We can't do this..."

She wasn't about to let him go—not now. She grabbed him and pulled him down. "Why not?"

They kissed again, mouths open, tongues entwined. They were half lying on the seat by this time, and when he began to unbutton her blouse, she strained up toward him. She couldn't wait to be free of her confining clothes; all she wanted was to feel his naked body against hers, for them to make love until they both collapsed of exhaustion. She felt an over-whelming need. He felt it, too. She knew by the way his hands were shaking, and the deep, gulping breaths he took.

"Here, let me," she said, reaching up to help him unbutton her blouse.

But just then, headlights swept the roof of the cab, and at the same time, there was the scrunch of tires on the gravel outside. At the sound, they bolted upright like guilty teenagers caught by the cops at some make-out spot. Horrified that someone would see her in this compromising position, Carla quickly arranged her clothes into some semblance of order.

"Who is it?" she gasped without looking up.

She expected him to tell her that one of the grooms had driven by on the way to the employees' quarters around back. Instead, he pointed to the rental car parked by the front porch. Still breathing hard himself, he said, "I think your mother's finally home."

The sight of Meredith going up the front steps brought everything back. Instantly, Carla's face darkened, and when he saw her expression, Wade opened the door and got out. Carla didn't wait for him to come around to her side; she met him by the hood of the truck.

"Wade, I—" He put a hand out to stop her.

"I'll see you tomorrow," he said. "If you feel like it, we can talk then."

She didn't want it to end like this, but she didn't see any other way out. As much as she wanted to prolong the moment, she had to go inside and confront her mother. They had, she thought harshly, a lot of things to talk about.

"Thanks for understanding," she said. She wanted to kiss him good-night, but thought better of it.

Wade apparently had second thoughts, too. He hesitated a moment before taking her hand and giving it a squeeze. "Good night, Carla."

"Good night," she said. Before she could change her mind, she turned and went into the house.

MEREDITH WAS in the front room by the bar when Carla came in. She had just poured two fingers of Scotch into a glass and was adding another when she obviously realized she wasn't alone. She turned, splashing some of the liquor onto the polished surface of the bar.

"Carla!" she exclaimed.

Carla was too upset for niceties. "Where have you been?"

Meredith stiffened at her tone. "I beg your pardon?"

"You heard me. Where have you been?"

Meredith stared at her for a moment, then she took a quick swallow of the Scotch. Carla noticed that her mother's movements were jerky, as though her nerves were on edge. Well, that was fine, she thought grimly. So were hers.

"I don't have to answer to you," Meredith said. She took another drink. "Let's just say... I was out."

"Oh, is that so? Well, it might interest you to know that *while you were out,* something happened."

Meredith paused with the glass halfway to her mouth. "What?"

Carla didn't feel like softening the blow. "Grandmother's in the hospital. She had a heart attack."

Meredith paled. "Is she... all right?"

"Do you care?"

"Of course I care! And don't take that tone with me! Just answer me—*is she all right?*"

"She's going to live, if that's what you mean. The doctor said it was mild. Hopefully, there won't be any damage." She paused. "No thanks to you."

Meredith groped for the back of the couch, then looked up sharply. "What does that mean?"

Carla lost what was left of her precarious control. "You know what it means! What did you do to her today, Mother? What did you say?"

Meredith looked at her as though Carla had lost her mind. "What did I *do?*" she repeated. "I didn't do anything to her! She was fine when I left. Maybe she choked on her own venom."

"What a terrible thing to say!"

"Oh, grow up." As always, Meredith was rapidly recovering her equilibrium. She took another sip of her drink. "You don't know her like I do."

"Is that so? Well, I don't think you know her at all!"

"May we please leave my relationship—or lack of it—with my mother out of it for the moment? I'd like to know what else the doctor said, if it's not too much to ask."

The sarcasm made Carla want to tell her mother to call the hospital herself. But then she saw the fear that Meredith couldn't quite conceal. "He told us that the next twenty-four hours will tell him more, but he feels now that there was little damage. Grandmother should make a full recovery, although because of her age, she'll have to be more careful in the future. And," Carla added pointedly, "And that means there are to be no more upsets or quarrels, or tension of any kind."

"We didn't quarrel," Meredith said. She put the glass down and reached for her cigarette case. She took out a cigarette and lighted it, expelling the smoke before adding, "In fact, we didn't say much about anything."

"I'm sorry, but I have trouble believing that. Something upset her, and you were here at the time."

Meredith took another drag on the cigarette. "I *told* you, I didn't have anything to do with it. Now, do you mind? I'm very tired. I think I'll go to bed." She paused. "Unless there's reason to go to the hospital, of course."

"Oh, no, there's no reason." Carla's sarcasm matched her mother's. She added, "No reason at all. The doctor told us he'd call if there was any change."

"You see, then? Everything's going to be fine. I'll see you in the morning." Meredith started out of the room, but just as she passed Carla, who was standing stiffly in the doorway, she said, "By the way, who was that man I saw you with a few minutes ago?"

Carla should have known this was coming. Her mother didn't miss a trick. She could feel her sudden flush betraying her, but she said, "His name is Wade Petrie." Defiantly, she added, "He's the barn manager here."

Meredith's nostrils flared. "I see. Well, don't you think it's a little beneath your dignity to be...necking in the front seat of a truck?" She paused significantly. "Especially with the hired help?"

"He saved Grandmother's life!"

Meredith lifted an eyebrow. "And that was your way of rewarding him for it?"

Carla was so furious she couldn't reply. Before she could gather her wits together enough to make a suitable scathing response, Meredith was gone. Carla was still standing there when she heard the decisive bang of the guest room door.

CHAPTER NINE

"I'M GOING HOME," Octavia stated after less than a week in the hospital. "And no one's going to stop me. Not you, Dr. Glassman, nor you, my darling grand-daughter. Now sign the papers, or whatever you have to do, Doc. And Carla, see to the bill, please. Oh, and nurse! What is your name?" She peered at the nurse's name tag. "Anna! Well, Anna, where are my clothes? I've been lying here like a lump long enough. I want to be where the action is."

Carla tried not to laugh when she saw the doctor's face. They were all gathered in Octavia's hospital room, and she assured him, "Don't worry, Dr. Glass-man, we have your instructions about rest and stress." She glared sternly at her grandmother. "And we'll see that she obeys them to the letter. *Won't* we, Grand-mother?"

Octavia was already involved with supervising the removal of her clothing from the hospital-room wardrobe. Flapping a hand in their direction, she said, "You two will have me dying of boredom instead of a heart attack if you're not careful."

"Grandmother—"

"Oh, all right, all right, whatever you say. I'll agree to anything as long as I can get out of here. Now, where did you put my shoes, Anna? I can't go anywhere without my shoes!"

"They're right here, Mrs. Dunleavy," the nurse said patiently.

"And my lace handkerchief! A real lady *never* goes anywhere without her lace handkerchief." Octavia looked at the scrap of linen Anna obediently handed her and wrinkled her nose. "Although *why,* I can't imagine. Useless things, these. Not like a man's handkerchief, I'll tell you. Now, *that's* a piece of cloth...."

Carla and the doctor stepped out of the room, leaving Octavia still chattering to Anna as the nurse helped her get dressed. Once in the hallway, Carla held out her hand.

"Thank you for everything, Doctor," she said.

"Oh, it's not over yet," he replied, smiling. He jerked his head in Octavia's direction. They could still hear her going on about something, and he said more seriously, "She's not going to be an easy patient, but it's imperative that you follow my instructions. As I said, this attack was mild, but it was a warning all the same. I'd hate to see Mrs. Dunleavy return in full cardiac arrest just because she wouldn't take an afternoon nap or follow her diet."

Carla shuddered at the thought. "I've mobilized everyone. She's going to toe the line, or else."

"Good luck. In the meantime, I'll see you at her appointment next week."

Carla watched him walk down the hall. Then she squared her shoulders and went back into the hospital room. Octavia was already dressed and sitting in a wheelchair.

"I see you're eager to go," Carla said dryly.

"If you're waiting on me, you're losing time," Octavia retorted. She put her purse in her lap, and with a wave of her hand indicated to the nurse to start pushing. Carla could only smile and follow.

"PLEASE FASTEN your seat belt," Carla said when they were in the car. She'd driven the Rolls because she knew Octavia would be more comfortable in it. Someone with foresight had had modern seat belts installed, and she added, "After the scare you gave us, I certainly don't want to lose you now."

"You're not going to lose me," Octavia said. She fastened the belt, anyway. "I'm not ready to go just yet."

Impulsively, Carla reached for her grandmother's hand and gave it a squeeze. "I'm glad to hear it," she said and then started the car.

"And I'm glad you and Wade came when you did," Octavia said. Her eyes took on a faraway glaze. "You know, I'm still not sure exactly what happened. One minute everything was fine. The next..." She shook her head. "I don't know. It was just so fast."

This was the opportunity Carla had been waiting for. With her mother still at the farm, this week had been a real strain. Beyond what communication was absolutely necessary, Meredith wasn't speaking to her—which was just as well, Carla thought grimly, because at this point, she didn't have much to say to her mother.

She wanted to believe Meredith's version, but her mother's deliberate evasiveness about what had happened between her and Octavia that afternoon, and where she'd disappeared to for so many hours afterward, made Carla distrustful. She hated the feeling, but when she had tried to discuss it, her mother had become angry.

No matter how Carla tried to put it out of her mind, questions about that afternoon lingered. And now that her grandmother had given her an opening, she asked cautiously, "You really don't remember anything that happened that day?"

"Well, I do recall that terrible pain," Octavia said with a wince. "It felt like my chest was being crushed. I tried to call Teresa, but I didn't have the breath. Then everything just went black."

Again, Carla proceeded warily. "Do you remember what you were doing right before you felt the pain?"

Octavia turned to look at her. "You're really asking, if your mother was responsible for this."

Embarrassed that her grandmother had seen through her, Carla felt her face turn red. "I wouldn't put it like that."

"Maybe not, but it's what you want to know, isn't it?"

She gave up the pretense. Sighing, she said, "I should have known you'd guess. All right, it *is* what I want to know. But it's a legitimate question, don't you think? Mother was alone in the room with you, and she left in a great hurry. The next thing we knew, Teresa was hysterical because you'd collapsed."

"Teresa has a tendency to overreact."

"She didn't this time. If Wade hadn't known CPR—"

"I know, and I'm more grateful to him than I can ever say. I told him so, too. But words are cheap. I'm going to reward him in a more substantial way."

"Wade doesn't want a reward, Grandmother."

"How do you know that?"

Carla didn't want to get into her relationship with Wade—if *relationship* was what she could call this little dance they'd been doing ever since the night Octavia had been taken to the hospital. The few times she'd seen him this week had been completely unsatisfactory. He hadn't had much to say, and she'd had too much on her mind.

"He told me," she said. "But that's beside the point. I thought we were talking about you and Mother."

"No, *you* were talking about that. And the answer to your question is that your mother didn't have anything to do with . . . what happened. It was my fault, pure and simple. I just got overexcited. After all, it's been years since Meredith and I have spoken. It was too much for me. That's all there is to it."

"I think there's more to it than that, but if you don't want to tell me—"

"I don't," Octavia answered crisply. Then she relented and put a hand on Carla's arm. "It's between Meredith and me, my dear. I know you mean well and that you're concerned. Don't think I'm ungrateful. But this is something she and I are just going to have to work out."

Carla started to reply, then gave another resigned sigh. "All right, if you say so. But may I ask you one more thing?"

"Go ahead."

"Do you think that you and Mother will ever work it out?"

Octavia turned to stare out the window. She waited so long to answer that Carla was beginning to think she had decided to ignore the question. Then Octavia said, "Only time will tell. But that's always the way of things, isn't it? Sometimes no matter how much you want something, it takes its own sweet time in coming."

Carla had to be satisfied with that. It was her turn to be quiet, and she was concentrating on her driving

again when Octavia said, "So. Tell me about you and
Wade."

"What do you mean?" she said as casually as she
could.

"You don't have to pretend to be so innocent, miss.
I know what's going on. I may be an old woman, but
I've still got eyes."

"I don't know what you're talking about. Nothing
is *going on*. Why, we hardly know each other."

"Oh, piddle. I've seen the way he looks at you when
you're not aware of it."

"That's ridic—how does he look at me?"

Octavia glanced at her slyly. "Are you saying you
don't know?"

"There's nothing to know. We're just friends."

"Friends," Octavia repeated. "I see."

Carla suddenly knew where this was coming from.
"What has Mother been telling you? Whatever it is,
it isn't true." Meredith had visited Octavia once during the older woman's stay in hospital.

"Meredith hasn't said anything. But as I mentioned, I've got eyes. I can see for myself. So can anyone who has half a brain. The man's in love with you.
It's obvious."

"In love! Why that's a . . ."

"Appalling? Amusing?" Octavia supplied help-
fully. She paused. "Apt?"

"*Absurd*," Carla stated firmly. "Now, please,
Grandmother, can we talk about something else?"

"Whatever you wish, dear. It was just an observation, after all. I had no idea you'd react so strongly."

"I didn't react at all!"

"But in that case, might I say just one more thing?"

"I doubt I can stop you. What is it?"

"Just that you could do a lot worse than Wade Petrie."

"Now, Grandmother..."

"It was just a comment, just a comment. You don't have to bristle like that."

"I'm not bristling!"

"All right, dear. Now, what did you wish to talk about?"

Carla gladly seized on the new topic. "I wanted to talk about two of the horses at the farm."

"Oh? And which two are those?"

"Well, the one that just came home—a colt named Done Cryin'. And the other I've only heard about and haven't seen yet, a filly named Never Done Dreamin'. She's been—"

"I know where she's been," Octavia said dryly. "Go on. What did you want to know?"

Carla turned eagerly to her. "I want them to go into race training, Grandmother. That colt and filly are directly related to Done Driftin'. If they're only half as good as he is—"

Octavia smiled. "I think they can be."

Carla couldn't believe it had been this easy. "Then you agree? They can go to Dwight? Oh, Grandmother, this is wonderful! I'm—"

"I didn't say that," Octavia told her. "I have plans for those two horses."

"Plans?" Carla was taken aback by a sudden horrible thought. "You're not going to *sell* them, are you?"

Octavia laughed. "Oh, my goodness, no!"

"Then, what plans are you talking about? If you're not going to sell them, and you aren't going to race them—"

"I didn't say they wouldn't race," Octavia said mysteriously. "It just isn't time yet."

"Time for what? Have I missed something?"

"No, you haven't missed anything, my sharp-eyed granddaughter. But remember what I said about things taking their own sweet time? Well, this is one of them. To find out, you'll just have to wait."

Carla could tell from Octavia's tone that she wasn't going to learn more, not right now, anyway. "I hate to tell you this, Grandmother, but I've never been very good at waiting."

"I know. Patience isn't a family trait, more's the pity, I think at times," Octavia said wistfully. "Now, I've a favor to ask of you. Please don't take this the wrong way, but would you mind if we didn't talk for a while? I'm a little tired, and after spending all that time in the hospital, it's so restful just looking at the scenery."

Carla gave her a suspicious look. She wondered if her clever, secretive little grandmother was manipulating her, but she couldn't ask. Octavia did look a little pale, she thought in guilty dismay. She shouldn't have asked all those questions; it was too soon; her grandmother wasn't strong enough. Quickly, she pressed down on the accelerator and the car surged forward.

"I'll have you home in a jiffy," she promised.

"Let's just make sure it's in one piece, my dear," Octavia said calmly. "As far as I know, we're not going to a fire."

Carla slowed to a more reasonable speed. But left to her own devices, she thought about Wade.

She was mortified by her behavior the night of her grandmother's heart attack. She hated to admit it, but she didn't know what she would have done—or how far she would have gone—if her mother's arrival home hadn't interrupted that little scene in the front seat of the truck.

Just thinking of it made her blush. There was no excuse for such behavior. She was no panting teenager incapable of controlling her desires; she was a woman with experience.

In fact, she'd always felt contempt for females who allowed their passions to overrule good taste and common sense. But her response to Wade had made her think twice about that narrow-minded outlook; maybe until she'd met Wade, she had never really known what *passion* meant. Had she been fooling herself? Was she actually inexperienced—in true love, at least?

What was she thinking? Why was she speculating about *love*, for heaven's sake? So she'd gone a little too far that night; so she'd let things get a bit out of hand. It had been a relief from the terrible worry and tension. Her fear for her grandmother had made her...vulnerable.

There was more to it. There was something about Wade Petrie, something she saw in him that she hadn't found in any other man. It wasn't just the look in his eyes at times, or the brooding way he stared off into the distance; it wasn't even the wariness she sensed in him that mimicked the way she herself had felt at times. She suspected that he'd probably been hurt by a woman at one time or another in his life, and that he was still carrying the scars. Well, if that had made him reserved, she understood. Her experiences had made her withdrawn, as well.

So what would happen if she and Wade did fall in love? Would she be ready to make a commitment? Would he? Their opposing life-styles would be just one obstacle. The biggest difficulty would be adjusting to the relationship itself. She'd been on her own for so long; she was accustomed to doing things on her own time, in her own way, on her own turf. She didn't know how—or if—she could make room for someone else.

AT THAT MOMENT, Wade wasn't thinking about relationships or any commitment other than the one he had made to Octavia Dunleavy and Dunleavy Farm.

As he sat at his desk, he suddenly realized that even
though he and Mrs. D. had never discussed it, he had
gradually taken over more and more of the responsi-
bilities around the farm. On larger and more financially stable establishments, there would be stallion
managers and foaling foremen and financial officers
and maintenance crews. Here at Dunleavy, with the
exception of Samson and two handymen/grooms, he
was it.

Not that he minded. It was just that he hated the
fact that, with money tight and Octavia's health fal-
tering, Dunleavy wasn't the place it had been. The
stallion barn, once filled with some of the greatest
racing stallions in the sport, stood empty now except
for old Done Roamin' and the other colts that Wade
had brought in from pasture at night. And the brood-
mare barn, which had once been filled with high-
quality mares and their babies now just gathered dust.
No foals were in evidence now, none since Done
Roamin's last crop three years ago. He missed having
a lot of youngsters around; he missed the sight of them
playing in the pastures or taking the first few stumbling steps that would eventually smooth out into the
awsome stride of the racing Thoroughbred.

But worst of all were the signs of neglect all around
the place that meant the farm was becoming more and
more like a grand old lady whose time had passed.
Wade had helped out as much as he could from his
own none-too-substantial funds without Octavia be-

ing aware of it. But it wasn't enough to stem the inevitable decline and he knew it.

The sale of those horses had brought in a much-needed infusion of cash, but it wouldn't last long. What Octavia needed was a big sale, with Done Roamin's foals at the top of the list. The sale of the two colts and their sister would bring in enough to pull the farm out of danger for a while. But over a month ago, when he'd gone to Mrs. D. with the idea, she'd said she had plans for those horses, and that's all there was to it.

Wade shook his head at the thought. His employer kept her secrets to herself and he hadn't pressed. But then Carla had arrived, and he'd found out what Mrs. D. intended for one of the horses, at least. He couldn't be sure about the other two, but he had an idea. It would be interesting, he thought in his less morose moods, to see how all this worked out.

In the meantime, he had a bigger problem on his hands, and that was Miss Carla Dunleavy herself. When he thought of the night he'd brought her home from the hospital, he cringed. He'd acted like an adolescent whose hormones had run amok. God knew what might have happened if Meredith hadn't come along; he'd been so lost in the taste and feel and scent of the woman that he might have made love to her right there in the front seat of the truck.

What has she done to you? he asked himself.

But he already knew the answer to that one. The truth was that, no matter how he tried to fight against it, he was falling in love with her.

He didn't want to fall in love, he thought angrily. He didn't want anything to do with it. He'd been in love before—or had imagined he was, and look what had happened. It had ruined his life, his reputation and his self-esteem. Oh, he'd learned firsthand how love could blind a man.

So if he knew the pitfalls, why couldn't he forget how warm and willing Carla had been that night? Every time he imagined her slender, pliant body in his arms, an ache started up below his belt. He could still smell her perfume, still see how beautiful she'd looked. Whenever he thought about it, he wished to hell Meredith hadn't come home that night.

"Well, there you are," someone said. "I've been wanting a chance to speak to you alone. Do you mind?"

The voice startled him, and he turned around. When he saw who was there, he immediately got to his feet. As though his thoughts had conjured her, Meredith Dunleavy was standing in the doorway. He was so surprised, all he could do was stare.

It was the first time he'd seen her up close, and his initial thought was how much Carla resembled her—and how much she didn't. Mother and daughter both had the strong family features and the green Dunleavy eyes, but Meredith had a hard edge to her that Carla lacked. Wondering what Meredith was doing here, he nodded warily and said, "Good afternoon, ma'am."

She didn't answer right away; she just looked him up and down as though he were a horse at auction. He didn't like the feeling, and he asked, "Is there anything I can do for you...ma'am?"

Meredith smiled coolly at his tone. "As a matter of fact, there is," she said. Like Carla's, her voice was low and sultry. But unlike Carla, she didn't evoke certain...images in his mind; she only made him feel more cautious. "I take it you're... Wade."

"I am," he said, touching his hat brim with two fingers. "Wade Petrie. At your service."

His ironic salute didn't escape her. "I certainly hope so, Mr. Petrie."

She came into the room with the same unconscious grace that Carla had inherited, walking right up to the desk where he was standing. She was wearing high heels, and their eyes were nearly on the same level. Her gaze direct, she said, "You can stay the hell away from my daughter."

The profanity was mild, but coming from this sophisticated woman with her designer-label clothes and her cultured air, it almost sounded like a gutter-level curse.

"I beg your pardon?"

"You heard me. I told you to stay away from my daughter."

"Your daughter is a grown woman. I think she can make up her own mind."

"I thought so, too—until I saw you together in the front seat of the truck the other night."

He could feel himself redden, but he said, "What happened is between Carla and me. You'll pardon my saying so, but it's none of your business."

"You're wrong, Mr. Petrie. My daughter is my business. She always has been, and she always will be. Especially—" she deliberately looked him up and down again "—where someone like you is concerned."

Just for an instant, he wondered if she had somehow found out what had happened in California. Then he told himself not to be absurd. His guilty conscience was probably working overtime.

Still, there was a look in her eyes he couldn't quite fathom, and he said, "Someone like me. Just what does that mean?"

"This isn't a subject open to discussion, Mr. Petrie. If you have problems with this, I suggest you take them elsewhere."

"Is that a threat?"

"No. It's a promise. I might have been gone a while, but I still have some influence, so be careful. If you leave Dunleavy Farm, you might not easily find work elsewhere."

He pushed his hat back to show that she didn't intimidate him, and drawled, "Well, ma'am, I'm not so sure that's true. But in any event, I take my orders from Mrs. D., not you."

The green eyes flashed. "Are you trying to be amusing, Mr. Petrie? Or just offensive?"

"Neither. I don't like being threatened. And I don't think Carla would appreciate your trying to regulate her life, any more than I cotton to your trying to do it to mine."

"My relationship with my daughter is none of your business."

"That's true. Still, I think I'll wait and find out what she thinks about this."

"If you were a gentleman, you wouldn't mention this conversation."

"Well, I think we've already established I'm no gentleman."

Angrily, she leaned across the desk. He had the feeling that if she were a man, she would have grabbed a fistful of his shirt and jerked him off his feet—or tried. As it was, she had to content herself with saying, "Don't trifle with me, Mr. Petrie. I can make life miserable for you if I wish. Do I make myself clear?"

"Oh, yeah," he said. "But I repeat. You're not my boss— Mrs. D. is. And she will be, until I quit, or she tells me to go. Is *that* clear?"

She flushed. "Are you *quite* finished?"

Thinking that he probably was—here, at least, he said, "Yes."

"I certainly hope so." Slowly, she straightened. "Well. I'm so glad we've had this little chat. Now at least, we know where we stand."

"Yeah, I guess we do."

She gave him a look that would have made him angry, if he wasn't already feeling foolish. Why had he defended his right to see Carla, when just moments before Meredith came in, he'd gone through all the reasons that he shouldn't have anything more to do with her?

"Don't think this is over," Meredith said as she went to the door. "You might as well know now. I'll do everything I can to sabotage this—" her lip curled contemptuously "—relationship. Carla deserves better than you. I haven't given her the best life had to offer, in experiences and education and travel, only to have her end up *here,* in this godforsaken place. She's destined for better things, and I'm determined to see that she gets them. *Now* do we understand each other?"

Before he could answer—before he could think of a reply he could make to a woman—she turned and walked out. He started to follow, then halted in mid-step.

Don't make things worse, he told himself, and sat down again. Meredith had given him an excuse, and he should take it. He and Carla weren't meant to be; that's all there was to it.

CHAPTER TEN

As CARLA HAD EXPECTED, Meredith wasn't waiting to greet them when they came home from the hospital. Teresa came out alone to help.

"Now, you don't have to treat me like I'm about to break," Octavia grumbled as they helped her from the car. But her face was pale when she said it, and Carla was so anxious to get her grandmother inside that she didn't have time to wonder where her mother was.

But a few minutes later, after Octavia was settled in bed and Carla was drawing the drapes, she saw Meredith emerge from the stallion barn. She stood at the window a moment in surprise, her hand still on the drapery cord. What on earth had her mother been doing in the barn? she wondered.

Then she remembered that Wade's office was there, and she quickly pulled the drapes shut. Octavia was just about asleep, so she left Teresa to finish up and tiptoed out. As soon as she closed the bedroom door behind her, she sprinted for the front door. When she got there, Meredith was coming in.

"Mother?"

Meredith had started toward the stairs. At Carla's peremptory tone, she stopped. "What is it?"

"Did I just see you coming out of the barn?"

"Yes, you did. What of it?"

Suddenly, Carla felt uncomfortable about demanding if Meredith had been talking to Wade, so she said, "Well, I . . . I mean . . . What were you doing in there?"

"If you must know, I was talking to your boyfriend."

"If you mean Wade, he's not my—"

"Oh, no? Then perhaps you shouldn't be dallying with him like a lovesick teenager."

Carla knew neither Teresa nor her grandmother could hear them from the bedroom, but she lowered her voice, anyway. "I thought we settled that."

"Did we?"

Meredith started for the stairs once more, but Carla couldn't let it go. She knew she was making a mistake, but she said, "Just a minute. What were you talking to Wade about?"

"If you're so interested, why don't you ask him?"

"Because I'm asking you."

Meredith paused, one elegant hand on the banister. She thought a moment, then seemed to have made up her mind. "All right, I'll tell you. Perhaps it will give you something to think about other than my relationship—or lack of it—with my mother. As I understand it, Mr. Petrie came here three years ago . . ."

Carla tensed. "Yes, so?"

Her mother looked directly at her. "Wasn't that about the time that Done Roamin' had his accident?"

IN THE DAYS that followed, Carla couldn't forget her mother's insinuation that Wade was somehow responsible for Done Roamin's accident. She had been so shocked the afternoon Meredith had suggested it that she hadn't been able to think of anything to say in response. Even a hot denial had been beyond her. Stunned, all she could do was watch as Meredith stared at her a moment before continuing up the stairs to the guest room. After what had seemed an aeon, Carla had made herself move, too.

In fact, she'd been a virtual perpetual-motion machine ever since, running from one thing to another so she wouldn't have to deal with her mother's veiled accusation. Despite Octavia's protests that she could eat in the dining room, Carla insisted on bringing her grandmother meal trays that Teresa fixed in the kitchen. She spent hours poring over the farm's accounts and finances. She ran errands into town and took care of all the mail. In short, she did everything she could so she wouldn't have to see, or think about, Wade.

But no matter what she did, the question kept returning to her mind. *Could* it be true? she'd wondered again and again, only to reassure herself quickly every time that even the idea was insane. What motive would Wade have? What reason?

He'd implied that she'd come to take advantage of Octavia, but what if *he* was the one with that plan in mind? Maybe he had insinuated himself into her grandmother's good graces in the hope that Octavia would be grateful enough to give him the farm.

Then she'd think: *No, no, it just can't be!* She recalled how comforting he'd been at the hospital, and how genuinely concerned he'd seemed; he couldn't be a con man out to get what he could from a lonely old woman.

She was still trying to convince herself about him when race day arrived. Determined to forget her problems, she wanted to simply enjoy the experience. It wasn't as difficult as she had imagined now that she was actually at the track and able to feel the undercurrent of excitement.

Carla had been to numerous horse tracks, or race courses, as they were called in England and on the Continent, but on the day Done Driftin' was scheduled to run, no track had ever seemed more exciting than Turfway Park in nearby Florence. It wasn't as famous as Churchill Downs, where the Kentucky Derby was run, but she was too thrilled to care. Dwight had transported Done Driftin', from his stable several days before.

After being cleared through the owner's gate, Carla headed directly to the backside to see her horse. The groom was giving Done Driftin's shiny coat a last brush when she got there; Dwight was checking the colt's legs. As she watched, Carla was sure a more beautiful horse had never lived. And, likely sensing something momentous was about to happen, Done Driftin' stamped and snorted in anticipation. He looked as if he were going to burst out of the starting gate and never look back.

"What do you think, Dwight?" she asked.

Dwight was grinning from ear to ear as he straightened from his inspection, but all he'd say was, "I think he's ready."

Wade had come ahead yesterday. Meredith had rented her own car, so Carla had come alone. Octavia had wanted to come, but the doctor had been adamant: she wasn't to leave the house yet, much less subject herself to the excitement of the racetrack. As much as Carla wanted to share this moment with her grandmother, she had reluctantly agreed with the doctor. But she had promised to bring Octavia a tape of the race.

Just as it was time to bring the horses for the upcoming race to the paddock, Wade emerged from the tack room.

"What do you think of the colt?" she asked.

"I think he looks just fine."

"Fine? Is that all you can say? He looks gorgeous!"

"Yes, but can he run?" Dwight teased her. "That's the question."

"He'll go wire to wire, that's how sure *I* am," she declared. "Any bets?"

"Hey, not me," Dwight said. "I never bet unless it's a sure thing."

"Then you'd better put your money down, because I guarantee you, this colt's going to win."

Ian McKenzie was at the saddling enclosure when they arrived; he was dressed in Dunleavy Farm's racing colors of royal blue and gold. Carla thought he looked spectacular. After the horses were checked in by the steward and saddled, Carla waited until Dwight issued his last-minute instructions and gave the jockey a leg up before she approached.

"Good luck, Ian," she said.

With Done Driftin' already prancing in place under him, Ian grinned down at her. "I don't think luck's going to have much to do with it, Miss Dunleavy. The way this horse feels today, he's going to head for the front and just improve his position."

"I hope you're right," Carla said fervently. She touched the jockey's boot. "Safe trip, then."

Ian saluted her with his whip, and then the outriders came to lead the horses to the track. Dwight had already indicated he was going to watch by the rail, and Carla hoped Wade would stay with him. But as he followed her up to the grandstand, she was too anxious about her colt to be nervous about Wade. It was almost post time, and she was already wound tighter than a drum.

"Relax," Wade said. "You've got a few minutes yet."

"That's the problem," Carla said, clasping her hands tightly together to stop them from trembling. "If the race doesn't start soon, I'll be a basket case."

Wade noticed that she was shaking. "Are you cold?"

"No, just nervous."

"He'll do just fine."

"I don't want him to do *fine!*" she said fiercely. "I want him to *win!*"

AND THAT'S what Done Driftin' did. By the time the colt passed under the finish line with almost contemptuous ease, he was six lengths ahead of the second-place finisher. The crowd went wild at the performance, and everyone who was anyone in racing was aware that a new star had been born.

Carla knew it, too. Almost hoarse from screaming her encouragement as Done Driftin' had rounded the final turn and headed for home, she forgot her doubts about Wade and turned excitedly to him.

"I told you, didn't I?" she cried. "Wire to wire! There wasn't a horse who could touch him!"

Wade looked a little dazed at what he'd just witnessed. Never had he seen anything like this. Done Driftin' had not only won the race; he had so easily outdistanced the competition that it was almost a disgrace.

He was just starting to say something, when another roar went up from the crowd. At the sound, he and Carla turned to look at the toteboard that was flashing a new track record.

"I'll be damned," Wade said when he saw the time posted. It was almost two seconds faster than the previous record.

"Do you see that?" Carla shouted. She was so elated that she threw her arms around Wade and kissed him hard.

Instantly, Wade forgot Done Driftin', the race and everything else. With Carla in his arms, all he could think about was her. With the sounds of the exhilarated crowd still ringing in his ears—or was that just the thundering of his pulse?—he grabbed her to him and kissed her right back.

For an electrified moment, it was as though they were the only two people alive. For Carla, there was only the strength of Wade's arms holding her close, and the glorious feel of his mouth on hers, demanding all she could give. For Wade, it was the sensation of Carla's pliant body pressed against his, and the ache in his loins that was quickly becoming an urge that wouldn't be denied. Her lips felt soft under his; the smell of her exotic perfume filled his nostrils, driving him wild. He wanted to crush her to him and make love to her there on the spot.

Then reason returned, and with a gasp, they pulled apart.

"Oh, Wade," Carla said breathlessly.

At the dazzled expression on her face, it was all he could do not to pull her to him again and . . .

Fiercely, he thrust away the powerful, erotic images that were filling his head. He had to think, and he couldn't do that with the feel of that beautiful body so close to him. He realized he was still holding her; reluctantly, he let her go. He tried to say something, but his voice was a croak. He cleared his throat and tried again.

"I think," he finally managed to say, "that you're wanted in the winner's circle."

For a moment, Carla looked blank. Then she glanced down at the track, at the horses coming back, at Ian and Done Driftin' cantering lazily down the stretch toward the waiting officials, and said, "Yes, I . . . guess you're right."

She looked up at him again, her hand to her lips. She looked so vulnerable that he was tempted to embrace her again. He didn't dare; he didn't trust himself. Already, he was dangerously close to the edge.

What is this woman doing to me? he wondered again. But even as he asked the question, he knew he didn't want her to stop.

THE EXCITEMENT of Done Driftin's spectacular win, coupled with that electrifying kiss, made Carla feel completely befuddled. *What's happening to me?* she wondered. She'd never felt like this before; she'd never acted like this. In fact, she'd never even *dreamed* that she was capable of screaming in public, or of passionately kissing a man in plain sight of a crowd. She was too sophisticated, too cultured, too aware of the proprieties to engage in such outrageous behavior. As her mother would have said, in their circle, it just wasn't done.

Then perhaps you should change circles.

At the moment, it sounded like an excellent idea. Before she could change her mind, she grabbed Wade's hand. "You have to come with me."

He pulled back. "To the winner's circle?"

"Where else? Come on. I'll—"

She couldn't stop him when he withdrew his hand from hers and gave her a little push forward. "You go ahead. This is your moment, Carla. Enjoy it."

She wanted to ask why he didn't want to come, but she didn't have time. She had to get down there; she owed it to Dwight, and to the jockey, and to her horse. But she said, "Wade, we have to talk—"

He gazed at her a long moment. Then he said, "I know. But now's not the time. You go ahead. I'll try to meet you later for a drink."

"You have to promise," she said. She couldn't stop herself from grinning with sheer pleasure. "You'll know me when you get there. I'll be the one buying everyone champagne."

CARLA WAS on cloud nine as she went upstairs to the VIP bar. To her surprise, Meredith was already there, sipping from a flute of champagne.

"Congratulations," she said when Carla came up. "That was quite a race."

"A one-horse race," Carla said, and laughed. "Did you see it?"

"I didn't come all this way to miss it. Of course I saw it. But I wasn't about to sit in the grandstand with everybody and his uncle. I much preferred the atmosphere up here. Dunleavys do, you know.''

"Now, Mother, don't start. I'm too happy to argue, and I don't want anything to ruin my day.''

"You're right. Let's get you a drink so we can have a proper toast to your horse.''

They headed toward the bar, Carla covertly checking the small groups of people that dotted the room in the hope that Wade would join her. When she didn't see him, she tried not to be disappointed. She knew he hated gatherings and parties and social events, but this was a special occasion, and he had almost promised.

She and Meredith were just raising their glasses in a toast when they were joined by the man Carla had met at the auction. "Trent Spencer!" she said as the tall, handsome banker with the silvered temples came up to them. "Did you see the race?''

"I did indeed.'' He smiled, his eyes twinkling. "Congratulations. That was a great run for your horse. A track record.''

"It's only the first of many," she boasted shamelessly. "Trent, do you know my mother, Meredith Dunleavy? Mother, this is Trent Spencer. He's a neighbor.''

"I know who he is, dear," she said. Her expression was guarded as she shook hands with Trent. "It's been a long time, Mr. Spencer.''

"Indeed it has. I'd heard you were at the farm and should have done the neighborly thing and come to welcome you back, but recently I've had some changes in my personal life, and things have been a little ... difficult.''

"I understand. But there was no need for a welcoming committee. I won't be staying long. In fact, now that Carla's horse has run his race, I'll probably be on my way.''

"That's too bad. After so many years away, it's a pity you can't stay longer to catch up.''

"I've done all the catching up I need to do, Mr. Spencer,'' Meredith said. "Now, if you will excuse me, I think I see some old friends across the room.''

"Of course,'' Trent said politely. "But before you go, may I say how nice it is to see you again. I was young when you all left, but I still remember the Dunleavy clan.''

Meredith shot a glance at Carla, who had turned to look at her mother in shock. Quickly, she said, "Thank you, Mr. Spencer. I've enjoyed this meeting too.''

She started off, leaving Carla behind, rooted to the spot.

Trent saw her expression and took her arm. "Are you all right?''

She tried to compose herself. "Yes, I ... I'm fine. It must be the excitement.''

"You have reason to be excited. Everyone on the backside is talking about that colt. They're already comparing him to the immortal Secretariat.''

Carla desperately wanted to find a chair and sit down, but she willed herself to stand there and make polite conversation. "I think it's too soon for that, don't you? After all, he's only run one race this year."

"Yes, but it's the way he ran it. And you know how racing people are. Everybody is always looking to grab that gold ring. Maybe you've found it."

Carla spoke without thinking, "That would be nice. Dunleavy Farm could use—"

She stopped midsentence, but it was too late. Trent said, "Yes, I know about the farm's financial troubles."

"You do?"

"I'm an investment banker, Ms. Dunleavy. It's what I do—look into things like that."

She didn't care for the idea that someone knew about the financial fix the farm was in, even if it was a man as nice as Trent Spencer seemed to be. She said, "I see. But why have you made it your concern to look into my grandmother's business?"

"Because I like Octavia," he said simply. "In fact, I wanted to approach her months ago with an offer to help."

There was no doubting his sincerity, and Carla was ashamed of her quick judgment. "I'm sorry. I didn't realize—"

"It's all right. As you've no doubt learned by now, we live in a small community. It's difficult to hide things. As I said, I would have called on Octavia long before now if I hadn't been certain she would have thrown me out on my ear."

Carla had to smile. "She probably would have. She does have her pride."

"Yes, and the last thing I wanted to do was offend her." He hesitated. "But the offer still stands. If you need my help, all you have to do is ask."

"Why would you do this?"

"Because a long time ago, when my family needed help, Octavia extended a hand," he said. "She accepted my grandfather into the racing world when no one else would." For the first time, a tinge of bitterness entered his voice. "After all, he was a man who owned the local feed store. He had no business aspiring to owning a racing farm."

"But he went ahead."

"Yes, he did. And maybe he would have pursued his dream, anyway, no matter what the cost, even if Octavia hadn't gone out of her way to help him. Now all these years later, I'm ready to return the favor."

Carla was touched. "Thank you, Trent," she said. "I'll tell her. At least, I'll try. Whether she'll accept or not—"

"It doesn't matter. I hope she will, but I want you to know that the offer is there, any time, open-ended. Now, I've monopolized you too long. I see some people over there who have been waiting to congratulate you. Goodbye, Carla. It was nice talking to you."

After Trent disappeared into the growing crowd, Carla was inundated with congratulations from everyone in the room, some of whom she had met, others whom she had never seen before. But the entire time she was laughing and smiling and accepting the best wishes, she was surreptitiously searching the throng for Wade. When she still didn't see him after an hour, she knew he wasn't coming and the party went flat. It was time to leave, but before that, she wanted to talk to her mother. She found Meredith just starting out.

"Wait a minute," she said. "I'll walk out with you."

"No need, darling."

"Oh, yes, there is," Carla said, linking arms so her mother couldn't hold back. "I found that comment Trent made very interesting."

"Which comment was that?" Meredith asked cautiously.

"Oh, the news that, in addition to the farm and a grandmother I never knew about, it seems I have an aunt and uncle you never told me about, as well."

Meredith tried to disengage her arm. "Yes, well, now you know."

Carla held on firmly. "Why didn't you ever tell me?"

Meredith gave up trying to free herself. Sullenly, she said, "Because we lost touch, and it would only have complicated things."

"Yes, I can imagine. Then you would have had to fill in the rest of the story, and we couldn't have that, could we? Not when you had gone to such great lengths to create the fiction that we were alone in the world."

"You're being melodramatic."

"Am I? I think I'm being quite calm about the whole thing. It's not every day that someone loses and finds an entire branch of a family she never knew existed."

"Oh, Carla, it was so long ago—"

"What's the matter? Didn't you get along with them, either?"

"I loved Gary and Jamie! They were my brother and sister—"

"Yes, and they were my uncle and aunt."

"You don't understand."

"Then tell me."

"I don't wish to speak about this in a public place!"

"Obviously you never wished to speak about it at all."

"If you're so interested, why don't you ask your beloved grandmother?"

"I will. But I can't right now. The doctor said she wasn't to have any stress—"

"Oh, of course. And it would be *so* stressful for her to remember that at one point she actually had three children."

"Do you really think you have a right to be sarcastic?"

"As a matter of fact, I do. But since you're so interested in protecting her, maybe you should think about this. Have you ever seen any pictures, mementos, or trophies around that mausoleum of a house—other than those concerning *horses*, of course?"

Carla began to deny it, but her mother was right. Aside from the painting of Alvah Dunleavy and the things from Octavia's grandmother and sister, she *hadn't* seen other evidence of family.

Meredith saw her expression and said, "I see you haven't. Well, let me tell you why. To your precious Octavia, the horses always came first. *We* were an afterthought, if we were thought of at all." She paused, her eyes cold. "It's something for you to remember, my darling daughter, in case you get any foolish ideas about how much your grandmother loves you."

"That's an awful thing to say!"

"Awful or not, I speak from experience. I've tried to tell you, maybe now you'll believe me. My brother, Gary, was a high school basketball star who led his team to a state championship. He was also a champion archer. My sister, a wonderful, sweet girl named Jamie, was an artist who had her own show at seventeen. She won numerous awards, too. Yet there's not even a picture. I wasn't as talented or adept as they were, but I did quite well at horse shows. Where are all my cups and blue ribbons? Don't you see? To Octavia, it's as though her three children didn't exist."

Carla felt as if someone had pulled the rug out from under her. "I don't understand."

"Don't bother trying. Everything was fine as long as we did what *Mother* approved of. The instant we didn't . . ." Meredith stopped and gave a weary shrug. "It doesn't matter now. It was a long time ago."

"You're wrong, Mother. It does matter."

"Not to me," Meredith said flatly. "Now, if you don't mind, I really don't want to discuss this anymore. It's been a long day and I'm tired."

She was gone before Carla could think of a way to stop her.

Carla followed slowly. There was still no sign of Wade, and as she drove back to the farm, she realized what an emotionally exhausting day it had been. All she wanted to do now was go home and climb into bed.

But when she finally drove through the big gates and saw that the lights were on in Wade's little house out by the main barn, she thought differently. He hadn't come for that drink, so maybe she'd simply take the drink to him.

WADE WAS SITTING in his living room, when someone rang his doorbell. When he'd come home, he'd tried watching television, but nothing could hold his interest, so he'd sat at his desk here to go over some paperwork. He couldn't concentrate. He knew Carla was going to be angry that he hadn't come to celebrate with her, but he just couldn't do it. Facing those people in the bar, some of whom had been his clients at one time, was too much to ask. Even if no one said anything, he would have seen the questions and doubts still in their eyes and in the awkward way they acted around him. In the end, he'd left without telling anyone, catching a ride from one of the grooms at a nearby farm.

But he couldn't stop thinking about Carla. After this latest stunt, how was he ever going to face her? He still didn't know when the doorbell sounded. Not even curious, he got up wearily and went to the door.

Carla was standing on the porch, a bottle of champagne in one hand and two glasses in the other. Before he could think what to say, she came in and said, "I thought about it a lot, Wade. And I decided that if the mountain won't come to Mohammed, well, then, Mohammed will just have to come to the mountain."

"Carla, I—"

"We'll talk about it later."

Her voice was low and husky, the look in her eyes unmistakable. He couldn't resist her. Without another word, he took her in his arms and closed the door with a well-placed kick.

CHAPTER ELEVEN

CARLA HAD TOLD HERSELF that the reason she was taking champagne to Wade was to share a celebration drink. But the instant he opened the door, she knew she'd been fooling herself. Before she could stop herself, she was in his arms and his mouth was on hers, and the way he was kissing her—as if he couldn't get enough of her—obliterated all else.

She never did know how they got to the bedroom, but all at once, he was taking the champagne bottle and glasses from her hands and setting them on the bureau, and then his arms were around her again and their mouths met, hungry for contact.

Dizzily, she thought she had never been kissed like this. The pressure of his lips sent desire raging through her, and she clung to him, wishing they could just fling their clothes away so she could feel him, skin against skin.

Those slim hips of his were pressed against her, pushing her back into the dresser, and when she felt his arousal between her thighs, an answering throbbing rose inside her, an ache begging to be appeased. Groping with one hand, she found him and cupped him through his jeans. When he felt her touch, he pulled her harder into him.

"It's about this denim," she murmured, her lips on his.

He drew back for a second, his eyes appearing almost black in the light that trickled in from the front room. On his face was a sheen of perspiration that made him more handsome and more desirable than ever.

"It's about these clothes," he said.

She stepped away from him and began to unbutton her blouse.

"Wait," he said as she came to the last button on the blouse. He hadn't taken his eyes off her. "Let me do it."

His hands were shaking as he reached for her. Gently, he pulled the tails of the blouse from her skirt. Slowly, as if hardly daring to believe this was happening, he pushed the two edges aside so that he could look at her.

She was wearing a lace bra that barely covered her, and when she saw his expression, she blessed the unknown impulse that had made her choose this particular style that morning. The look in his eyes gave her a rush of feminine pleasure, and he was just reaching for the bra's straps when she caught his hand.

"My turn," she said huskily, and began unbuttoning his shirt.

His chest was even more powerful and broad than she had envisioned, and she put her hands on his shoulders before tracing a line down his torso to his belt. His warm skin felt sensuous under her hand, and she closed her eyes, enjoying the feel of his body.

As though it was a cue, he pulled her gently to him. She barely noticed the caress of the silk as her blouse fell to the floor; when the bra followed, she pressed against him. The sensation of his skin against her breasts was exquisite and she wanted it to last forever, but he tipped her head up and began to kiss her again, and she realized she wanted—needed—much more.

She hadn't a clue how the rest of their clothes followed the others; she was lost in the bliss of the moment. Finally, Wade pulled back a little. Tenderly, he took one of her breasts in his hand and sighed from the depths of his soul.

"What is it about you . . . ?" he murmured.

What was it about you? she wondered dizzily when he ran a thumb over her nipple. The simple caress sent a shock of desire through her, and she tried to bring him closer. Instead, he dropped his head and gently tongued her nipple until she didn't think she could bear the ache that inundated her. She wanted him, and she couldn't wait.

"Wade . . ."

They were still standing by the bed, and with one hand he reached down and jerked the bedclothes to the floor. The blankets landed in a tangled pile, but neither of them noticed. Mouths clinging, hands seeking, bodies yearning, they fell on top of the sheets.

After a few moments, she managed to gasp, "Wait! I didn't bring anything."

"I'll take care of it," he murmured, kissing her eyelids, her earlobes, the line of her jaw, her throat.

Swept away in the sensations he was evoking with every touch and caress, she didn't think any more about it. Instead, she closed her eyes and ran her hands down his strong back. Then she wound her fingers in his thick hair and kissed him, hard.

Carla had never made love—or been made love to— quite this way before. With Wade's naked body against hers, and his hands caressing her and touching her in places that made her desperate for more, she surrendered completely to pleasure. With other lovers, she had held something back. Mistrustful of men, she'd wanted to retain some control even during lovemaking. But tonight, she gave herself completely to this man, and he repaid her trust by taking her to heights she had never dreamed of.

She wanted to savor every moment, from the slow movements of his hips after he entered her, to the increasingly wild pitch that carried them away before they knew it.

"Wade!" she cried, beginning the ride, and wanting him to take it with her.

"I'm right here," he said hoarsely, lifting his head just for a second so he could look down at her.

She wanted to watch him, but couldn't. Pleasure was flooding her, taking her to another plane, and she closed her eyes and went with it, feeling him soar with her. Up and away they went, into an indescribable place where passion and desire met with a roar. Just when she thought she wouldn't be able to bear this exquisite agony any longer, it was over. She tried to hold on, but the whirlwind died to a gentle breeze, and left them soon after.

A long time later, when she could speak again, she said, "Well. That was quite a welcome."

Wade had collapsed by her side. As he held her, he tried to catch his breath. "That was quite an entrance."

"If I'd known I'd get that reaction, I would have made it sooner."

"And if I'd known you were so inclined, I would have worn a sign saying I was available."

She had never seen him this way, relaxed and at ease with himself and with her. Something tight inside him had loosened with their intense lovemaking. She could see it in his face and feel it in his body. Even in the dark, she saw that the shadows were gone from his eyes.

For good? she wondered. It was too soon to tell. Maybe she should enjoy this glimpse of him, she told herself, resting her head on his chest. The comforting sound of his heart warmed her and made her feel safe.

As I understand it, Mr. Petrie came here three years ago... Wasn't that about the time that Done Roamin' had his accident?

The warm glow Carla had been feeling vanished as her mother's words flashed into her head. *Damn it!*

Why did her mother have to plant suspicions in her mind?

Wade must have felt the change in her, for he asked, "Did I say something wrong?"

She didn't want the evening to end on a bitter note, so she forced a laugh and said, "No, I was just thinking about Done Driftin'."

"Thinking what?" he asked sleepily.

"That if Done Driftin' is superior to his dad, I won't remark on it to Octavia. You know how much my grandmother loves that horse."

"They've been through a lot together. I think, in a way, he helped her get through some tough times. And I know he helped me."

Maybe this was an opportunity to clear things up. She said, "He did? How?"

"It was a long time ago, Carla. It's all history."

"Not to me."

He glanced at her, and just for a moment, she thought she saw something in his face. Then he looked away again.

Or was it to avoid her eyes?

"Do you really want to hear this?" he asked.

More than anything in the world, she realized. She said, "Yes, I do."

He was silent for a few seconds, then he said, "A long time ago, I trained horses at Santa Anita racetrack, in California. I had a client named Annabelle Renfrow—"

"I know her."

"You do?"

"We've met." She waved her hand distastefully. "She came to England, supposedly on holiday, but really to marry a title. Apparently, it was the only thing in her life she didn't have."

He grunted. "Yeah, that's probably true."

"What about her, though?"

The shadows had returned to his eyes. "It was my fault," he said, his voice low. "I knew it was wrong to get involved with a client, but I went ahead and did it, anyway."

She was beginning to wish she'd never started this. "You mean, you had an affair?"

"Yes. But I'm not going to lie to you. It was more than that. At one point, God help me, I thought I wanted to marry her." His jaw tightened. "Even if things hadn't gone so wrong, I see now just how idiotic that idea was. I certainly had no title."

Carla felt a ridiculous stab of jealousy. She tried to make light of it by saying, "So you fell in love. That's not a crime."

"I know. But that's not all. Because I fancied myself in love with her, I did some things I shouldn't have, things against my better judgment, things I knew were wrong."

She was silent, part of her wondering if she wanted him to go on.

"What things?" she made herself ask.

He was silent again. Finally, he said, "There was a horse that belonged to Annabelle. A filly that came back from a workout with a filled ankle right before she was due to enter a big race. I didn't want her to run, but Annabelle insisted." His jaw tightened. "She wanted to show off the filly to her friends."

Carla knew by the look on his face that it would be a mistake to ask how this story ended, but she couldn't help herself. "What happened?" she asked.

"The horse went down with a spiral fracture on the backstretch. We had to destroy her."

Carla drew in a sharp breath. "How awful!"

As though he hadn't heard her, he said, "The filly was good, one of the best. I should have listened to my instincts and not the vet."

She knew where this was going. "It wasn't your fault, Wade."

"The hell it wasn't. I was the trainer. I was responsible. It was my call, and...oh, to hell with it. It doesn't matter now. It's all in the past."

Carla knew by his expression that it still mattered a great deal. "Is that why you gave up training and came out here?"

"I didn't *give it up*," he said angrily. "Annabelle owned thirty horses. When she took them to another trainer, my other clients followed her. Rumors started flying around about my being involved in an insurance scam. By the time the smoke cleared, it was pretty obvious that it was time to get out." His lip curled. "I didn't really have a choice. By then, I didn't have anything left."

"But you said—"

"I know what I said, Carla. But what it boils down to is the fact that I was responsible. It was my call and I blew it."

She couldn't let it go. "I still don't understand. If the vet said—"

"It was an insurance scam," Wade said. "No one knew it at the time, but Annabelle was financially strapped. She agreed to split the money with the vet if he'd substitute normal X rays for the ones he took on the filly that morning."

"So there *was* something wrong with the horse."

"Yeah, that filled ankle she came back with after her morning work turned out to be a warning of the fracture to come. If I'd known—"

"It wasn't your fault. If the vet substituted the X rays, how could you be responsible?"

"I know horses," he said. "I *knew* something was wrong."

"But what could you have done?"

"I should have gone to the stewards—anything to stop her from racing that horse that afternoon. But I didn't do that. Against my better judgment, the horse ran. When Queen Mab broke down on the backstretch, Annabelle had hysterics. Oh, it was a great show. You would have thought she'd lost a beloved companion instead of a horse she hardly recognized. But she got the money, the racing world lost a greathearted filly, and I gave up training. And now you know the whole sordid story."

Angrily, he threw the sheet back and reached for his jeans. "This was a mistake, Carla. We never should have allowed things to go this far. You ask too many questions."

She knew he was angry and embarrassed about what he'd told her, but she wasn't going to let him get away now. She snatched up the sheet and wrapped it around her before she got out of bed.

"I know how you feel—" she began.

He looked at her furiously. "You don't have the slightest idea how I feel, so don't give me any mock sympathy."

She stiffened angrily. "All right, fine. Since we're on the subject of horses, this has been on my mind, too. Someone pointed out to me recently that you came to the farm just about the time of Done Roamin's accident—"

She hadn't meant to sound so accusatory. She wouldn't have, if her doubts about him weren't so close to the surface. But the way he was acting—

He had just reached for his boot when she mentioned Done Roamin'. For a tense second or two, he froze. Then he grabbed the boot and slowly stood.

"Do you think I had something to do with that?"

At the look on his face, it took all her courage to answer. "You tell me."

His face was like a mask. "Why should I tell you anything? You know what happened. Octavia told you."

But Octavia's words weren't enough for Carla. After all that had been said between her and Wade, everything depended on his denying that he'd had anything to do with the stallion's accident.

When something bad happens, and there seems no reason for it, ask yourself who had the most to gain. The answer will tell you who's responsible.

Her stepfather had said that to her more than once. So had her mother, who had raised all these doubts in her mind. It was true that Wade had come to the farm just before the stallion was hurt. In fact, she remembered Octavia telling her that he'd been the one to find the horse that terrible morning. Now she'd learned from Wade himself that at that time, he'd lost everything: his stable, his livelihood, his profession, his reputation. He'd also admitted that there had been some suspicion of his being involved in an insurance scam in California.

Done Roamin' had been insured; Carla had seen the papers herself. And Octavia was so fond of Wade; she depended on him for everything. If he had tried to recoup his losses by accepting money to injure the stallion he'd certainly had the opportunity.

In fact, Octavia had also mentioned he'd been sleeping in the groom's apartment above the barn at that time because the barn manager's house was being painted. Why hadn't he heard anything? A horse who was so seriously injured would certainly have made noise, yet Wade claimed not to have heard a sound that night.

But the horse hadn't been put down, a desperate little voice said inside Carla's head. *If Wade was guilty, and his plan had gone awry, why is he still around? What would he have to gain now?*

The farm, Carla thought suddenly. If Wade *was* responsible for the stallion's injury, he could only enhance himself in Octavia's eyes by taking care of the horse after the animal's surgeries. Wade might not have planned on Octavia's being willing to spend everything to save the stallion, but once he realized what she intended, it would have been to his advantage to do everything he could to assist in the horse's recovery. Octavia, lonely and old and so dependent upon him, would have rewarded him handsomely.

But then Octavia had sent that letter and an inconvenient granddaughter had arrived to throw a wrench in Wade's plans. No wonder he was so resentful when she came, Carla realized. He regarded her as an adversary.

Was that why he'd made love to her tonight? Maybe he'd decided that if she was going to stay at Dunleavy Farm, it would behoove him to get into her good graces.

Not to mention her bed, she thought, suddenly. He wasn't going to get away with it, she vowed, and looked at him furiously.

"Grandmother told me what *you* told her," she said, her voice steely. "I'm asking you what *really* happened. A horse like Done Roamin' doesn't just . . . break his leg. Not like that. It's too serious an injury. It's too—''

Wade looked at her incredulously. "You think *I'm* responsible?"

"I didn't say that."

"You didn't have to. I don't believe this. You actually think—"

"I just want to know what happened!"

He looked at her so contemptuously that she wanted to shrivel. Was she wrong? She didn't have time to decide, for he said, "To hell with you, *Miss* Dunleavy. I told you what happened. If you don't believe me, so be it. I'm out of here. Say goodbye to Mrs. D. for me."

"What? You can't go!"

"Yes, I can. It's obvious what you think of *me,* so I'm not going to stick around. The next thing I know, you'll be accusing me of faking the hay invoices or fixing the sale of those horses. Hell, I'm so bad that maybe I'll just go all the way one day and kidnap the old lady for ransom."

"You're not being fair!"

"Fair? *Fair!* You've got a lot of nerve saying that. Goodbye, Carla. Oh, and since I'm giving such short notice, don't worry about my two weeks' severance pay, I'll forfeit. Believe me, it'll be worth it."

She couldn't believe this was happening. As he started toward the door, she cried, "But where are you going?"

"What do you care?"

Carla knew she'd acted hastily, but her pride wouldn't let her apologize. He'd hurt her, so she wanted to hurt him back. "I don't. But Grandmother will ask. What am I going to tell her?"

A look of regret passed over his face. "Tell her I'm sorry." He turned and left.

When she heard the front door slam, she clenched her hands. If she hadn't been so furious, she would have run after him and told him...what?

Now threading its way through her fury was doubt. She shouldn't have let him go, she thought. What was her grandmother going to think?

Then she lifted her chin in defiance. What was the big deal? What did Wade really do here that anyone familiar with the business couldn't do just as well? There were so few horses on the farm now, and since she'd taken over the books, she knew there was so little money that it wouldn't be long before the farm would have to shut down, anyway. Then Octavia could retire to a smaller more manageable place.

But was that what her grandmother wanted?

Carla knew in her heart it was not, but she had to persuade Octavia this was best. They didn't need Wade. If she couldn't find anyone to run the farm, well, they'd just have to put it up for sale—assuming they could find a buyer. Trent Spencer had said he would help, she remembered suddenly. But if not him, maybe someone else. Because it was certain that *she* wasn't suited to this type of life. She had tried, but obviously it just wasn't her style.

But Octavia was depending on her.

She cringed at the thought. Octavia had been the heart and soul of the farm for all her adult life. How could Carla ask...demand...*expect* her to give up Dunleavy Farm just because she was old and couldn't manage by herself anymore? It was obvious now that Octavia had hoped Carla would find roots here. She knew it was her grandmother's dream that her visit would become permanent, giving the farm, and herself, new life.

Could she stay on? She was tempted, she had to admit it. But she rejected the idea. If she'd ever needed a lesson in exactly how wrong it was, she'd had it tonight. She'd always known it was a mistake to get involved with Wade, but she had gone ahead, anyway, and now everyone would have to pay the price.

At the thought, she realized that she'd have to explain to Octavia why Wade had left. How could she confess to her grandmother that she'd practically accused him of being responsible for Done Roamin's injury? Octavia would be horrified, appalled and furious—and she'd have every right to be.

She was still standing there debating how to handle the situation when she heard an engine roar. She turned and watched as Wade flashed by the house on his motorcycle, and before she knew it, she was running to the window to watch his taillight disappear.

He really was going. Until she saw him head out on that bike, she'd believed . . .

What? That he'd come back? That he'd say he'd changed his mind? That he'd go down on his knees and swear he was innocent of any wrongdoing so she wouldn't have to suspect he had a hidden agenda?

"Oh, what have I done?" she whispered, her hand to her mouth as the sound of the bike faded.

LATER, AS SHE STOOD on Wade's porch, the night air cooling her flushed face, she had no doubt that she'd just made one of the biggest mistakes of her life.

Oh, God, what a mess! she thought, her hand to her head. She wasn't ready to go up to the main house yet, so she went down the steps and headed toward the stallion barn. She'd say good-night to Done Roamin' and give a pat or two to his son. Then she'd go and face her grandmother.

The big old barn was warm and redolent of horses and leather and hay. The grooms always left a light burning at either end, and as she walked toward Done Roamin's double stall, one of the three resident barn cats came to rub against her leg.

"I'm about as low as I can go," she said as the feline, duty done, sauntered away. He jumped up onto a pile of hay bales, where two more glowing eyes looked eerily down at her from the shadows. Carla tried to smile at the sight, but felt the tears begin to flow instead. Her steps dragging, she went to say good-night to Done Roamin'.

The aged horse was half-asleep when she crept up quietly, but stallions, no matter how old, always seemed to be on watch. His ears twitched at her approach, and he came to the stall bars when she looked in.

"How're you doing, old man?" she asked tearfully. She carefully slipped her hand through the bars to rub his forehead, a gesture he usually accepted only from Octavia.

As though he sensed her low spirits, Done Roamin' permitted the caress, and even allowed her to pet his gray-haired muzzle. But instead of buoying her up, the gesture made her feel more depressed. After a few moments she moved on to see Done Cryin'.

This other son of Done Roamin's was looking for a last bit of hay from his dinner when she came to his stall. The light at this end of the barn glimmered on his dark bay coat. As she watched him, she thought that he was—almost—as good as his half brother, Done Driftin'.

As though he sensed her thoughts, Done Cryin' lifted his head and gave her an arrogant stare. Trying to distract herself from that horrible scene with Wade, she leaned against the stall door, wondering if she should talk to her grandmother again about starting this colt in race training. The vet had pronounced the horse fit, but Octavia still wouldn't say what her plans were for him.

"What do you think, boy?" she said as Done Cryin' finally gave in and meandered casually over to the bars to put his nose through. She stroked his silky muzzle. "Would you like to go into race training with your brother?"

After snuffling her hand a moment to make sure she hadn't brought him a treat, he turned his back to her. Normally, Carla would have laughed at the sight. Tonight, she thought sadly, it seemed symbolic.

CHAPTER TWELVE

CIGARETTE IN HAND, Meredith was pacing the living room that night, wondering where Carla had gone, when Octavia appeared in the doorway. At the sight of her mother, she stopped midstride and said, "Should you be out of bed?"

Octavia came into the room. "I'm tired of being in bed. That's all I've done for a week."

"How stupid of me. You never have done anything you didn't want to. Why should you start now, just because the doctor gave orders for you to rest?"

Octavia sat down in her favorite chair, the high-backed Queen Anne with the carved arms and the rose-colored upholstery. She looked very tiny sitting there, her slippered feet barely able to touch the floor. Meredith stared at her a moment longer, then looked away and took another drag on her cigarette.

"Like mother, like daughter, I suppose," Octavia said pointedly. She added, "You know I don't like anyone to smoke in the house."

"Oh, yes, how could I have forgotten? Well, fine. In that case, I'll go elsewhere."

"Please don't leave. I'd like to talk to you."

Meredith was heading toward the door. "I beg your pardon? A 'please' and a request to talk, practically in the same sentence. Wonders will never cease."

Wearily, Octavia closed her eyes and rested her head against the chair. Suddenly, she looked old and frail to Meredith, who came back and sat down again. Grudgingly, she said, "All right. What did you want to talk about *now?*"

Her eyes still closed, Octavia smiled faintly. "You always were hard-edged, Merry. Even when you were a child."

"Please don't call me by that ridiculous nickname. You know I hate it. I always did, ever since Jamie invented it."

"I thought Gary was the first one to call you that, not your sister."

"Does it matter?" Meredith asked impatiently. "The point is that I don't like it. I never have, and I still don't."

Octavia lifted her head. "It doesn't seem to fit, does it? Especially now. If you don't mind my saying so, you don't seem to be a happy woman."

"Oh, really?" Meredith took another furious drag on her cigarette. "And whose fault is that, I wonder."

"I know I made some mistakes, Meredith."

"Some?"

"All right, many. But you're a grown woman. You can't blame everything on me. At some point, you have to take responsibility for your own life."

Meredith looked at her coldly. "Is that what you wanted to talk to me about?"

"In a way, yes. We haven't had a chance to talk yet. If I didn't know better, I'd think you were avoiding me."

"I came to see you in the hospital."

"Yes, you did. But I suspect it was because you knew we couldn't talk there."

"And we can here? Since when? I don't seem to recall our ever having a real conversation at any time in our lives. Why start now?"

"Because this estrangement between us has affected Carla, that's why."

Meredith's voice rose. "What do you know about Carla? She's *my* daughter."

"And one of my granddaughters. And since she came, we've gotten to know each other quite well." Octavia paused. "Perhaps better than you and I ever did."

"And I suppose that was my fault, too! Well, if I were you, I'd consider this. If you hadn't been so busy with the farm, you might have had more time for your children. Gary and Jamie and I were far down on your list, weren't we? The horses always came first."

"That's not true."

"Isn't it?" Meredith waved her hand, a bitter gesture encompassing the room, the house, the farm beyond. "If that's so, where are your other two children? Why do you think we all left, Mother? No, that's the wrong expression. We didn't *leave*. We were *driven* away. By you!''

''I didn't drive you away—''

''The hell you didn't!'' Meredith was furious now, her composure gone, her face red. ''We always had to do everything you said—or else!''

''I was a widow, trying to raise three children the only way I knew how. I admit I made mistakes. But I always tried to give all three of you what you needed. Why do you think I worked so hard to make the farm a success after your father died? I wanted you to have all the things I never had. I wanted—''

''Oh, you *wanted*, all right. But it wasn't anything for us! Why don't you admit it? You enjoyed the limelight. You loved being in the winner's circle with Dunleavy horses. Sometimes I think if you could have arranged it without causing talk, you would have put us in the barn and let your precious horses sleep in the house!''

''You go too far! I admit that I've always loved the horses. But they were separate from you. I loved you children—''

''Did you? You certainly picked a strange way of showing it. You turned my husband against me, you disinherited Gary and as for poor Jamie—''

Octavia banged her cane on the floor. ''Your sister was a fool! She didn't know what she was doing, she never did. She always had her head in the clouds. What was I to do?''

"You could have let her live her own life!" Meredith shouted. "Just like you could have done for Gary and for me! At least then, if we made mistakes, they would have been *our* mistakes, not yours!"

Octavia's face paled. "I didn't know you hated me that much."

Meredith looked at her in a rage. Then she turned away. "It's obvious that we'll never see eye to eye about this. You have your way of thinking about what happened, I have mine. But there's one thing I'm going to insist on...."

"What? I'll do anything to make it up to you."

"It's too late for that," Meredith said pitilessly. "The best we can hope for now is that Carla won't be dragged into this feud. I don't want her subjected to all this ancient history."

"But don't you think you should tell her about—"

"I did. At least as much as I'm going to tell her. And if you—"

Tiredly, Octavia raised her arm in a gesture of submission. "There's no need for threats. I haven't said anything, and I won't. As you pointed out a few minutes ago, Carla is *your* daughter."

"Yes, she is. You made your choices, Mother. So will I. And I'm not going to allow you to try and rectify past mistakes with your children through mine." She turned sharply toward her mother. "But perhaps Carla isn't the only grandchild you plan on trying to inveigle into taking your side. Tell me, have you tried to contact Nan and Seth?"

"You know about them?"

"Oh, please. You don't think I'd find out about my own brother's and sister's children? Of course I know. Before I came back, I made it my business to find out. You're not the only one who can hire a private investigator, you know."

"Does Carla know about her cousins?"

"Not unless you've told her."

"Oh, Meredith!"

"Don't give me that! Why would I tell her about them when I never told her about you and the farm? I decided long ago it was better for her to grow up thinking she and I were alone in the world."

"Then tell me, Meredith, why did you come home?"

Meredith stiffened. "This isn't my home! It hasn't been for a long time."

"You'll never forgive me, will you?"

"Why should I? I was married, Mother. I was pregnant with Carla. Everything would have been fine if you hadn't interfered!"

"Do you really believe that?"

"I have to believe it!" Meredith cried. "Alan—"

She stopped, obviously realizing too late just what she had said. After a long, tense silence, Octavia reached for her cane. Slowly, she got up and started toward the door. She was at the threshold when she paused and looked back.

"I'm sorry it turned out this way," she said quietly.

Meredith wouldn't look at her. As she took another drag on the cigarette, she said, "So am I."

Octavia waited a moment longer, but when her daughter said nothing more, she went out.

Meredith waited until she heard the bedroom door close before she angrily switched off the living room lights. She was about to go up to her own room, when she heard the sound of a motorcycle. She went to the window and looked out just as Wade Petrie roared by on a big bike. She knew it was him; despite the helmet, she recognized those boots and saw a flash of light on the large silver belt buckle he wore.

At almost that same moment, a light came on down at the barn manager's house. When Meredith saw that, her lips tightened. Now she knew where Carla had gone tonight. Angrily, she sat down to wait. Obviously it was past time for them to have another of those productive mother-daughter chats.

THE MAIN HOUSE was dark when Carla said goodnight to the horses and began the trek up the path to the front porch. She hadn't realized it was late until she glanced at her watch and saw that it was almost midnight. She was exhausted, but she had to find a way to explain the situation to Octavia. She climbed the porch steps and opened the front door.

"Well, I see you finally found your way home."

The voice coming out of the darkened living room startled her. She switched on the wall light and saw

Meredith sitting on the couch. Angrily, she said, "What are you doing sitting here in the dark?"

"Waiting for you, of course," Meredith said, her eyes as cold as the look on her face. "Did you have fun tonight down in the servants' quarters, making love to the help?"

Outraged, she said, "I can't believe you were spying on me!"

"I didn't have to spy. You were there in plain sight. I thought we agreed you weren't going to have anything to do with that man."

"*That man's* name is Wade Petrie, Mother. And *we* didn't agree to anything."

Meredith stubbed out her cigarette in a crystal ashtray and stood. "I'm only thinking of your own good, Carla."

Aware of the irony of defending Wade to her mother when she herself had hurled accusations at him tonight, Carla said, "I'm a grown woman, Mother. I make my own decisions. But now that we're on the subject, why do you dislike Wade so much? You don't even know him!"

"I know enough. He's like all such people—"

"What do you mean by *that?*"

"Never mind. I didn't mean to say that."

"Well, you said it. Now, explain yourself."

"Oh, Carla, can't you just trust me on this?"

"No, I can't, Mother. All these innuendos and secrets are—" Carla stopped midsentence. "This has something to do with why you left Dunleavy Farm, doesn't it?''

"No—"

"Yes it does." Suddenly, she was certain. "What was it, Mother? You got involved with the 'help' too. That's why you're so opposed to Wade."

"You're being ridiculous."

"Am I? Maybe you're hiding something else from me."

"I'm not hiding anything! Carla, believe me. Oh, I knew we never should have come here. I want to leave immediately."

"You're not leaving until I know what this is all about. I mean it, Mother. If you don't tell me now, we won't have anything to talk about—ever."

Meredith paled. "You can't be serious!"

"Yes, I am. This has gone far enough. First there was the grandmother I never knew existed, then I find out about an aunt and uncle you neglected to mention. For all I know, I have cousins somewhere—maybe even an entire extended family. I never would have known any of it if Grandmother hadn't written that letter!"

Suddenly, Meredith crumpled. "I told you what your precious grandmother did to me. Alan and I never had a chance. I can never be sure whether he loved me or, as Mother insisted, he was simply after the Dunleavy money. He certainly didn't stick around to fight for you and me."

Trembling, Meredith reached for her cigarette case. She pulled out a cigarette and tried to light it, but her hand was shaking so badly that she couldn't touch the flame to the end. Carla took the lighter from her mother's hand. Meredith looked at the cigarette, then threw it down.

"I hope you're happy," she said bitterly. "All your life, I've tried to spare you that story. I didn't want you to have the doubts about your father that I had! Now you know. Does it make you think more kindly of your grandmother?"

Carla didn't reply. She couldn't help thinking that if her father had really loved Meredith, nothing could have separated them.

But maybe she was being unjust, she told herself. How could she judge, when she didn't know her father's side of the story?

You judged Wade, and you didn't know his.

The realization sobered her, and instead of erupting with anger at her mother, she sat down beside Meredith. "I'm sorry," she said. "I know how painful that was for you, but I'm glad you told me."

Meredith wouldn't look at her. "Oh, Carla," she said. "I wish—"

"So do I," Carla said quietly. "But it's over and done now. Somehow we have to put it behind us."

"I can't."

"Yes, you can. Now, come on." She helped Meredith to her feet. "Go upstairs and get some rest. Things will look better in the morning."

But after Carla was ready for bed herself, she turned off the light and went to her bedroom window. Her arms crossed at the waist, she stared out at the quiet moonlit night and thought wearily what a day it had been. She'd gone from the heights of joy when Done Driftin' won his race, to the ecstatic pleasures of making love with a man she realized now she was beginning to love, to a quarrel and denouement with her mother about which she still wasn't sure how she felt. The emotional roller coaster had left her weary, but she couldn't rest.

She felt so confused in those lonely hours as she stood by her window, her eyes involuntarily going to Wade's dark house. It was almost four in the morning before she finally went to bed, but even then she couldn't sleep. She'd hoped against hope, but in all that time, Wade hadn't come back.

WADE HADN'T reached the front gates of Dunleavy Farm earlier that night before he felt like a fool for running away. He was tempted to turn back, but then pride got the best of him and he gunned the bike. His expression grim under the helmet, he roared out to the main road, heading toward . . . he didn't know where.

The interstate to Louisville suddenly loomed before him and he took the on-ramp at a fast clip. Whenever he had problems in the past, being at the track seemed to clear his head. *And God only knew,* he thought, *his head could use a little clearing tonight.*

What had he been thinking of earlier? Until he opened the door this evening and saw Carla, he hadn't had any intention of making love to her. But the instant he saw her, everything but how much he desired her fled from his mind. Then, when she spoke to him in that husky voice of hers, he completely lost his head.

Or was that an excuse? He might as well admit it: he'd been tempted long before tonight. In fact, the thought had crossed his mind that very afternoon at the track. When Done Driftin' had won his race, the usually controlled Carla had been so excited that her face was luminous. It was all he could do not to drag her off to some dark, private spot.

At the memory, he unconsciously throttled down a little harder. The powerful motorcycle surged forward, reminding him again how much things had changed—how much *he* had changed. After the debacle in California, he had impulsively bought the Triumph with some vague intention of taking a solo trip across the country. He'd planned to camp wherever he stopped, stay as long as he wanted and move along again when he chose. He thought it would give him time to think, but he'd only made it to Arizona before he realized the arid truth behind that old saying, *No matter where you go, there you are.*

He hadn't been able to get away from himself then, and he couldn't now. So, why didn't he go back and set the record straight? All he had to do was turn around....

His hands tightened on the handlebars, but then the upcoming freeway exit flashed by and it was too late.

Just like it was too late for a lot of things, he thought. It was better to leave it as it was. Carla would despise him, but after all the harsh words they'd exchanged tonight, they probably couldn't even go back to the way they'd been when she'd first come to the farm. So it was pointless to think of her expressive green eyes, or the shape of her mouth, or how beautiful her body was, rounded in all the right places, moving sensuously against him....

Memories of their lovemaking caused an ache to start in his groin, and he gripped the bike harder. *None of it mattered,* he told himself fiercely. He had quit, and that was that. Maybe later—a long time later— he'd write to Octavia and tell her how sorry he was that he'd skipped out on her. But right now, he needed a drink.

THE BETTING LINE WAS a gathering spot for racetrack people, and as Wade sat at the bar a few minutes later nursing a beer, someone clapped him on the shoulder.

"Hey, Wade! I thought that was you. It's been a long time, buddy. Where've you been?"

Wade looked at the man who had heaved his bulk onto the stool beside him. It was Bobby Watkins, a trainer he'd known a lifetime ago in California.

"Hi, Bobby," he said unenthusiastically. "What are you doing so far from home?"

"Oh, I came for an owner who wants me to check out a Derby prospect," Bobby said, signaling the bartender for a drink. "The guy thinks he can buy a Triple Crown winner like he does everything else."

"Maybe he can," Wade said. He wished the man would go away.

"Say, you're working out at Dunleavy, aren't you?"

Wade nodded because it was easier than explaining that he'd left.

"I saw that Done Driftin' colt run today," Bobby said. "He sure put it away."

So much had happened that it seemed aeons since the colt had raced. Was it only this afternoon? Wade wondered. But he didn't want to think of Done Driftin', because then he'd think of the colt's owner, and he most definitely did not want to dwell on her.

"He sure did," he said.

"Say," Bobby said. "You don't think that colt's for sale, do you?"

Wade thought of Carla's face this afternoon when Done Driftin' had won his race and shook his head. "I doubt it."

"Aw, come on. Everything's for sale. A man just has to find the right price."

"I don't think so, Bobby. I know the owner, and she has quite an interest in that colt."

"You know the owner, eh? What's her name? I saw it on the program...no, don't tell me...I got it! Carla Dunleavy, right?"

"Right."

"Is she some relation to the old lady?"

Wade shifted impatiently on the stool. "If you mean, is she related to Octavia Dunleavy, the answer is yes. Carla is her granddaughter."

Bobby squinted at him. "Well, you always did like those socialites, Wade, I'll give you that. When you were out in California, it was that Annalisa Benbow. Or was that her name? It's been so long now, I kind of forgot."

Wade wondered if the name had really slipped Bobby's mind, then decided he didn't care. "Not that it matters, but her name was Annabelle Renfrow."

"Yeah, well, whatever she's called, she sure gave you a rotten deal. Everyone I know shudders to think it coulda happened to any one of us."

Wade had learned a long time ago that it was pointless to deny or explain; it only made things worse. So he said, "Only if you were as stupid as I was."

"Aw, don't be so hard on yourself, man. You fell for a pretty face and she tricked you into doing something you didn't want to do. Like I said, it coulda happened to anyone."

Wade drained the last of his beer. Suddenly he was anxious to get out of here. As he got up from the stool, he said, "Yeah, but it happened to me. See you, Bobby. Good luck in finding a horse."

"Thanks. Hey, you want another brew?"

"No, thanks."

"Wait a minute. Where are you going?"

"I don't know," Wade said, and walked out of the bar. As he got on the bike again, he knew he had some decisions to make. And uppermost in his mind as he drove away, was the certainty that if Carla was going to stay at Dunleavy Farm, he'd best be on his way.

CHAPTER THIRTEEN

IT WAS ALMOST ten o'clock the next morning before Carla dressed and went downstairs. She'd managed to fall asleep sometime around dawn, but even after a hot shower, she still felt tired and groggy and out of sorts.

She felt even worse when she remembered she had to find a way to explain Wade's absence without upsetting her grandmother. In the light of day, her accusation seemed even more inexcusable than it had last night. She knew Octavia would have every right to be angry, and she wasn't looking forward to the necessity of making a confession.

She decided that she needed a cup of coffee before she did anything, so she was sitting in the breakfast nook when Teresa entered the kitchen carrying a bed tray.

"Good morning, Miss Carla," the housekeeper said. "Did you sleep well?"

"Oh, yes," Carla lied. She eyed the tray. "I see my grandmother is awake."

"Mrs. Dunleavy has been up for hours. She had breakfast in the sun room this morning. Would you like me to take a tray there for you, as well?"

The last thing Carla wanted to do was eat. Her stomach was already in knots. "No, thank you," she said. "I'll just take this coffee with me."

As Teresa had indicated, Octavia was in the solarium at the side of the house. In this warm room, adobe tiles covered the floor and the walls and ceiling were made of glass. White wicker furniture padded with green-and-white-striped cushions were scattered around, and several tall ficus trees in brass pots gave the cozy area a junglelike atmosphere even when it was cold outside. Octavia was sitting in one of the chairs, her feet on an ottoman, reading a newspaper when Carla came in.

When Octavia saw her, she immediately put the paper aside. "Well, good morning. Or perhaps I should say good afternoon, instead?"

Carla wasn't able to tell her just yet what a disaster last night had been, so she said, "Now, don't start. I had a right to sleep in. After all, my horse won his first race yesterday. I had to celebrate, didn't I?"

"Indeed you did." Carla had already told her about the race when she'd come home the day before, but Octavia's eyes glowed with the memory. "It sounded so exciting. I wished I could have been there."

"Well, you'll see it on the tape when it comes, and you can be on hand for the next one."

"Is that a promise?"

Carla saw where this was going, and said, "Only if the doctor agrees."

"Oh, piddle. What does he know?"

"More than you or I do. How are you feeling today?"

"Like a fool, if you want to know the truth. All that fuss and bother over a little upset."

"It was hardly that. You did have a heart attack."

"It was probably just gas," Octavia grumbled. "Those doctors don't know what they're doing, so they just guess."

Carla smiled. Then she said, "I wanted to talk to you about something. Mother told me about my father."

"I see. Did she tell you my part?"

"She said you didn't approve, and had the marriage annulled."

"It's true. I did."

"Why?"

"It's a long story. But the main reason is that I knew Alan was all wrong for her, and I didn't want to see her hurt."

"But she was."

"Yes, she was. I often wish I'd never interferred. But it seems I made so many mistakes."

"What was he like, my father?"

Octavia sighed. "Alan was . . . charming. It was his stock in trade. And he knew horses, I'll give him that. But . . . I'm sorry, Carla, I have to say it—he was an opportunist. I never thought he wanted Meredith as much as he coveted the farm." She shook her head. "But perhaps I was wrong about that, too. I don't know anymore. It was so long ago."

When Carla was silent, Octavia reached for her hand. "I'm so sorry dear."

Carla was sorry, too. But as Octavia had said, it had all happened so long ago and she had so many things to think about.

During the long, seemingly endless nighttime hours, when sleep eluded her, she'd had plenty of time to wonder about the farm. Since it was her fault that Wade was no longer part of the operation, it was her duty to replace him. Another responsibility was to find a way to shore up the place financially so Octavia wouldn't have to declare bankruptcy.

The problem was how. She'd gone over the books with the proverbial fine-tooth comb. But no matter how she figured it, she'd come to the reluctant conclusion that even if she could sign over a major portion of her trust fund, it wouldn't be enough to lift the farm out of its fiscal morass; all it would do was temporarily stave off the inevitable.

Then she remembered Trent Spencer. Trent had offered his help as a banker and businessman—and yes, as a friend of the family. And even though she suspected what Octavia's reaction would be to allowing some Yankee *outsiders* a glimpse into Dunleavy's dismal monetary state, it would be foolish to turn Trent down. She'd have to convince Octavia that the farm needed Trent's help to survive.

So maybe she had a way to sort out the finances. That still left the problem of who would manage the operation. She couldn't leave her grandmother to do it all alone. Octavia needed an administrator; *pots* of money wouldn't help if things weren't restructured. As fond as Carla was of her grandmother, Octavia wasn't the person to manage such a big enterprise, not anymore. No, it had to be another person, someone who would be committed to the farm. Someone like—

Octavia's granddaughter.

No matter how many ways she tried to get around it, she always came back to this point. And always, she had the same question. Was it what she wanted? She never stayed in one place for long: she would have been gone long before now if it hadn't been for Done Driftin's first race. But now that was over, and she was free to move on.

Just then, Octavia said, "Tell me again about the race yesterday. I wish I could have been there to see him run!"

Carla was glad enough to put away her gloomy thoughts and turn to something else. "I do, too. Grandmother, it was wonderful. I've seen all sorts of races before, but never one like this. Maybe it was because my very own colt was racing."

"It does make a difference. I always felt the same way when one of our horses was running. Especially Done Roamin'. In his day, no one could catch him. When the race started, it was almost as if he were alone on the track. As soon as the gate opened, the rest of the field was battling for second place."

"I wish I could have seen him."

"I wish you could have, too. He was something, all right."

Overcome with sudden emotion, Octavia wiped her eyes, then waved her hand impatiently. "Listen to me, an old woman rambling on about the past when it's the present we should be celebrating. So, when is Dwight planning to race him again? We have to prep him for the Derby, you know. And then, after that, the Preakness, and the Belmont. Who knows? We could have another Triple Crown winner in the family. Wouldn't that be wonderful?"

Carla felt a thrill at the thought. "Do you really think he's that good?"

Octavia laughed. "If he lives up to his promise, yes, he could be good enough."

Carla thought of Done Driftin' and how he'd looked before the race: ears pricked, eyes bright, his entire body practically vibrating with eagerness to get out there and do what he'd been born to do. And when he had crossed the finish line so far ahead of the other horses, she knew she'd never again feel another thrill quite like it.

But did that mean she wanted to stay on? And what if she did stay? What would happen in June, after the Belmont was run? Would she kiss her grandmother goodbye and thank her for a great time? Would she hand Done Driftin' off to someone else to race and train, while she went off to...what?

"Grandmother," she said suddenly, aware that she couldn't put it off any longer. "There's something I have to tell you."

"What is it, my dear?" Octavia asked, sounding concerned.

Carla was just answering, when Meredith walked into the room. She was dressed in a suit and heels, and in addition to her purse, she was carrying her jewelry case, something she only did when she traveled.

"Oh, good," Meredith said tersely. "You're both here. I came to tell you I'm leaving on a flight out of Louisville at two this afternoon."

"Where are you going?" Carla asked.

Meredith was probably one of the half dozen women left in the world who wore a hat and gloves while traveling. Smoothing one of her paper-thin leather gloves now, she said, "Back to London, of course. Surely, it can't be a surprise, Carla. I told you I was leaving."

Carla didn't want to explain to her grandmother about the argument she and Meredith had had last night. "Yes, but I didn't think it would be so soon," she said pointedly. "Don't you think we should talk about it?"

Meredith met her eyes. "I think we've said all there is to say, don't you?"

Carla flushed. Aware that Octavia was closely following the conversation, she said in a low voice she hoped her grandmother couldn't hear, "I'm not sure. Perhaps we should discuss it in private."

Apparently, Octavia heard her, after all. "Oh, don't mind me," she said. She picked up the paper again. "You go right ahead, I'll just read."

Meredith flashed a glare in her mother's direction, but Octavia just smiled. Her lips tight, Meredith turned her back and asked Carla, "You haven't changed *your* mind, have you? Because if you have, there's room on the flight. I've already checked. We could pick up your ticket at the counter. In fact, we could send for your luggage later. I'm sure Teresa will be glad to pack for you."

Carla could see her grandmother over Meredith's shoulder. Octavia was slowly lowering the paper she'd put up in front of her face. Her eyes were fixed on Carla.

"I told you, Mother," Carla said, "I'm not ready to leave yet."

"What you *told* me was that you'd stay just long enough to see that colt race. Well, he raced. It's time to leave."

Desperately, Carla said, "Try to understand, Mother, please. I—"

"Oh, I understand, all right." Meredith turned to look at her mother. "Well, you were successful, weren't you?" she said. "Not only did you lure my daughter here, you managed to turn her against me. That's what you intended all along, isn't it? Well, let me tell you something—"

But Teresa interrupted whatever Meredith had been about to say. "There's a call for you, Miss Carla,"

Teresa said, obviously upset. "It's Dwight Connor, the trainer. He says it's an emergency."

Carla's heart plummeted. Her hand was shaking when she picked up the phone on the nearby table. "Dwight? It's Carla Dunleavy." Her pulse was beginning to pound, and she had to force herself to be calm. "What's happened?"

When the normally unflappable trainer took a moment to answer, Carla feared the worst. When Dwight finally replied, his voice was so choked that Carla could hardly understand him.

"It's Done Driftin', Ms. Dunleavy," he said. "There's been . . . an accident."

With her other hand, Carla gripped the back of a chair for support. Somehow, she managed to say, "What kind of accident?"

"It's kind of . . . bad, Ms. Dunleavy. I think you should get down here to the track. The vet says . . . he says there's some decisions we might have to make."

Swaying, Carla closed her eyes. Dwight didn't have to spell it out for her to know what kind of decisions he was talking about. "I'll leave at once," she said. "Please don't do anything until I get there."

Dwight sounded about to cry. "I won't," he promised, and hung up.

Meredith and Octavia were still staring at her when she dropped the receiver into the cradle with nerveless fingers. She knew they were waiting for her to tell them what had happened, but for a few seconds, she couldn't speak. Finally, her voice under tight control, she said, "There's been some kind of accident with Done Driftin'. Dwight says the vet is there and wants me to come immediately."

Like Carla, both women knew what that meant. Octavia drew in a sharp breath, while Meredith looked at Carla's pale face and said immediately, "I'll drive you. I don't think you're in any condition to drive by yourself."

"I want to come, too." Octavia said.

As anxious as she was about her horse, Carla couldn't allow that. She tried to say, "Grandmother, you can't—"

Even Meredith protested. "I don't think that's a good idea—"

Octavia shushed them both with an imperious wave of her hand. "I'm going. I'll be more anxious here than I would be if I were doing something. Don't worry, I'll stay in the car if you like. Let's just get going and find out what happened."

CARLA WAS SO TENSE by the time they got to Done Driftin's stall that at first she didn't comprehend the awful news. The colt looked so . . . so *normal* standing there, she thought. It was only when she looked down and saw his grotesquely swollen front leg that she thought she might be sick.

"How did this happen?" she asked. If there hadn't been so many people around, she would have burst into tears. Her beautiful horse! she thought desperately. Was he ever going to race again?

The question seemed to be: would he even walk? Carla knew a few things about horses, but she was in such a state that words like *snapped ligaments* and *chipped sesamoids* and *strained tendons* seemed to fly around uselessly in her brain. Finally, she held up her hand, halting the veterinarian in midflow.

"Just give me the bottom line," she said. "Will he ever race again?"

There was an exchange of glances. Carla saw it and she clamped her lips shut on the wail of grief that was rising inside her like a fast wave. "Never mind," she said tightly. "Just tell me... will he have to be put down?"

Put down... put to sleep... euthanized... killed.

The veterinarian, a strong-featured, no-nonsense blond woman named Krista Vallon, shook her head. To Carla's relief, she said, "No, that's not necessary. We can patch him up, if that's what you want. And maybe someday, he might even be okay as a general riding horse. And, he's still a colt, which is good, so he can be put to stud. That race he ran the other day, well... You'll probably get a lot of bookings on that alone."

"Thank you," Carla said. She was aware that the vet was trying to be encouraging, but right now, all she could think of was that she'd never see her magnificent colt race again. Now she knew how her grandmother had felt when Done Roamin' had broken his leg. Both sire and son had been born to run. To deprive them of the chance seemed cruel beyond anything Carla could imagine.

"Please, Dr. Vallon," she said. She felt close to tears again. "Do what you must. I don't care what it costs. I don't want him to suffer unnecessarily, but I want you to save him."

The vet put her hand on Carla's arm. "I promise, I'll do what I can."

As much as Carla wanted to stay close to her horse, she knew she'd only be in the way as Dr. Vallon and her assistant went to work. Trying to stop her lip from quivering, she gave her colt a last pat. Then, with Meredith following, she gestured to Dwight and led the way to his office. As soon as they were inside with the door shut, she turned to him.

"All right," she said. "Tell me exactly what happened."

Dwight looked both angry and uncomfortable, as though he wanted to let out a string of vivid curses, but was prevented from doing so by their presence. He glanced at Meredith, who had gracefully taken a seat on the only chair other than the one behind his desk.

"I'm not really sure what happened," he said. "I saw it, and we got witnesses all over the place, but it went so fast. Fernando—that's the groom—took the horse outside the barn to give him a little sun, and a chance to eat some grass. We thought he deserved it after the race yesterday—"

"Just get to the point, will you, please, Mr....

Connor, is it?'' Meredith said. ''As I'm sure you can see, my daughter is extremely upset, and we'd like a clear, concise account of what happened.''

Carla was grateful for her mother's support, but she knew Dwight needed to tell the story his way. She understood her mother's impatience. Before she'd come to Kentucky, Carla herself wouldn't have considered Dwight's feelings. *But I'm a different woman now,* she thought, and said, ''Thank you, Mother. Go ahead, Dwight. What happened then?''

''Well, it was the damnedest thing—beggin' your pardon, ladies. I've gone over it a thousand times in my mind since, but I'll never know where that motorcycle came from. One minute, the path outside the barn was nice and clear, the next...that big bike came barreling along, scaring the bejesus out of both the groom and the horse.''

Carla tensed at the mention of a big bike. Trying not to let her expression betray her, she happened to glance in her mother's direction and saw a strange look on Meredith's face. For a moment, she wondered wildly if her mother had had the same thought. She shook her head. She was letting the tension get to her, and she turned back to Dwight.

''Go on,'' she said.

''Well, like I told you, it all happened so fast. I don't want to say it, but it seems that the biker was *aiming* for the horse. I don't know, maybe I'm crazy or something. Who'd want to hurt Done Driftin'? It had to be an accident. But whatever it was, it was a damned fool thing to do. And I'll tell you another thing, with no apology, either," he finished angrily. "I wish to hell it had been the guy on the bike who was hurt, and not that colt."

Her mind screaming, Carla refused to think about the motorcycle and who might have been driving it. *Take it one step at a time,* she told herself, and forced a stiff, "What happened next?"

Clearly agitated, Dwight ran a hand through his hair. "Well, naturally, the colt panicked. What horse wouldn't, seeing something like that heading right toward him? Fernando had a stud chain on him, of course, and he tried to hold him. But you know that not even Godzilla is going to hold a scared horse whose only thought is to get away and run like hell."

Carla tried to brace herself. "And then?"

"Well, and then…the colt took off down the road, Fernando chasing him. People heard the ruckus, and everyone came running out, trying to catch him. It only made matters worse, it usually does, but what choice do you have? And when the colt found the entrance to the track, well, he took off like a bat out of hell. They were dragging it after the workouts this morning, and—" He broke off. "Are you sure you want to hear this?"

Carla couldn't remember when she'd wanted to hear anything less. But she nodded jerkily and said, "I need to know, Dwight—all of it."

Dwight clenched his jaw. Then he said, "When the colt came across that big tractor rig out there in the middle of nowhere, he tried to . . . jump it."

"Oh my God." Carla closed her eyes again, thinking it was a miracle Done Driftin' hadn't been killed.

Now that she'd pressed him for the story, Dwight seemed compulsively determined to finish it right to the end.

"We think that's when he did the most damage— trying to jump the thing, but we're not sure. He could have hammered that leg any number of places. But his leg caught on something. The guy who was driving the tractor can't tell us, 'cause he bailed out when he realized the horse was heading toward him."

Carla felt dizzy and caught hold of the back of her mother's chair. She sensed Meredith looking up at her, but she had to keep her mind on details or she'd lose what little composure she had left.

"Did they catch the man on the bike?" she asked.

Dwight looked even more angry. "No, the guy escaped in all the confusion. By the time we caught the horse, and people started looking for the biker, he was long gone."

Carla didn't want to think what she was thinking. Trying to thrust away the image of Wade roaring away last night on his motorcycle, she asked shakily, "Did anyone recognize him?"

When Dwight shook his head again, Carla almost sagged in relief. Then she caught herself. What was she thinking? If Wade *had* done this terrible thing, she wanted him caught and punished. She wanted *whoever* had done it caught and punished.

It wasn't Wade! she told herself fiercely. He'd never hurt a horse; he had too much feeling for them to do that.

But if it hadn't been Wade, who had it been?

"What about the gate man?" she asked abruptly. "Where was he? Why did he let someone in who was riding a motorcycle?"

"He didn't," Dwight said. "We already questioned him, it was the first thing we thought of. But he swears that no one riding a bike came through the backside gate, or anywhere else."

Carla was getting angry. She welcomed the feeling because it helped her focus on something besides the terrible injury Done Driftin' had suffered.

"Well, Dwight," she said, "obviously *someone* came in on a motorcycle. You all saw it, didn't you?"

"Yeah, but what I meant was, no one came in *riding* a bike. I don't know, maybe the guy had it hidden in the back of a van, or a trailer or something." He ran his hand through his hair again, making it stick up in points. "The stewards will look into it, you can be sure. But in the meantime..."

Carla knew about the meantime. She said it for him. "In the meantime, it isn't going to help my horse."

"No." He sounded choked up again. "It isn't. I'm sorry, Ms. Dunleavy, I swear to God I am. When I think of the promise that colt had..." He stopped to control himself. "If there's anything I can do—"

The old Carla would have told him nastily that he'd already done the most damage he could. For good measure, she might even have added that he'd be hearing from her lawyer.

But this new person she seemed to have become had more empathy. "It's all right, Dwight," she said. "No one could have predicted something like this. I don't blame you, and I don't want you to blame yourself. These things . . . happen."

Dwight's expression said that things like this didn't happen in his stable, but he remained silent. What could any of them change now? The damage had been done. All they could do was leave it in the hands of the authorities and hope that the culprit would be found and dealt with appropriately.

But insidious doubts followed Carla as she said goodbye to Dwight and left the little office, her mother following. How would she feel if someone proved the person responsible had been Wade? Would she believe it then?

"You go ahead," she said to Meredith as they started toward the car. "I'll meet you in a few minutes. I just want to see how Done Driftin' is doing."

"Carla—"

"What?"

Meredith looked as if she wanted to say something, but then changed her mind. "I . . . er . . . what do you want me to say to your grandmother?"

"Don't upset her more than necessary. Tell her I'm still talking to the vet. Tell her we don't know anything for sure yet. Tell her—"

"There's no need to tell me anything," Octavia said. Meredith and Carla whirled around. Octavia was standing behind them, leaning on her cane, looking at them sternly. "Since you've been gone so long, I decided to find out what was going on myself."

Hurrying to her grandmother's side, Carla said, "You shouldn't have left the car! You know you're not supposed to exert yourself. You promised!"

"Yes, Mother," Meredith said. "Remember what the doctor said—"

Octavia silenced them both. "I know what I can do, and what I can't. Now stop fussing over me, I don't need it. We have more important things to worry about than whether I'm going to have another heart attack or not."

"But Grandmother—"

Octavia rapped her cane sharply on the ground. "We know what happened. What we have to find out is why." She looked around. "Where's Wade? Why haven't I seen him?"

"Wade?" Carla repeated. In all the tension and strain, she hadn't had a chance to tell her grandmother about the quarrel she and Wade had had last night, and how it had ended. She knew she didn't have the strength to explain now, so she said, "I... don't know."

"Yes," Meredith said as though just thinking of it herself. "Where *is* Wade? I'd like to know. As I recall, last night I thought I heard him driving away from the farm . . . on a motorcycle."

Carla glared at her mother. It was one thing to wonder about Wade herself, another to have Meredith implicate him. "What are you implying?" she asked.

"It's a logical question, isn't it? We all know he drives a motorcycle." She paused. "Don't we, Mother?"

"It wasn't Wade," Octavia stated flatly.

Nastily, Meredith said, "Are you sure of that?"

"Yes, I am." Octavia stared directly at her daughter. "Perhaps a better question might be, what do *you* know about this, Meredith?"

Carla gasped. "Grandmother!"

Meredith's face turned crimson. "How can you ask me such a question?"

Octavia's eyes never left Meredith's face. "I think you know why."

Meredith didn't answer for a long, tense moment. Then she said clearly and precisely, "Go to hell, Mother."

Carla was still staring in complete shock when Meredith turned and stalked off.

CHAPTER FOURTEEN

TWO DAYS LATER, Wade was in a diner near St. Louis, Missouri, when he heard the news about Done Driftin'. It was lunchtime and the place was crowded and noisy, the two waitresses shouting back and forth and trading ribald remarks with the customers. The din was so loud that he wasn't listening to the television mounted up behind the counter until he heard something about a racing tragedy in Kentucky. When he looked up to the screen and saw a tense-looking Carla being interviewed, Dwight frowning behind her, he sat up.

"Hey, honey, you all right?" the waitress asked. Carafe in hand, she'd come to pour him another cup of coffee.

She was standing in his line of sight, and he said, "Turn that thing up, will you?"

"What?"

When she just stood there looking at him, he pointed at the television. "It's so damned noisy in here that I can't hear it. Turn it up, will you?"

Annoyance flashed across her face at his tone, but she obliged. The newsperson had apparently just asked about the colt's future, for Carla was saying,

"It's too soon to tell if he'll race again. We're taking it one day at a time."

"Are there any leads as to who might be responsible?"

"You'll have to ask the authorities about that."

"Early reports indicate that the accident was caused by someone on a motorcycle. Is that true?"

Tight-lipped, Carla replied, "That's correct."

"Do you know who it was, or how this person managed to get by the gate man on a big bike like that?"

Carla looked into the camera. To the stunned Wade, it seemed as if she were looking straight at him. She said, "The police are investigating. But you may be sure that *when* this person is caught, he will be tried and punished. That's all I have to say."

"Wait—"

The reporter started after Carla when she began to walk away, but Dwight stepped in front of him. "Ms. Dunleavy isn't going to answer any more questions," the trainer said. He nearly dwarfed the other man with his bulk, but the announcer was after news. Without hesitation—or much regard for his personal safety— he stuck his microphone under Dwight's nose.

"Then perhaps *you* won't mind answering a few questions," the reporter said eagerly. "I understand you're the colt's trainer, Dwight Connor, is that correct? And if that's so, isn't is your responsibility to see to the safety of your charges? How could you have let this happen?"

Watching, Wade thought Dwight was going to explode. The trainer's face turned crimson, and he seemed to swell. "Why, you—"

The announcer quickly moved back. On the way, he said into the camera, "And there you have it from Louisville, Kentucky, the tragic tale of a horse named Done Driftin', whose brilliant racing career was recently cut short by a mysterious behind-the-scenes accident. We'll be following this story and releasing details as soon as they're available. But for now, this is Jimson O'Herlihy, reporting live from Sports on WKNB. Curt, Barbara, back to you."

Wade had heard enough. As the reporter's idiotic smiling face filled the screen, Wade stood up and pulled a couple of bills from his pocket. He slapped them onto the counter and was out the door before the waitress could reach him.

"Hey, mister!" she called.

He'd already started the bike. Seconds later, he roared onto the highway.

BACK AT THE FARM, Carla couldn't sit still. She should never have agreed to do that interview, she thought for the tenth time. But the publicity people at the track had finally persuaded her. Rumors were flying around that had little to do with what had actually happened, and they'd wanted to clear up the speculation. They'd said they were worried about her horse, but she knew they were more concerned about damage control. Done Driftin's accident was big news, and when they'd pointed out that maybe someone watching would be able to provide information, she'd finally agreed. She'd do anything to help catch the person responsible for ending her colt's racing career.

Another point that had swayed her was the fact that after almost two days of exhaustive investigation by the stewards, the police and other officials, they had nothing to go on. It was as if the man on the motorcycle had materialized out of thin air, taken a run at her horse and then disappeared without a trace.

And where was Wade? One of the reasons she'd consented to the interview was that she'd hoped Wade would be watching. But there had been no word. Where was he?

The question kept coming at her until she thought she was going to scream.

"It wasn't him, I know it wasn't," she said to herself over and over again. But she had nightmares about the terrible "accident" old Done Roamin' had suffered not long after Wade had come to work at the farm, and she couldn't forget that when she had accused Wade, he hadn't denied it.

She had to know what her grandmother thought. Octavia had been uncharacteristically silent on the way home from the track the day of the accident. In fact, none of them had said a word the entire drive. As soon as they'd pulled up to the front door, Meredith got out and went inside without looking back. It had been up to Carla to help her grandmother into the house, but finally, she couldn't bear the suspense any longer.

"Grandmother, you don't think Wade could have done this, do you?" she asked.

Octavia didn't reply for a second or two. Finally, she leveled her gaze at Carla and said, "I thought you had learned something about people during your stay here, Carla. Apparently, I was wrong."

Every word had been like a knife in her heart. She knew Octavia was right, but she said, "I just—"

"No excuses," Octavia had told her. "If you have to ask that about such a man, then I'm afraid you don't deserve an answer. By the way, where *is* Wade? I haven't seen him. Why hasn't he been around?"

Carla knew she didn't have anything left to lose at this point, so she said miserably, "I don't know where he is, Grandmother. We had a fight and he . . . left."

"Left? What do you mean, left? You're not saying . . . for good?"

"It seems so," Carla said. She couldn't look her grandmother in the eye. "I'm sorry. It's all my fault."

"I see."

It would have been better if Octavia had ranted and raved and yelled. But that mild tone was too much. Tears filled Carla's eyes, and her voice shook with pent-up emotion. "I know I had no right to let him go. Believe me, if I knew where he was, I'd go to him and tell him I was wrong. But I've tried everything to find him, asked everyone and no one knows where he is. I'm so sorry, Grandmother. I had no right to interfere."

"What did you say to him?"

Carla would have given anything not to confess. Wringing her hands, she said, "I asked him to tell me what really happened to Done Roamin'."

Octavia drew in a sharp breath. "Why did you do that?"

"I can't explain. It just came out. I didn't mean to say it."

"Then why did you? Surely you can't believe that Wade had anything to do with Done Roamin's accident!"

"I don't know what I thought that night. One minute, everything was fine. The next—" Her expression tragic, Carla looked up. "Can you ever forgive me?"

Octavia had given her a look that made her cringe. "Wade is a very dear friend. I simply don't understand how you could have said what you did." Octavia had brushed Carla aside, summoned Teresa and went directly to her room, where she'd been ever since.

Now, as she had been for the past two days, Carla was pacing the front room. She'd done everything she could think of to find Wade, but nothing worked.

Now what? she asked herself mournfully. Was it going to end like this? Would she always wonder what had happened to him, where he had gone . . . if he had done this terrible thing?

"He didn't do it, I know it," she said again.

But if he hadn't, why hadn't he come back? He had to have found out about the accident by now. It was in newspapers across the country, she'd been told. Unless he had crawled into a cave somewhere, he'd heard the terrible news. Why hadn't he at least called?

And what was she going to do about her grandmother?

She had tried to talk to Octavia through the closed bedroom door, but there had been no answer. She had even bribed Teresa to let her take in a breakfast or dinner tray, but as soon as Octavia heard that it was Carla at the door, she'd refused permission to enter.

Suddenly, she stopped pacing and decided to try again. Once more, she found herself standing before her grandmother's closed bedroom door. What was she going to do if Octavia refused to answer her, wouldn't let her in? She almost lost courage. Then she bit her lip and knocked. As before, there was no answer.

"Grandmother, please listen to me!" she begged from the hallway. "I can't bear this silence any longer. I didn't mean it. I know Wade wouldn't do such a thing. I was wrong and I'm sorry. Please say you'll forgive me."

At last—at last!—the door opened. When she saw her grandmother standing there, tiny but ramrod straight, she was so relieved she nearly started to cry. But when she bent to give her a hug, Octavia was stiff in her arms, and she straightened again.

"I know you're angry," Carla said in a low voice. "Can we at least discuss it?"

Octavia stared at her for what seemed an aeon. Then to Carla's relief, she said, "Yes, I think it's time we talked. Come in."

The big master suite comprised a sitting room with the bedroom beyond. Octavia went to a chair grouping by the window and sat down. On pins and needles, Carla followed and took the opposite chair.

Octavia began to speak. "I can't believe you actually thought I'd have anyone around who would hurt a horse—any horse, much less one like Done Roamin'. Don't you think I had the incident investigated? Don't you think I did everything I could to prove—to myself most of all—that what happened was an accident?"

"Yes . . . no . . . oh, Grandmother, I don't know!" Carla could hardly bear the disappointment in Octavia's face. "It's just that Wade is so difficult to understand. When he became so angry and defensive, I got angry, too. I felt so . . . protective of Dunleavy Farm—of everything here that I . . . that I . . ."

Her tears finally spilled over. "I'm sorry," she said, her voice muffled as she put her face in her hands. "I'd do anything in my power to undo what I said."

"Carla, you said you felt . . . protective. What did you mean?"

Wiping tears away with the heels of her hands, she said, "I don't know when it happened, but for the first time in my life I started to feel that at Dunleavy Farm I really had a home. And when Wade implied that the only reason I'd come was because . . . because . . ."

She couldn't go on. Breaking down completely, she began to sob again. Octavia let her cry for a moment, then she pushed a lace handkerchief into her hand. In utter misery, she left her chair and threw herself at her grandmother's feet. Her head in Octavia's lap, she said, "I didn't mean for any of this to happen!"

Carla's unhappiness was so overwhelming that her grandmother's gentle touch on her hair only made her tears flow faster. Finally, Octavia said quietly, "Don't cry, sweetheart. Everything will be all right."

"But how? Wade is gone, you and my mother hate each other, the farm is in trouble, and my beautiful horse will never run again. Oh, I just want to die!"

Octavia smiled sadly, one hand on Carla's shiny hair. "I know it seems impossible now, but things have a way of working out."

"Not this time!" Her face red and splotched, Carla looked up. "When I first came here, I thought I'd stay a few days—maybe even an hour or two, and then I'd be off. I never expected the farm to grow on me."

Octavia smiled again. "It has a way of doing that."

"So do you," Carla said shakily. "Oh, Grandmother, I love it here. I love you. I don't want to leave."

"You don't have to leave. Whatever gave you that idea?"

"But I thought—"

"We've all made mistakes, my dear. And it took me a long time, but I think I've finally learned my lesson." She looked into Carla's eyes. "I'd like to give you time to learn yours."

"But I have learned my lesson. I know I treated Wade badly, and if I ever see him again, I'll...I'll apologize from the bottom of my heart. In the meantime, I want to help. I want to make Dunleavy the place it used to be. But as much as I want to, I can't do it on my own."

As Carla bowed her head again, Octavia closed her eyes as if in thanks. Then she reached down with one hand and tipped up her granddaughter's chin. "Maybe you won't have to."

"What do you mean?"

"Yours wasn't the only letter I wrote, you know," Octavia said. "I think it's time I told you about your cousins."

Carla sat up. "I have cousins?"

"Indeed, you do. In fact, I sent them letters at the same time I sent yours to you."

"Why didn't you tell me?"

"Because I thought I'd hear from them before now. Nan is the daughter of my son, Gary. She's in Montana, but I haven't heard from her yet. Seth is the son of my other daughter, Jamie. He's married to a woman named Honey and they follow the fair circuit. I'm hoping the reason I haven't heard from them is that they move around so much and their letter is chasing them."

"Do you think they'll come?" Carla asked eagerly.

Octavia hesitated. "I don't know," she said. Then, when Carla's face fell, she added, "But I didn't think you'd come, and you did. So we'll just have to wait and see what happens. I wanted Nan to have Done Cryin'—"

"Done Cryin'!"

Moved by what her grandmother had told her, and suddenly full of hope, Carla rose to her feet. All at once, what had seemed so irreparable before didn't seem so desperate. Thoughts of Trent Spencer's offer of financial help vied with images of Done Cryin' in race training again—and those mixed with ideas for breeding the wounded Done Driftin'. And, she thought excitedly, there was yet another Done Roamin' offspring waiting in the wings—the supposedly spectacular Never Done Dreamin'.

Now that she wasn't alone, now that she had a chance to rectify her mistakes, she had to seize the opportunity. Everybody had always said what a good business head she had on her shoulders; this was her chance to use it.

"What's her number, do you know?" she asked Octavia.

"Her number? Who?"

"Nan, of course!"

"Why, I don't know. I didn't call, I wrote her a letter. But the address is in my book by my bedside.... Where are you going?"

Carla ran into the bedroom. When she emerged seconds later, she was waving a battered address book. "Is this it?"

"Yes, it is, but what are you—"

"I'm going to call her and ask why she hasn't replied to your letter. I want to ask her what she intends to do about Done Cryin'!"

"What?"

Carla gave her grandmother a hug. "Oh, it's all going to work out, you'll see! With two of us here, it'll be different, I guarantee."

"But what if Nan doesn't want to come?"

Carla refused even to consider it. "She'll come," she said. "Even if I have to fly to Montana and bring her here myself!"

In the living room, she quickly dialed Nan's number. At the other end, the phone rang once…twice… When it rang a third time without being answered on the other end, she wanted to scream. What if Nan wasn't home? What would she do then?

Just then there was a click, and a wary voice said, "Hello?"

Carla was so relieved, she sank into the desk chair. "Hello…Nan?"

The voice turned even more cautious. "Yes. Who's this?"

"This is your cousin, Carla. I'm calling from Kentucky to find out if you ever received a letter from a woman named Octavia Dunleavy. Our...grand mother.''

The voice became hostile and defensive. ''And if I have?''

This wasn't going well, but she pushed on.

''I know we don't know each other, but Nan, please listen,'' she pleaded. ''I'm calling to find out if you'll accept Grandmother's offer to visit Dunleavy Farm.''

''Oh, I—''

''I know it sounds crazy. That's what I thought, too, when I received my letter—''

''She sent you a letter, too?''·

''Yes. She wanted to give me a colt called Done Driftin'—'' She was so eager to convince Nan to come that she laughed almost hysterically. ''Little did I know how appropriate that name was going to be!''

''What?''

With an effort, she got hold of herself. ''Never mind. We can talk about it when you get here. Because, you see, something happened to my colt and he can't... Oh, we can talk about that later, too. The point is, now there's Done Cryin'—''

''Done Cryin'?''

''The colt Grandmother wants to give you. Oh, Nan, I don't know if you know anything about horses, but he's going to be one of the great ones, I just know it. You have to come! We don't want to race him without you, and he does so want to run!''

"I still don't know what you're talking about. How do I know you're who you say you are? This could be some kind of trick."

"It's no trick, please believe me. If you come, I promise you won't regret it. I didn't."

There was a silence. Then Nan said, "Well, I don't know. Will you be there if I do?"

"Oh, I'll be here," Carla said fervently. "I didn't realize it for a long while, but this is my home now."

Carla was just hanging up on Nan's cautious agreement to think about the offer to visit when she realized her mother was at the door. In Meredith's hands were two suitcases, which she set on the polished entryway floor. When she saw that, Carla said, "You're leaving after all? I thought you changed your mind and decided to stay."

"We both know it's for the best. But before I go, I'd like to talk to you."

"If it's about my leaving here, please save your breath. I'm not going."

"I know you won't come now—"

"No. I'm not leaving, period."

"You can't mean that. I don't want to remind you of a painful subject, but you told me you wanted to stay and watch your horse run. Now that he...that his racing career looks to be over, why do you want to stay on?"

"Because I realize that I've found the one thing I've been looking for all my life."

"And what's that, pray tell?"

"My home."

Meredith didn't answer for a moment. Then something seemed to sag inside her. "I should have known," she murmured.

"Mother, please don't ruin this," Carla said. "I know how you feel about Grandmother and the farm and everything, but I just don't feel that way."

"I know." Meredith came into the living room. "I realize that I can't change your mind."

"No, you can't."

Meredith took a deep breath. "I'm sorry, Carla. I know all this has been difficult for you. I know I should have told you long ago about your father, but I was trying to protect you."

"Protect me? From what? What possible harm could there be in my knowing about my father? Unless—" A thought occurred to her and she looked at her mother sharply. "Unless . . . he's not dead. Is that it, Mother? Is he still alive?"

"I don't know," Meredith said. But she wouldn't meet Carla's eyes. "I haven't seen Alan since."

"Are you sure about that, Meredith?" Octavia asked from the doorway.

Carla and Meredith both jumped. Meredith's expression hardened.

"You just can't let it rest, can you, Mother?" she said.

"Nor can you, Meredith. Don't you think it's time to put the past to rest?"

"I'll never forgive you, Mother. You know that."

"Oh, I'm aware of that," Octavia said. "You've made that quite clear."

"Then—"

"You know, I was never surprised that you fell in love with Alan. He seemed to be quite a catch in those days."

Meredith looked at her bitterly. "Even if he was only a farm manager?"

"His job had nothing to do with it. I respect any kind of work, and you know it. No, the problem was Alan himself. He was an opportunist and he proved it."

"Did he?" Meredith's eyes were like green ice. "A man would have to be a saint to take what you dished out in those days, Mother. And as much as I loved him, I knew Alan was no saint."

Octavia was silent for a moment, then said, "I made a mistake. I should have let things run their course. But instead—"

"Instead, you had to take matters into your own hands, just like you always did," Meredith interrupted. "You did it with me, and with Gary and with Jamie, too. It's no wonder we all left here. The wonder is that we all stayed as long as we did."

"You never did want to know the whole story, did you?"

Meredith snatched her purse off the table where she had put it. "No, and I don't want to know it now. I should have known it was a waste of time to come here. Well, this is the last you'll see of me. Goodbye,

Mother. And goodbye, Carla. I'll be in London if you want to contact me."

"Mother, wait!" Carla exclaimed as Meredith turned and started toward the door. Her mother turned back.

"Are you going to change your mind?" Meredith asked.

Carla looked from her mother to her grandmother. She felt torn. But then, from out on his pasture, she heard Done Roamin's now-familiar shrill whinny. It was crazy, she thought, but he seemed to be telling her that eventually everything would work out. Hoping her mother would some day understand, she said, "I'm sorry. But I have to stay."

"Fine. You know where I'll be."

"Mother, can't we—"

But Meredith had already gone.

Carla went over to the window in time to see the taxi pull away. As she stood there dejectedly, her grandmother joined her. Quietly, Octavia said, "It'll be all right, you'll see."

"How can you be so sure?"

"I'm an old woman. I've seen a lot through the years."

Carla suddenly knew. "There's more to this story than either you or Mother have said, isn't there?"

Octavia hesitated. Then she said, "Yes, there is."

"Tell me. I have a right to know."

"Yes, you do. But your mother and I still have some things to work out."

"But how will you do that? She's gone, Grand-mother. And I don't think she's coming back."

"Oh, she'll be back."

"You sound so certain."

"I am. Your mother might hate me, but she loves you. As long as you're here, she'll come back to see you."

"I wish I could be as sure as—"

Just then, Carla was interrupted by the sound of a vehicle on the long driveway. For an instant, she thought it was the cab coming back, but then she knew it wasn't a car. Quickly, she looked at her grand-mother, then she rushed onto the porch and shaded her eyes. Yes, there it was—a motorcycle coming fast up the driveway.

"Grandmother, is that—"

Octavia came out, too. When she saw the bike, she smiled. Satisfaction in her voice, she said, "I knew he hadn't left for good."

Then, with a glance at Carla, she slowly backed away and went inside.

Carla hardly noticed her grandmother's departure. Her senses were so attuned to that bike and the man who was driving it, that she felt almost light-headed from the strain. Her heart pounding crazily, she waited until Wade stopped the Triumph in front of the house and took off his helmet. She hadn't the faintest idea what she was going to say to him—or if she could say anything at all. Her lips were too stiff and her throat didn't seem to be working. She could only stand there, breathing hard and drinking in the sight of him. Until now, she hadn't allowed herself to think how bleak and empty her life would be if she never saw him again.

"I came as soon as I heard," he said, using his booted heel to bring the bike stand down into place. He swung his leg over the seat and got off, tossing his helmet casually onto one of the hand grips. He looked up at her, his black hair tousled, his eyes like blue stars, and Carla knew then as she'd never known anything before, that no matter what had happened, or what might take place in the future, this man would always be the only one for her.

"Is he all right?" Wade asked.

"We don't know yet," she said. "It's still touch and go."

"Have they found the guy who caused it?"

Her eyes went to the big, heavy bike before she looked at him again. Then she said, "You mean the man on the motorcycle?"

"Yeah," Wade said evenly, watching her face. "Him."

The air was so electric with tension that Carla felt the hair on her nape stir. Her heart was thudding against her ribs, and she knew that one wrong word from her would destroy everything.

"No, they haven't found him," she said.

Wade's glance hadn't left her face. His voice strained, he said, "It wasn't me, Carla."

Every muscle in her ached to close the distance between them and feel his strong arms around her and his lips on hers.

"I know," she said evenly. "You drive a Triumph. The man responsible was on a Harley."

Anger flooded his face. "Is that the only reason you don't think I did it?"

"No it isn't." She held his eyes a second or two before she added, "I know, because the man I love would never hurt a horse just to hurt me."

She couldn't stand it anymore. She flung herself down the steps and ran to his embrace. As his arms closed tightly around her and their lips met with a clash, she pressed herself against him with all her might.

"Oh, Wade, I missed you!" she said, her mouth under his. "Don't leave me alone like that, ever again!"

Instead of answering, he pulled her even harder against him. Desire and want and need were like steam boiling off him. As Carla curled her fingers in his thick hair, her nostrils took in the pungent smells of the road, the heat and the oil and the gas and the sweat, all mingled into one. She breathed in the aroma deeply, telling herself never to forget it. She never wanted to smell it again.

Finally, she pulled back. "I'm so glad we're both home."

He smiled and cocked an eyebrow. But he didn't let go of her as he said, "Don't tell me you're finally going to settle down. You, the woman with the peripatetic life-style who said she wouldn't stay in one place longer than five minutes?"

She hugged him, too. "I've changed, Wade. I've learned a lot about things...about myself—and you. I never want us to be apart again. I never want us to be far away from Dunleavy Farm."

"Amen to that," he said fervently. "But does that mean—"

She smiled up at him with love shining in her distinctive green eyes. Then she said, "Grandmother named my horse better than she knew. After all these years, I'm done drifting. I searched all over, and finally found you."

EPILOGUE

THE SUN WAS just going down behind the hills when Octavia came out of the house and began to walk slowly toward the paddock area. After all the fuss and confusion of the past few days, it was quiet at last, and, with the exception of her still-tattered relationship with Meredith, she felt more at peace than she had for a long while. But she wouldn't think of Meredith right now, for she hadn't given up hope that they would work things out. The last rays of the sun were gilding the trees, and the sleepy birds beginning to fly back to their nests. It was her favorite time of day and she was going to enjoy it.

As always, from high on the hill in his paddock, Done Roamin' saw her heading toward the gate. For a moment as he stood there, silhouetted against the skyline, he looked as he had so many years ago—strong and powerful, and oh so fleet. As she watched him, Octavia felt a lump in her throat. Without warning, she was transported back in time to that once-in-a-lifetime thrill when he had won the Belmont, the last leg of the Triple Crown.

Suddenly, she could hear, as though he were right beside her, the announcer's voice that day. Even over the loudspeaker, he'd had to shout to be heard. The roar of the grandstand crowd was deafening as the field of eight turned for home. As always when her stallion ran, the other horses were battling for second place. Done Roamin' had surged out of the gate and stayed ahead. Even on this third race of that grueling contest, it had been his race all the way.

"And it's Done Roamin' pulling away all by himself!" the announcer had cried. *"Done Roamin' by three lengths, four... by ten lengths now! It's Done Roamin', on a hand ride by jockey Reynaldo Morales, Done Roamin' driving to the wire... Done Roamin' all alone...!"*

And then came the words she had waited and prayed and planned for so many years to hear: *"Ladies and gentlemen, Done Roamin' has just won the Triple Crown!"*

She would never forget that feeling, she thought, even if she lived a hundred years. She still saw as clear as could be that horse of her dreams, the jockey so elated that he'd almost fallen out of the stirrups on the way to the winner's circle. And Done Roamin', triumphant and victorious, prancing still, as though he knew what he had accomplished. In all these years, eleven horses had earned that crown, and her beloved stallion was one of them. She knew what it was like to have a dream come true.

As though he'd sensed her memories of past glories, Done Roamin' let out another whinny before starting down the hill toward her. As quickly as they'd overtaken her, the sights and sounds of that glorious Belmont day faded from Octavia's mind, and she laughed as the stallion lurched up to the fence and put his head over. This horse might be old now, with a slight swayback and gray hairs in his mane, but to her, he was still the most beautiful horse she had ever seen. Tenderly, she reached up and stroked his muzzle, then laughed again when he nuzzled her palm.

"You fair-weather friend," she scolded fondly as she pulled his carrot out with her other hand. "Sometimes I think you wouldn't come to say good-night to me if I didn't bring you a treat."

Done Roamin' was too busy chewing to answer, and as Octavia stood there, listening contentedly to the crunching sounds he made, she looked up at the glowing sunset and sighed.

"Well, Meredith left today," she said conversationally, as if the horse could understand. "But Carla is going to stay. And Wade came back—but then, we always knew he would, didn't we?"

Done Roamin' snorted.

"But we still don't know who hurt Done Driftin'," Octavia went on. "I could cry when I think of it, and of course, Carla was devastated. But she's strong, and she'll carry on." She paused a moment, then brightened. "And even if Done Driftin' can't run, he'll make a fine stud, especially after that one race. You should be proud of him, Roamy. After all, he's your son."

Done Roamin' snorted again and rooted for another piece of carrot, just like a grumpy old man.

"You know," Octavia said thoughtfully, "I think Meredith knows more than she's saying about all this. There was something in her eyes... But maybe I'm wrong. Why would she know anything? She's been gone so long. Then again, one never knows about Meredith, does one?"

Done Roamin' finished the carrot. It was time for both of them to go in. Octavia gave the horse a final pat on the neck. But then, before she started back to the house, she looked around at him again.

"We did what we could for one of my grandchildren, and it worked out pretty well, didn't it, old man?" she said to the stallion. "I guess now we'll just have to wait and see what Done Cryin' can do for Nan."

* * * * *

Be sure to read Nan's story in the next exciting installment of the Dunleavy Legacy

DONE CRYIN'
by Janis Flores

Available in September wherever Harlequin books are sold.

HARLEQUIN SUPERROMANCE®

WOMEN WHO DARE
They take chances, make changes
and follow their hearts!

The Father Factor
by Kathryn Shay

Amanda Carson has helped many parents in her job as
guidance counsellor but never has she come across one who
challenges her as much as Nick DiMarco. The single father of
two is determined to prove he can handle everything—even
his difficult teenager. Fiercely proud, he wants no help from
"outsiders." But the DiMarco kids—and their stubborn
father—have found a special place in Amanda's heart. Now
all she has to do is convince Nick to let her into his.

**Watch for *The Father Factor*
by Kathryn Shay**

**Available in September 1995 wherever
Harlequin books are sold.**

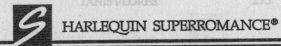

HARLEQUIN SUPERROMANCE®

The Dunleavy Legacy
by Janis Flores

For more than a century, the Dunleavy name stood behind the winners of horseracing's most prestigious prizes. The family's wealth and fame was recognized in the most powerful circles.

But times are different now, and the new generation of Dunleavys is about to claim its legacy. Meet the three grandchildren of Octavia Dunleavy, matriarch of the family, as they deal with old feuds and jealousies, with family pride and betrayal, in their struggle to restore the Dunleavy dynasty to its former glory.

Follow the fortunes of Carla, Nan and Seth
in three dramatic, involving love stories.

#654 DONE DRIFTIN' (August 1995)
#658 DONE CRYIN' (September 1995)
#662 NEVER DONE DREAMIN' (October 1995)

This eagerly awaited trilogy by critically acclaimed writer Janis Flores—a veteran author of both mainstream and romance novels—is available wherever Harlequin books are sold.

DLL-1

HARLEQUIN SUPERROMANCE®

**He's sexy, he's single...and he's a father.
Can any woman resist?**

FAMILY MAN

JACOB'S GIRLS
by Tara Taylor Quinn

Girl trouble. Jacob Ryan has it in triplicate. Seven-year-old Allie is organizing her teacher to death. Seven-year-old Jessie is crying in class. Seven-year-old Meggie is becoming almost reclusive. Jacob's told that what the triplets need is a woman in their lives— and maybe they do. But that's the last thing *Jacob* needs.

Woman trouble. He's gone that route before. All it did was get his daughters' hopes up—*his* hopes up—and then the lady left. Maybe the answer is to enlist the help of a friend, someone like his partner, Michelle....

**Watch for *JACOB'S GIRLS* by Tara Taylor Quinn.
Available in September 1995,
wherever Harlequin books are sold.**

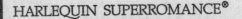

HARLEQUIN SUPERROMANCE®

Pregnant...and on her own!

THREE FOR THE ROAD
by Shannon Waverly

Mary Elizabeth Drummond: She's a sheltered "good girl" with a pedigree a mile long. She's three months pregnant. She has no intention of marrying her baby's father. She's lost her credit cards, her driver's license and her money. She's on her own for the first time in her life.

Then she meets Pete Mitchell—tough, sexy, a confirmed bachelor.

Things are looking up.

Watch for *Three for the Road* by Shannon Waverly.
Available in September 1995,
wherever Harlequin books are sold.

PRIZE SURPRISE SWEEPSTAKES!

This month's prize:

BEAUTIFUL WEDGWOOD CHINA!

This month, as a special surprise, we're giving away a bone china dinner service for eight by Wedgwood**, one of England's most prestigious manufacturers!

Think how beautiful your table will look, set with lovely Wedgwood china in the casual Countryware pattern! Each five-piece place setting includes dinner plate, salad plate, soup bowl and cup and saucer.

The facing page contains two Entry Coupons (as does every book you received this shipment). Complete and return *all* the entry coupons; **the more times you enter, the better your chances of winning!**

Then keep your fingers crossed, because you'll find out by September 15, 1995 if you're the winner!

Remember: The more times you enter, the better your chances of winning!*

PWW KAL

PRIZE SURPRISE
SWEEPSTAKES

OFFICIAL ENTRY COUPON

This entry must be received by: AUGUST 30, 1995
This month's winner will be notified by: SEPTEMBER 15, 1995

YES, I want to win the Wedgwood china service for eight! Please enter me in the drawing and let me know if I've won!

Name_____

Address _____ Apt. _____

City   State/Prov.   Zip/Postal Code

Account #_____

Return entry with Invoice in reply envelope.

© 1995 HARLEQUIN ENTERPRISES LTD.   CWW KAL

PRIZE SURPRISE
SWEEPSTAKES

OFFICIAL ENTRY COUPON

This entry must be received by: AUGUST 30, 1995
This month's winner will be notified by: SEPTEMBER 15, 1995

YES, I want to win the Wedgwood china service for eight! Please enter me in the drawing and let me know if I've won!

Name_____

Address _____ Apt. _____

City   State/Prov.   Zip/Postal Code

Account #_____

Return entry with Invoice in reply envelope.

© 1995 HARLEQUIN ENTERPRISES LTD.   CWW KAL

OFFICIAL RULES
PRIZE SURPRISE SWEEPSTAKES 3448
NO PURCHASE OR OBLIGATION NECESSARY

Three Harlequin Reader Service 1995 shipments will contain respectively, coupons for entry into three different prize drawings, one for a Panasonic 31" wide-screen TV, another for a 5-piece Wedgwood china service for eight and the third for a Sharp ViewCam camcorder. To enter any drawing using an Entry Coupon, simply complete and mail according to directions.

There is no obligation to continue using the Reader Service to enter and be eligible for any prize drawing. You may also enter any drawing by hand printing the words "Prize Surprise," your name and address on a 3"x5" card and the name of the prize you wish that entry to be considered for (i.e., Panasonic wide-screen TV, Wedgwood china or Sharp ViewCam). Send your 3"x5" entries via first-class mail (limit: one per envelope) to: Prize Surprise Sweepstakes 3448, c/o the prize you wish that entry to be considered for, P.O. Box 1315, Buffalo, NY 14269-1315, USA or P.O. Box 610, Fort Erie, Ontario L2A 5X3, Canada.

To be eligible for the Panasonic wide-screen TV, entries must be received by 6/30/95; for the Wedgwood china, 8/30/95; and for the Sharp ViewCam, 10/30/95.

Winners will be determined in random drawings conducted under the supervision of D.L. Blair, Inc., an independent judging organization whose decisions are final, from among all eligible entries received for that drawing. Approximate prize values are as follows: Panasonic wide-screen TV ($1,800); Wedgwood china ($840) and Sharp ViewCam ($2,000). Sweepstakes open to residents of the U.S. (except Puerto Rico) and Canada, 18 years of age or older. Employees and immediate family members of Harlequin Enterprises, Ltd., D.L. Blair, Inc., their affiliates, subsidiaries and all other agencies, entities and persons connected with the use, marketing or conduct of this sweepstakes are not eligible. Odds of winning a prize are dependent upon the number of eligible entries received for that drawing. Prize drawing and winner notification for each drawing will occur no later than 15 days after deadline for entry eligibility for that drawing. Limit: one prize to an individual, family or organization. All applicable laws and regulations apply. Sweepstakes offer void wherever prohibited by law. Any litigation within the province of Quebec respecting the conduct and awarding of the prizes in this sweepstakes must be submitted to the Regies des loteries et Courses du Quebec. In order to win a prize, residents of Canada will be required to correctly answer a time-limited arithmetical skill-testing question. Value of prizes are in U.S. currency.

Winners will be obligated to sign and return an Affidavit of Eligibility within 30 days of notification. In the event of noncompliance within this time period, prize may not be awarded. If any prize or prize notification is returned as undeliverable, that prize will not be awarded. By acceptance of a prize, winner consents to use of his/her name, photograph or other likeness for purposes of advertising, trade and promotion on behalf of Harlequin Enterprises, Ltd., without further compensation, unless prohibited by law.

For the names of prizewinners (available after 12/31/95), send a self-addressed, stamped envelope to: Prize Surprise Sweepstakes 3448 Winners, P.O. Box 4200, Blair, NE 68009.

RPZ KAL